TO BE A CHAMPION

Pat Eddery

with Alan Lee

Hodder & Stoughton
LONDON SYDNEY AUCKLAND TORONTO

Many of the photographs in this book are from the author's private albums. It has not always been possible to trace copyright. The publishers apologise for any inadvertent infringement and will be happy to include an acknowledgment in any future edition.

British Library Cataloguing in Publication Data

Eddery, Pat
  To be a Champion
  I. Title II. Lee, Alan
  798.40092

  ISBN 0-340-485647

Published by Hodder and Stoughton, a division of Hodder and Stoughton Ltd, Mill Road, Dunton Green, Sevenoaks, Kent TN13 2YA Editorial Office: 47 Bedford Square, London WC1B 3DP

Photoset by SX Composing Ltd, Rayleigh, Essex

Printed in Great Britain by St. Edmundsbury Press, Bury St. Edmunds, Suffolk.

To Frenchie Nicholson
my guide and support
in the days when it all began

Illustrations

[1] Agence APRH, P Bertrand et Fils
[2] Allsport
[3] Author's private collection
[4] Bespix
[5] Ed Byrne
[6] J Cashman
[7] Gerry Cranham
[8] Peter Deighan, portrait
[9] Wallis Doncaster
[10] Tony Edenden
[11] E L Gibbs
[12] Trevor Jones
[13] Press Association
[14] George Selwyn

Permission to reprint the illustrations has been kindly granted by the above. The publishers wish to thank them and *The Racing Post* for all their help in providing photographs.

Contents

Introduction

by Alan Lee

Out of the patchy, playful clouds of late March, the Cessna began its descent heading, apparently, for nothing more grand than a farmer's field decorated with a windsock. And so it was: a patch of grass in rural Buckinghamshire, somewhere between Thame and Aylesbury and utterly undistinguished but for being the launchpad of a remarkable champion, the improbable daily starting-point for the pursuit of winners which consumes Patrick James Eddery, seven days a week, eight months of every year.

At the controls, Jan Bussell eased gently back on the throttle, lowered the landing gear and, with a light chuckle, swooped mischievously across the roof of the silver Mercedes nosing into the field below. Bussell was born in north London of Devonian stock, spent most of his working years in Malaysia and, to his knowledge, has not a trace of the Scandinavian blood his Christian name suggests. Until 1987, he had only been to one race meeting in his life, and that was the other side of the world, half a lifetime ago. Now, he goes every day of the flat-racing year. Call him the transport manager, call him the pilot, he is the man who gets the champion to the course on time to ride, and home in time to relax; he is an indispensable part of the Eddery team and proud of the fact that, in the four years since he began the job, he has flown the Cessna for 1200 hours. It is the equivalent of flying ten times around the world.

Eddery himself jumps from the passenger seat of the Mercedes, short, wiry and with the remains of a Caribbean suntan. Stepping slightly more deliberately from the driver's side, the anxiety of a new season much more prevalent on his creased features than on the jockey's, is Terry Ellis. Terry is Pat's brother-in-law but very much more besides. If Jan Bussell is responsible for getting Eddery to the course, Ellis is responsible for making sure he has something to make the journey worthwhile. He is the manager, the formbook student, the booker of rides, the shield from the media and constant shadow. He is, to many who go racing regularly, the public face of a private man.

Pat and Terry have had their quiet months and enjoyed them. They have been, independently, to the West Indies, Terry returning first to begin the business with which he is now so familiar: the endless conversations with trainers, seeking rides and seeking inspiration. Now it is time for a resumption of operations – Doncaster, the traditional first venue, for another defence of the jockey's title which Eddery had retained in 1990, at first unfussily and then historically, as he became the first flat rider since Sir Gordon Richards to partner 200 winners in a season.

Whatever anyone else in his line of work felt about the opening of the perceived summer racing season in distinctly wintry March weather, Eddery was ready for it. With twenty-two years of race-riding behind him and uncharted territory increasingly difficult to locate, he still found the adrenalin coursing strongly through his veins on his first morning of many.

Most days in the season start in the same way, even if few are comparable at the business end of affairs. Bussell drives from his home in Chipping Norton to the busy little airfield at Kidlington, where the Eddery Cessna is housed. He might first hose down the plane before attacking his mobile telephone, checking arrangements with Ellis, phoning ahead for a taxi to meet the plane if it cannot land on the targeted racecourse. On a clipboard, he will have carefully written out his flight-plan for the day. An instrument check, contact made with air-traffic control and then out onto the runway for the short hop to the grassy field which, to all intents, is Eddery's private airstrip, a mere few minutes' drive from his farm home.

He flies almost everywhere these days. He gave up driving himself long ago, a decision not unconnected with some consistent brushes with the motorway police, and for some years Terry drove his client and friend and relation to every meeting. It was Willie Carson, not just a fierce rival but a friend as well, who pioneered the use of a private plane and Eddery, persuaded by the freshness with which he could daily arrive at the racecourse compared to the weariness of those confined to the roads, laid out the equivalent of a Derby winner's purse on his own plane. He has never for a moment regretted it and nor has Terry, after overcoming his own fear of flying so totally that he now sits habitually up front next to Jan and is tempted to take out a licence himself.

The manager clambers now into his accustomed seat and slides on a set of headphones so he can talk to the pilot. The jockey spreads himself in the comfortable rear section, where there is room for four to sit; there is also a drinks cabinet containing a beer or two but, more conspicuously, supplies of Lucozade, which is the only drink Pat will allow himself before his dinner. Breakfast, as usual, has been a slice of toast and a cup of sugarless tea and the one luxury Eddery permits himself during working hours is regular puffs of a cigarette. He has smoked since his early teens and is not proud of the fact, but on the one occasion when he managed to kick the habit for all of six weeks, his weight became uncontrollable. So now, although the doctors at his annual BUPA pre-season medical will shake their heads disapprovingly, Pat smokes a packet of twenty each day, including a couple on each leg of the aircraft journey and a habitual, reviving couple of drags in the weighing-room between races.

There are days, before racing, when Eddery will become withdrawn, preferring the silence of his own company to any forced attempts at conversational wit. Terry, too, can be anxious until the outcome of his meticulous planning is known and Jan has observed the symptoms and learned to treat them with respect. 'I have never once seen Pat angry about racing,' he reports; 'only when he is playing cards! But he can be quiet, even a little grim in the mornings, especially if he has been wasting. As soon as racing is over he is relaxed and conversational.'

This morning, however, there is no obvious anxiety, probably because there are no lofty expectations. The season is to start busily enough, with four booked mounts, but their quality reflects the standard of racing at what is, by peculiar custom, a low-key overture to the flat season. On Saturday, day three, the Lincoln Handicap will be run and Eddery will be aboard one of the favourites. Until then, there is little to stir the blood.

Eddery is never concerned by this phenomenon. Indeed, he positively welcomes the slow start in the belief that launching directly into a full book of rides each day would be a health hazard. He is not among those unfortunate jockeys whose weight swells extravagantly in winter recess so that returning to a racing poundage becomes a regime of depressing self-deprivation, but then neither is he as biologically blessed as, for instance, Carson, who continually eats and drinks as he chooses and has not the slightest difficulty in riding at well below eight stone. Pat spends upwards of half an hour, every morning of the season, in the saunas he has had built at his homes in Buckinghamshire and Newmarket, and he does not do so for the fun of it. This year, his pre-season routine has also involved running a three-mile course near his home, mostly uphill, plus use of a stationary bike and a rowing machine. Feeling rather pleased with himself, he flew to France, two days before the start of the Doncaster meeting, to partner a heavily-backed horse. The ground was bottomless and, although the horse won, Pat had to work hard enough to realise that, though he might be physically fit in the normal acceptance of the term, he was not race-fit. 'Nothing,' he is fond of saying, 'compensates for riding, and I know I will not be at my sharpest until, perhaps, the Craven meeting at Newmarket at the end of April, when most of the major trainers start getting serious about the season.'

The flight from Aylesbury to Doncaster takes just forty minutes, perhaps a quarter of the driving time and, just as important, giving only a fraction of the stress. It is an hour before the start of racing when the Cessna makes a smooth landing on a slightly scruffy airstrip close to the newly modernised course. A taxi waits on the approach road, Jan Bussell's forward planning proving faultless, and Pat casts an eye around the airfield before commenting that Willie, as usual, would be late. 'He always arrives in a tearing hurry with only a few minutes to spare,' he laughs.

Once inside the course, Pat and Terry go their separate ways, the jockey disappearing inside the weighing-room, the sanctuary from which he will emerge only in colours, purposefully businesslike prior to each ride, the manager setting off on his ritualistic tour of duty. 'I don't spend much time in the bars,' he says, and indeed he does not. Ellis is in perpetual motion, broken only for conversations with trainers or owners about future plans. He makes mental notes throughout each afternoon, not only during but between races, and his fund of knowledge will be shared with Eddery's own later in the evening.

The day goes no better and no worse than expected. Pat does not ride a winner, but then he did not expect to. Of his four mounts, one finishes third, one fourth and one fifth. In the day's final event, a three-year-old maiden race, he is stone last. He jumps off his horse just before 4.45 p.m.; less than twenty-five minutes later, the party is airborne again, heading back to base.

Eddery's first winner of the 1991 season arrived in race one the following day, a two-year-old selling event which his mount turned swiftly into a no-contest. On the Saturday he did not win the Lincoln but he did win a three-year-old race on what he called the first 'nice horse' he had sat on that season.

Trained by Barry Hills at Lambourn, the horse was owned by Prince Khalid Abdullah, by whom Eddery has been retained for the past four years. When combined with a second retainer from another Arab giant, Maktoum al-Maktoum, this gives Pat a notional pool of around 350 well-bred horses to ride during the season ahead. He knows, however, that some will never reach the racecourse, some will necessarily be ridden by other jockeys, many will turn out to be no better than moderate and a few could be the special sort which give each season its dreams. For now, however, he has to linger on the success of Bandol, for it is to be his last winner for more than three weeks, more than thirty rides. For the champion, it is an uncomfortably long wait, but then he long ago conquered the art of patience.

1

EARLY YEARS: Family and a Start with Seamus McGrath

For longer than I care to admit, my riding career was as keen to start as an ancient car on a winter's morning. While other young jockeys were off and running, riding winners at will, so it seemed to my eyes, I required seventy rides and countless deflating setbacks to earn my first visit to the winner's enclosure. I rode all of one English season and part of another waiting for that elusive break and there were inevitable low times when the feeling of prolonged failure became oppressive. Never once, however, did it occur to me that I was in the wrong job, for this was all I had ever wanted out of life and, no matter how long it needed, I was prepared to wait for the success.

When it came, and in quantities beyond my imagination, it did not alter my outlook or, I trust, my personality. I might have been able to add a few luxuries to my lifestyle and a few refinements to my manner but I remain, at heart, the Irish country boy who grew up in an environment dominated by and dependent upon racing and who knew, long before the age when most young people choose their career, that he would never seek or discover anything to surpass the exhilaration of riding thoroughbred racehorses.

Deciding on a course is one thing; being able to follow it is quite another. There are any number of budding young Lester Piggotts flocking through the gates of racing stables on an annual basis, their heads full of the very same dreams that I had as a young boy. Precious few of them will make the grade sufficiently to earn a living, let alone approach the dizzy heights scaled by the incomparable Lester. But in starting out on this precarious road, I was greatly helped by having a father who had been an accomplished and fearless jockey, and a caring mother who, while she had never in her life had the desire to sit on a horse, was bred into horseracing and disinclined to steer me on to a safer bet.

We were a Catholic family, and a large one. Jimmy, my father, was one of twelve children. Not to be outdone, he then had thirteen of his own, although the first-born, James, died at the age of nineteen months. Of the surviving twelve, I was fifth in line, and the youngest, David, was born in the year I left home to come to England. Consequently, although I think of us as having been a close family during my boyhood, the children never were all together and, these days, a complete reunion seems virtually impossible, so farflung are we all.

I was born on March 18th, 1952, on the outskirts of The Curragh racecourse, south of Dublin. Jimmy was still riding then, and did so until I was seven years old. He retired, it seemed to me, much too young, for by then I was hooked, going racing with him and my mother, Josephine, every Saturday and scuttling in and out of the weighing-room whenever I was allowed. Only much later did I hear the real reason for Jimmy Eddery's retirement.

My father always has been a fiery man. He has a quick temper which, when matched with the ruthless desire to win which marked his riding, apparently made him a dangerous opponent as a jockey. I am told he would do almost anything to win a race and his rough-house style undoubtedly had an early influence on me which, thankfully, I was to outgrow. It was the undoing of Jimmy, though, and I believe that the authorities were, shall we say, anxious for him to pack up when, at thirty-eight, he showed no sign of mellowing in his race-riding style.

By the end of his career, Jimmy was attached to Seamus McGrath's prestigious stable, near Leopardstown racecourse. Seamus might well have been among those who persuaded him to retire but he was not trying to ditch him. Instead, he took him on as assistant trainer, an arrangement which worked well enough for my Dad and more than well for yours truly. We had moved to a six-bedroomed house at Blackrock, not more than three miles from the McGrath yard, and at eight years old, with a head full of fanciful notions about winning Derbys and becoming champion jockey, I could begin to indulge my fantasies by surrounding myself with the creatures and paraphernalia of horseracing every spare moment of the day.

Jimmy had not wanted to stop riding, that much was obvious. He had been champion jockey of Ireland once, and was generally in the top few jockeys each year. In 1955, he was second in the English Derby on Panaslipper, the 100–1 outsider of two McGrath runners; I remember watching the race on TV back home. I'm told, though, that Dad's first classic winner had come eleven years earlier, when he dead-heated in the Irish 2,000 Guineas at The Curragh. The horse was called Good Morning and it was not only Dad's first classic winner but also his first classic ride. Coincidentally, the other horse in the dead-heat was ridden by another accomplished and experienced rider called Jack Moylan. He and Dad lived near each other and went to the same church for Mass. It was there that Dad met Jack's daughter, Josephine, who was to become his wife and my mother.

They were in many ways opposites, our Mum and Dad. Mum has always been serene, even-tempered, very difficult to upset. Probably she needed to be this way to cope with some of Dad's rages. Eventually, their differences were to prove insurmountable and they separated, but it was a far from unhappy household in which I grew up.

Mum was extremely hard-working, as you would expect with twelve children to look after. She was a very good cook, something which was the undoing of me in early life. As a boy I had an incurable sweet tooth and, consequently, devoured everything Mum put in front of me and plenty that she didn't. It may seem odd now, but I became quite fat.

The odd thing about my mother is that she was very frightened of horses and would not, by choice, go anywhere near them. Yet she loved watching racing and, when she went to the races most weekends, she would always have a bet. She still enjoys a flutter now, for all my warnings about filling the satchels of the bookmakers!

If I have a regret about my childhood it would be that I failed to make anything of my education. I was no good academically, through no fault of my parents, both of whom wanted the best possible schooling for me and were far from pleased to see me spurn it. But to me, the hours spent behind a desk were nothing more than mandatory wasted time, a penance I had to endure between the important things in life.

To Be a Champion

I was not a self-confident child. Indeed, I was pretty shy with people. When it came to riding, though, I was different. I had no fear of horses, even at an age when I was dwarfed by them, and on horseback I was instilled with a conviction and self-belief I never felt at other times. It first became evident when I was given a pony and, rather than contenting myself with gymkhanas and suchlike, I rode him on Mr McGrath's gallops with the racehorses.

This was a very good pony, naughty but quick, and he gave me my first experience of the exhilaration that can come from travelling at speed on horseback. The racehorses would work on the five-furlong gallop and I would wait with the pony at the four-furlong pole, ready to wing him in upsides them as they came past. He held his own, too, and far from resenting the intrusion of this improbable small boy, the jockeys thought it was hilarious.

I was only eight years old when I graduated to riding racehorses at the McGrath yard, and I went on riding out there for the next seven years before leaving home to go to England. For the first five of those years, of course, I was still at school, the encumbrance which, with a shameful lack of regret, I shed at least a year earlier than planned after my brother Michael and I were caught cheating in exams.

Michael was a year older than me but very much tougher. He, too, was keen to be a jockey and he became a very capable rider over jumps until, in 1972, he had a terrible fall at Newcastle. His right leg was amputated below the knee but even this tragedy did not turn him totally against the game. Nowadays, he travels the country selling horse vitamin foods to trainers. It is a respectable, responsible job for a brother who, in schooldays, was a self-confessed rogue and bully.

I suppose it was natural that, of all my brothers and sisters, I should feel closest to Michael. At home, we shared a bedroom; at school, we ended up in the same class when he was sent down a year for some misdemeanour or other. We were not at all alike, however. I was quiet and withdrawn, whereas Michael was the fearless extrovert. If I said anything bad to him I knew I had to get out of town a bit quick or expect a good hiding. But although we occasionally scrapped, with only one result I might add, Michael was also very protective towards me. I would back out of fights at school but if ever I did get involved through those around me, I would never get hurt because Michael would be there, taking my side and taking on allcomers to help out his kid brother.

Our school, Oaklands Junior, was in Stellorgan, just a mile from home. We walked there each schoolday, and rarely with any enthusiasm. I could not say I hated school because I could never summon such strong feelings about it. It just kind of passed by and, although I started out with the disadvantage of not being bright, I never made any attempt to compensate by putting in more work. I never bothered doing much at all; homework was ignored and the lessons passed in a haze, or more accurately in a daydream. I could think of nothing but my dreams of becoming a jockey, and the gathering of knowledge about history, geography or mathematics seemed absurdly irrelevant to my purpose in life. If I give myself credit for anything, it must be for being single-minded.

Games periods offered me some respite but, to be honest, I did not excel at them either. I was poor at running and never did enjoy it much; funnily enough, the one game I did really enjoy was cricket. This has never been a mainline sport in Ireland but for some obscure reason we played a lot of it at school and, although I am sure I was useless, I got quite a buzz out of it. I batted, and bowled a bit of spin, but my last cricket match at Oaklands was also the last in my life.

Each summer holiday we would go down to Cork, where Jimmy was brought up, and stay with my grandmother, a very religious lady who lived to be ninety-four. I have good memories of those holidays – carefree times with the sun seemingly ever present and the countryside green and enchanting. But for all the fun of it, I was forever anxious to get back to the yard and resume my riding.

At that time, only three of us children were really interested in riding. John, my eldest brother, was too heavy to be a jockey anyway and although he did eventually race-ride for a while, going to England for a spell with that grand old jumping trainer Arthur Stephenson, he never conquered the weight problems and returned to Ireland where he took a job as a barman. Nowadays, he runs the unpublicised side of my life for me, in charge of the stud farm at home.

Mary, the eldest of the girls, was a very good rider who won a lot at show-jumping. Lady riders were not allowed in Irish racing and so she never did race-ride, but I am sure she would have been capable. Her daughter now mops up a lot of prizes around the Northern Ireland shows.

This left Michael and me. We might have been very different in terms of size and temperament but there was nothing between us when it came to a passion for horses. There was a healthy rivalry between us but, being a year older, Michael would probably have advanced the quicker but for an accident, when he got hung up on his pony. He didn't ride at all for a time after that and so Dad turned his attentions to me, not exactly pushing me but certainly setting me stiffer challenges than a boy of my age would normally expect.

He would put me up on any of the McGrath horses, no matter their reputation. The stable's head lad was also a member of the Eddery family, my Uncle Connie, and he frequently told Jimmy he was mad to give me such hairy rides. On reflection, Uncle Connie might have been right; it was only later in life that Frenchie Nicholson taught me the right way for a lad to progress in riding. But although I would often be run away with, and I had my share of heavy falls, I never once complained. Tough initiation it might have been, but through it I gained in confidence and grew to recognise and adapt to the feel of individual horses.

Mum never saw Michael and me with the horses and we made certain she did not get to know of the mishaps. She knew we were excited about riding out, because we would talk of nothing else, and if she felt fear or concern for our safety, she never let on. She would never try to mollycoddle us and was keen that we should do what our instincts told us – which, she well knew, meant endless hours with the horses.

And so, in our blissfully rural part of Ireland (not so nowadays) the months and years passed contentedly as I daydreamed of the time when I would leave school and begin my apprenticeship as a jockey. It came, however, slightly sooner than planned.

I was thirteen years old when my education, such as I had allowed it to be, came to an abrupt end. Michael and I were not exactly expelled from Oaklands but we were disqualified dishonourably from our examinations and it was made pretty plain to us that the school would get along better for our absence.

It all came about because Michael was especially bad at Irish and I was well behind the rest of the class at English. Each of us was at least adequate at the opposite subject and so it made perfect sense for us to pool our resources. We swapped papers in the exam rooms and the teacher caught us in the act.

Justice was swift. We were both thrown out of the exams and sent to the headmaster's study. We got the cane, which was not a new experience to either of us and could be tolerated much more easily than the dreadful thought of what awaited us at home. Even if our mother accepted this disgrace with her customary calmness, it was an odds-on shot that Jimmy would go berserk when he was told. We tried to lie low when he came home but, of course, it was useless. He sought us out, in one of his blackest tempers, and gave us both a good hiding which I cannot claim we did not deserve.

I never went back to school in Ireland and, although under Irish Law I had to wait until my fourteenth birthday to sign the indentures which formally began my apprenticeship under Seamus McGrath, I was now to all intents and purposes full-time at the yard. As this was the fulfilment of my wishes I might easily have fallen to thinking that cheats really do prosper but, in all honesty, I was not proud of what I had done at school and, in the ensuing years, I have increasingly regretted it. I should have done one more year at school, and although at the time it would have seemed like the extension of a prison sentence I am sure it would have done me no harm. I left school having learned precious little, and although racing is full of lads who did exactly the same, I wish now that I had not been quite so narrow-minded.

It was March 1966 when I signed my name on the indenture form in the imposing presence of Mr McGrath. A rich man, and a very nice man too, Seamus was also a private person and we never did see very much of him. Most of his time was spent in the house or the office but I do remember that, as a boy, if I ever saw him coming into the yard when I was there, I would turn tail and run. I imagined that he had never spotted me before I reached a safe hiding place in some empty box or tack-room, but he probably found it all faintly amusing.

No, Seamus was no trouble to me. The problem for young Patrick was that the day-to-day running of the massive yard was in the hands of two members of the Eddery family. With Dad as assistant trainer and Uncle Connie as head lad the atmosphere could become uncomfortably claustrophobic. Michael had now signed apprentice forms, too, and with so many of the family living in each other's pockets, arguments were inevitable and frequent.

For any apprentice, the head lad is the most difficult man to get along with because he issues the orders and administers the discipline. Probably to avoid any suspicion of family favours, Uncle Connie seemed to pick me out for especially harsh attention. He watched me like a hawk, just waiting to pounce on anything I did wrong.

At first, these family niggles were no more than a mild irritation as I set about enjoying the life I had always craved. No one should ever pretend that the duties of an apprentice are the stuff of dreams, but the long hours and the menial tasks seemed to me a small price to pay for the joy of riding exercise three times a day on horses which, I convinced myself, I would soon be in line to partner on the racecourse.

I was not foolish enough to believe that I would walk straight into a jockey's position. Bill Williamson was the stable jockey and a master of the craft; other experienced riders were also used and Seamus appeared to give the apprentices a ride in rotation . . . except that, when my turn came, I missed out.

The horse I missed out on was an old handicapper called Vale of Cliona. I thought he was likely to be my first ride as he seemed a good, safe conveyance for a boy. The other lads in the yard all made their racecourse debuts in turn and Vale of Cliona was entered for a race at Leopardstown at just the time when I began to think I must be next in line. But Mr McGrath had other ideas and that lovely old horse won as he liked with one of the other kids on board. My Dad got quite upset about this and, although I was careful not to show my feelings, I was terribly disappointed inside.

I said nothing to Jimmy, because he was too closely connected with the yard. But I did confide in my mother. I told her how upset I was to be overlooked, unfairly as I saw it, and said that I was becoming unhappy at McGrath's. I wanted to get out and find a racing job in England which, ever since I sat and watched the TV racing as a young boy, had impressed me as the end of the rainbow so far as my dreams were concerned.

Mum thought I was too young. She might have been right. She

also felt I was being impulsive and that I would soon cheer up and begin to enjoy life again at home. For the time being, I allowed her to talk me out of the idea. But I never did abandon the thought, simply filed it away in the mental pending tray.

I carried on uncomplainingly and eventually, of course, my chance did come. Mr McGrath put me down for a ride at The Curragh in mid-August 1967, eighteen months after my apprenticeship had begun. I was to ride True Time, who had won a maiden event only a few days earlier; but this was a handicap, and it was a jockeys' race, not one confined to apprentices. And it was at The Curragh, home of the Irish classics. Outwardly I may have retained my mother's serenity. Inside, I was churning with nerves.

The first thing to strike me, as the race got under way, was the sheer speed of the action. It was a six-furlong race and they seemed to go a hell of a gallop. Too fast, anyway, for my fellow. He was never in the race with a chance and finished stone last, tailed off some way behind the other half-dozen runners. I walked him back to unsaddle, feeling very little of the expected thrill; there was a sense of deflation and, irrationally, of failure. It was heightened at morning exercise the next day when the rest of the lads took the piss out of me unmercifully. I should probably have seen the joke; instead it was the final straw. I was now quite determined to leave.

When I went home later that day I told my mother I would not be going back. This time she did not really try to dissuade me. She must have seen what I had gone through over that first ride and I am sure she sympathised. Next morning, she took me to the yard herself to see Seamus who, of course, was under no obligation whatever to release me from my indentures. He listened carefully to what I had to say and then told me he would give the matter some thought.

Two days later, he gave Mum a list of five or six trainers in England who might be suitable and willing to take me on. They included Doug Smith and Sir Gordon Richards. They also included the man who was to drag me into the adult world, teach me everything about riding and much more besides, and become a firm and respected friend until his death. When Frenchie Nicholson agreed to add me to his apprentices' academy, it was the luckiest break of my young life.

2

FRENCHIE NICHOLSON: A Great Trainer of Horses and Boys

Cheltenham, to me, was merely the place the Irish descended upon each March and a racecourse I occasionally saw on television back home in Blackrock. Given an unmarked map of England, I would not have had the first idea what part of the country the town was in, much less how to get there. But, having been accepted as the latest new boy in the Frenchie Nicholson jockey academy, Cheltenham was to become my home for a good many years and, to this day, it has a special place in my heart, for it was here that my career was properly launched.

If, looking back now, the memories are good, Cheltenham was not, however, an instant Shangri-la for this frustrated, young would-be jockey. I wondered for a while exactly what I had let myself in for and, given the chance, I would have made a rapid return to Ireland, never to return. Homesickness can be a painful condition for a boy who has hardly been outside his home village.

My Dad did not resent me wanting to go – in fact privately I think he was pleased I had taken the plunge – but I am sure he was a bit scared for me. As for Mum, now fully occupied with nappies again following the birth of my youngest brother, David, there was, I think, an acceptance that I was doing the right thing mixed with the emotional whirl of a mother's usual feelings when one of her brood flies the nest. There were, inevitably, tears from her when I set off with a single suitcase one weekday morning in September 1967. If I kept mine under control, it was touch and go.

I was to fly from Dublin to Birmingham and then take a train down to the Cotswold town where Frenchie trained horses, and men. It was my first time on a plane and I was glad to have my father with me for moral support. Had I known how I was to feel after a few days in England I might not have let him go home without me.

Mine had been a sheltered upbringing, for all the fresh air and freedom. I was sheltered by the small, close community in which I had lived; sheltered by a large and protective family; sheltered, if ever anything physically unpleasant threatened, by an elder brother who was bigger and tougher than me. But for the derision of the lads at Seamus McGrath's yard when I finished last on my debut race-ride at The Curragh, I might have been much slower and less impulsive in abandoning the cosy nest for the unknown. As I stood, shy and shaking, in the front room of the Nicholsons' house while an evidently terrifying man looked me critically up and down, England suddenly seemed not only unknown but also unwelcoming. Rapidly, I longed for the home comforts of Blackrock, Mother's cooking and the familiar routine I had left behind.

Frenchie, having completed his assessment of my build and concluded, as he was to tell me much later, that I was too fat, brusquely told me to get off to my digs, change into working clothes and report back in time for evening stables. I went, in some trepidation, a feeling that did not improve at the first sight of what was to become my home for the foreseeable future. The house was cold and depressing. The food, I was soon to discover, might easily have been designed for the purpose of slimming me down as rapidly as possible. 'My' room was shared with two other lads, privacy non-existent, home comforts a thing of the nostalgic past.

For the first week, I was desperate to be away. I might happily have traded in whatever fanciful dreams I had of riding stardom for a ticket back to Dublin. The work was tough, the guv'nor was frightening and the digs were desolate. Then, one morning, something happened which made me feel it might not be such a dead-end after all.

I had been there a week, maybe two. Frenchie selected four of us boys, myself included, to ride work on some two-year-olds. The other kids had only just started riding but, from my time at Seamus McGrath's, I knew how to spin one along. Already, that much came naturally to me. I gave mine a crack and won the gallop by five or six lengths. As we turned and walked back I caught Frenchie giving me another of those assessing looks of his. He said nothing at the time, but he had noticed I could ride. From that day forward, he began to map out a career for me.

Having arrived at Prestbury in September, with the flat season virtually over, I had a winter to get through before I could entertain any prospects of seeing my name on the racecourse number-boards. I cannot pretend it was an easy winter. Indeed, although it became increasingly obvious that Frenchie had spotted enough in my riding to mark me down as one who might make the grade, the greatest effect he had on me was one of intimidation.

Frenchie was one of those men whose essential kindness is forever cloaked in a gruff, abrasive wrapping. He was, in time, to teach me very much more than how to ride a race. He was to teach me manners, civility, call it what you will. He taught me how to behave, and in the long term that was just as important to my career as any refinement in riding style. His way of teaching, however, was the iron fist without too much of the velvet glove; it could be resented at the time for its uncompromising expectations. Only much later did I come to appreciate exactly what he had done for me.

So, that first winter, I would still have packed it all in on umpteen occasions, if only I had been mentally tough enough to do so. There were bleak times when I felt that nothing about the life was worthwhile, that I hated the work, the place and the guv'nor. But, somehow, it was less frightening to stay and see it through than to march in and tell Frenchie I was quitting.

Then, and right to the end, the day's agenda was as predictable as it was all-consuming. We arrived at the yard at 7 a.m. for mucking out; half an hour later we would pull out for first lot. We would ride out three lots, with a brief break for breakfast, and at 12.30 there was an hour for lunch. Most stable-lads would then have the rest of the afternoon free before evening stables, but not us. Frenchie had us gardening until four o'clock, before reporting back to the yard, where our duties finished at 6.30. Officially, that was the end of our day, but any thoughts of indulging in the nightlife of Cheltenham, drinking quantities of beer or chasing women were very soon banished from the minds of the newcomers. Frenchie would always want to know where you would be during the evening and, if it was anywhere other than at home in your digs, or occasionally at the cinema, he would not look kindly on it.

The unwary, or those who might fleetingly underestimate the man, tried to pull the wool over Frenchie's eyes by telling him they would be at home and then ducking off to a pub or nightclub. He was never fooled. Not only would he randomly check up at your digs, he also knew the town so well that word inevitably got back to him if any of his charges had been seen out late or, much worse, misbehaving. Life for the miscreants would not be pleasant for a while.

If all of this conjures up a picture of a Scrooge-like figure intent that the young should not enjoy their youth, then it must be said that is just how some of us regarded Frenchie at times. It was not true, though. Frenchie was no hermit or killjoy. He had his own social routine, which revolved around drinking his regulation two pints of beer in the Plough at Prestbury each evening, and he was very much a creature of habit. In the training of his brood, however, he considered it would have been all too easy for us to slip into bad habits if he did not keep us under close observation. He was probably right.

The gardening might seem an eccentric demand of boys trying to make their way in horseracing, but Frenchie believed it helped to keep us motivated, staving off boredom and lethargy. In an odd sort of way, some of us almost grew to enjoy tending the vegetable plot, too. The same aversion to all forms of laziness was behind Frenchie's insistence that everyone either walked or cycled to work. When I bought my first car he would not allow me to drive it to the yard. I seethed silently, but in retrospect, it was a good discipline.

Although Frenchie was in all respects the boss, the 'academy', as it became known, had been more the brainchild of Mrs Nicholson. Paul Cook was the first flat jockey to graduate from Lake Street, Prestbury, and his tutor had apparently been David Nicholson, Frenchie's son; Diana Nicholson shrewdly saw that this was a potential sideline to the business of training horses and the scheme developed quickly and naturally from there. They selected their pupils from an ever-growing number of applicants and they plainly chose well for, over the years, twenty-five of the Nicholson apprentices rode winners, the last but far from the least of them being Walter Swinburn.

Every one of them will have gone through the same somewhat daunting regime that I did and, at times, they will have resented it. Quite possibly they will have been scared of Frenchie who, as a guv'nor in those days, was at liberty to give you a whack if you stepped out of line. Almost certainly, they grew up to be better-behaved and better-dressed people, never mind better jockeys, than they could possibly have been without the man.

Fussiness about dress standards was not exclusive to the Nicholson yard. In those days, lads were expected to dress in a smarter, more uniform manner than they do nowadays. The first horse I was required to take racing was one of Lord Sefton's and, in my shirt and tie, tweed jacket and cap, jodhpurs and boots, I might have been straight off the cover of *Horse and Hound*. It rather spoiled the effect that it was pouring with rain and the Kempton Park parade ring was a mudbath, but I was undeniably smart, and woe betide me if I had not been.

The most remarkable aspect of Frenchie's success in producing flat-race jockeys was that by design and preference he was primarily a trainer of jumping horses. That first horse I led up, at Kempton, was a steeplechaser and so were the great majority of those in the yard. During my time at Prestbury I don't think Frenchie ever had as many as half a dozen flat horses, which naturally meant that we apprentices had to ride the jumpers at work. These were chasers used to carrying something between 11 and 12 stone on their back, and they must have thought they were loose with a seven-stone kid in the saddle. Occasionally one would take control of his rider and bolt, but the great thing was that we became so much stronger by riding them every day.

David was the stable jockey at the time, but he would usually ride out only when there was schooling to be done. Otherwise, the only times we saw him were when we led up his mounts at the races, but I came to know that he was someone I could speak to and that he would offer any advice possible, even though he was busy enough with his own riding commitments.

When he started training, David would often give me rides on his few flat horses, who were usually fit from hurdling and would often go well on what were then mixed cards at the Aintree Grand National meeting. And it was at this meeting that, on

March 30th, 1968, the long first winter at Frenchie's ended for me and I had my first ride in England.

At the McGrath stable back home in Ireland the youngsters were given rides in turn. It did not work that way at Prestbury. Frenchie would not book you a ride until he felt you were ready to do justice to yourself and, I suppose, to him. So when he called me aside one morning and told me I would be riding a filly at Liverpool, it was more an honour than a natural progression. I was excited when he told me and I did not stop feeling excited until long after the race had run its singularly eventful course.

The trainer to book me was Tim Molony, previously a champion jump jockey and the winner of four successive Champion Hurdles. He had not specifically sought me out to ride, for how could he? Like many other trainers, before and since, he had telephoned Frenchie and asked him to nominate a promising apprentice, totally confident in the man's judgement. Frenchie, who may have been seeking such an opportunity for me anyway, put forward my name. Tim Molony agreed and so, on that Friday morning, we set off from Prestbury after the first lot, with Mrs Nicholson in her usual place behind the wheel and Frenchie in the passenger's seat issuing me with my instructions.

I was to hear this particular car speech on many more occasions, for Frenchie was always of the view that if you told a boy something once it was all the better for telling him a few more times as well. It involved making certain I did not miss the break. 'If you get left,' Frenchie would say, time and again, 'it's nobody's fault but your own.' These words were still in my mind when Frenchie walked me round the course before racing and, an hour or so later, when we went down to post for the Hylton Handicap Stakes over six furlongs.

The filly's name was Dido's Dowry and the trainer had told me in the paddock that she was quite lively and liable to get excited. This, of course, made two of us, but she behaved impeccably down to the start. This, at least, helped to calm my nerves, which had been jangling since my initial sight of the vast Aintree course where, twenty-four hours later, Red Alligator was to win the Grand National.

Naturally enough, I have never ridden in the National, but I can align myself with the majority of jump jockeys in saying that I have had a fall at Aintree. In my case, however, it was not at an obstacle nor even with the race in progress.

The indignity came about partly through the temperament of my filly, partly through the old-fashioned barrier start and partly through my own determination to give Frenchie no chance to criticise me for being left at the gate. When one of the other runners charged the tape, Dido's Dowry and I followed. My filly hit the tape and, when it didn't rise, she wiggled to get her head free and I was deposited on the Liverpool turf, while she pranced off to do a furlong alone.

It was just about the worst start imaginable to a boy's English riding career but, thankfully, Dido's Dowry was caught without doing herself any damage and without running too far. We were reunited, the second attempt at a start went off smoothly and, for a 20–1 outsider, she ran a respectable race to finish sixth. One that did not finish at all was the favourite, from whom Lester Piggott had a nasty fall when the horse stumbled, giving me something in common with my lifelong hero, the very first time we rode in the same race.

Tim Molony seemed pleased enough. An hour later, I guess he was still more satisfied for, in another flat race, a lowly-rated three-year-old of his ran second with Lester riding. His name was Red Rum and, like me, he had been set on the path to greater things that afternoon.

3

CHAFING AT THE BIT: Learning the Ropes and Tasting Success

If I imagined that my first ride in England would lead quickly and naturally to the first of many winners, I was disabused at painful length. It was 390 days after my Aintree debut aboard Dido's Dowry that my duck was at last broken. It may have been a little more than a year but, to a teenager in a hurry, it seemed like a lifetime.

Of the seventy rides I had before that initial success, any number were placed and I admit there were moments when I bleakly doubted if I would ever end up in the winner's enclosure. Other kids in Frenchie's care were riding winners but, despite plenty of encouragement from the guv'nor and no shortage of opportunities, my mounts stubbornly refused to put their head in front.

This was the time when Frenchie's influence was at its strongest. Naturally, there were days when my inclination was to feel pretty sorry for myself if not to have a good sulk at the injustice of it all. Frenchie would not permit any such malingering. Even if another of his lads had won a race in which I had looked to have the better chance, he would say something to give me a boost, never letting me get down about it. He would be quick enough to tell me if he thought I had made an elementary error during a race, and he would do so without any obvious concern for my finer feelings. But at the same time he had a way of imparting confidence. I might not fully have appreciated it at the time but even in the midst of that apparently endless run of losers – a run which, if it happened now, would probably leave me sleepless with self-doubt – I never worried about my riding ability. That must have been down to the one man with whom I discussed riding, day after barren day.

It all came right on April 24th, 1969, and, rather like a golfer who finally settles on the right club after constantly underhitting, my mounts just kept going in after that. By the end of the 1969 season I had clocked up twenty-three winners and stood fourth in the apprentices' table. I had even ridden a winner at Royal Ascot, a prize for which I would have gladly given all the clothes off my back a few months earlier.

The Ascot win came from the same source as my first, a man named Major Michael Pope, who trained at Streatley in Berkshire. He, like many another trainer, had been alerted to my name by Frenchie and Diana, who had continued to push me, apparently without embarrassment, despite my prolonged failure to deliver any dividends. The Major, whom I came to know as a smashing man, kind and friendly, had bought a horse called Alvaro at Ascot Sales. He was a relatively cheap buy, not only because his form was modest but because he was listed as a wind-sucker, which is not usually designed to help a horse give of his best.

Somehow, the Major cured the complaint. I am told he stripped Alvaro's box completely and then put a wire around it with a mild electric charge, just enough to discourage the horse from grabbing hold of anything. The treatment worked and he had already won a two-mile race at Ascot when the Major entered him for an apprentices' event over the Derby course at Epsom. He remembered that Frenchie had recommended a young man called Eddery and had me down to his yard to ride work a few times before the race came around. I evidently did nothing on the gallops to dissuade him and I duly arrived in the parade ring at Epsom to receive some of the most confident instructions I had ever heard.

Having stood dutifully awaiting the Major's advice, and received none, I eventually asked him how he would like his horse ridden. I can clearly recall his words even now: 'Just guide him. He'll win.'

For a teenager who had begun to despair of ever riding a winner to hear this was to set off a confusion of emotions. If Michael Pope was right, and even I knew he had been right quite frequently before, then this was the big opening and I could not afford to mess it up. If he was wrong, there were likely to be some gloomy faces when I came back beaten.

But the longer the race went on, the more the Major's confidence transmitted itself to me. Alvaro was a very easy horse to ride because he did everything for you, on the bridle. He won by three lengths without me having to ask him a question and, quite naturally I suppose, my overwhelming feeling on passing the post was one of relief. It had, after all, been a very long time coming. It was also a nice race to win, not only because it was over the Derby course and distance, with all that this evoked, but because it was on television. As I walked Alvaro back towards the winner's enclosure, that previously out-of-bounds haven, I had a mental picture of my Mum and Dad watching, back home in Ireland. I fancy my grin became even wider at that moment.

Business, as I had quickly learned, was business whether in victory or defeat and I wasted no time asking the Major where and when he might consider running Alvaro again. Presumptuous, maybe, but even at that age it was very plain to me that you get nothing in this game without asking. Fortunately, the Major was aleady thinking along similar lines and, anxious to cash in while the horse was in good heart, not to mention being well handicapped, he said I could ride him again in a two-mile race six days later, this time at Newmarket.

This was not a restricted apprentices' event. Indeed, my win at Epsom was the first and last time I ever rode in an apprentices' race, not because the opportunities did not arise but because Frenchie was adamant that I must keep my claim as long as possible for the valuable handicaps, in which I might, he insisted, soon be in demand. Frenchie, you see, had never lost faith in me and when, after that first winner, I had time to be pleased for anyone other than myself, I was truly delighted for him.

So it was next stop Newmarket, and a continuation of the trend whereby the Major placed Alvaro in handicaps on the major courses. He had next to no weight and I remember the Major, who loved a bet, saying afterwards that he had considered him a good thing at 100–30, even though this was roughly half the price he had been a week earlier at Epsom.

He certainly won like a good thing, this time by six lengths, and it made victory a whole lot sweeter to have Lester Piggott beaten into second place. Once again, the horse was given only a week's grace before being asked to run again but, in truth, this was never likely to inconvenience him. He won all his races cosily, doing only what was necessary to beat the others, and as such he did not take as much out of himself as most horses.

Win number three came at Kempton Park, again over two miles, and I rode him pretty much the same as I had in the two previous races, only this time he cantered home by eight lengths. As the winning sequence extended, the partnership of Alvaro and the young Irishman began to attract some favourable attention. Apart from the natural injection of confidence I don't suppose I was riding any better or worse than I had been during the interminable losing run, but everybody loves a winner and, as Frenchie had always promised would happen, I now heard that the Nicholsons' telephone had begun to ring pretty regularly with requests for my services. Frenchie, however, was not only loyal to his boys, he was also loyal to trainers who had supported them. There was, for instance, a day on which I could have ridden four horses at Folkestone but Frenchie turned them all away so that I could partner one for Major Pope at the other meeting.

One of the Major's great charms, and he had many, was his sanguine mood both before and after a race. In the parade ring he would seldom deliver any detailed instructions bar saying something like: 'Go out and enjoy yourself and make sure you give the horse a chance.' Afterwards, he would be much the same, win or lose, except that, during this golden spell, I only seemed to see him as someone with another winner in the bank.

Alvaro's run went on and on. At Salisbury, in a decent sort of handicap over a mile and three-quarters, he won unchallenged, starting odds-on. Then we went north to Doncaster where, with his customary absence of fuss or frills, he recorded his fifth win in twenty-nine days. A month earlier I had been wondering when I might at last shake off my maiden tag. Now, the fickleness of the game epitomised, I could do no wrong; that day at Doncaster I also won on Pheidippides for the Major, completing the first double of my career.

I doubt that there is a jockey riding who could not instantaneously tell you the name of his first winner, but I guess there are few who feel such an affinity as I do with Alvaro. He and the Major did not just give me one off the mark; they gave me a run of winners which got me going in a way I had begun to believe could never happen.

The sequence had to end, of course, but I wish it had been on another day. Mum and Dad had been keenly following my progress back home, and decided to fly over during June to coincide with another of Alvaro's runs. He was in the London Gold Cup on the now extinct Alexandra Palace course. I remember it was a night meeting and we were short-priced favourites but it turned out to be the first defeat we had suffered together – and it had to be with my folks watching!

In fact, the handicapper had now caught up with Alvaro and he was again beaten into second place on his next start at Newcastle. The Major wisely decided the horse had done enough and gave him a rest but, later in the summer, he joined some horses of David Nicholson's for a jaunt to Deauville. Away from Streatley, and the Major's ingenious electrical deterrents, he apparently began crib-biting and wind-sucking again. On the racecourse, he simply did not look the same horse who had won six races with such ease.

The link between the Major and myself was now quite a strong one and I would often be required to ride work for him. This meant an overnight stop and I would be quite happy to stay in his lads' hostel. I don't suppose that I ever went there without some cautionary words from Frenchie ringing in my ears, to the effect that I would not be doing my job properly if I was not in bed by a certain time and that he did not want to hear of me going into local pubs. There was, as he well knew, very little danger of it, not because I didn't want to go out with the other lads but because he made sure I never had the money to do so. By this time, however, things were going well and I was aware that Frenchie's regime was designed for my future good and I intended to do nothing to jeopardise it.

During that 1969 season, nine of my twenty-nine winners were for Major Pope. Aside from the success, however, he was responsible for increasing my racing education by involving me in the planning for his horses and the tactics when they ran. He would always listen to what I had to say and, on occasions, he would act on it. The most notable occasion was before the Royal Ascot meeting that June, when I was to ride my first big-race winner.

To Be a Champion

The Major had bought a horse called Sky Rocket at the Newmarket Sales. His original hope had been that the horse would go jumping, but it was clear from a couple of abortive schooling sessions that Sky Rocket was not the hurdling type. I finished second on him at Alexandra Palace in April and I think it was then that the Major first thought we might have a horse for the Wokingham at the royal meeting.

Sky Rocket was owned by the Major's father and I think there was a bit of family money on him at Ascot in what is all too often a pin-sticker's race, a cavalry charge of thirty 'good things' in which all manner of trouble can occur in running.

It was because of this, and because we had been drawn one, right over on the stands side, that I suggested to the Major the night before the race that I should bounce Sky Rocket out and try to make all. I think he had other plans at first, but he listened and agreed. The plan duly worked, nothing got to us and we won by three-quarters of a length at 20–1.

I don't believe I was adversely affected by sudden success. Partly, this was because I had had to wait for it so long, but largely it was down to my training with Frenchie – training not as a jockey but as a person. He had first taught me how to cope with failure and now he was equally shrewd about keeping my feet firmly on the ground amid success. It was not that difficult. The taste of a few winners was sweet but I had no thoughts in my head other than maintaining my progress and building on the start.

It would be quite wrong to suggest that 1969 was an endless gravy train. There were still many more losers than winners. There was one injury scare, when I escaped relatively unharmed after being brought down in the thick of flying hooves during a seven-furlong handicap. And, the biggest blot on the horizon: there was a constant weight problem to conquer.

Quite simply, I was too fat. It was not that I over-indulged – Frenchie pretty much saw to that – so much as the fundamental fact that I was at an age when my body was growing more quickly than I would have liked. I had to eat for strength and there was no convenient sauna on hand to sweat off the excess poundage.

Mondays were always the worst. I enjoyed my Sunday lunch and, although I did not compound the crime by drinking quantities of beer (fortunately, I never developed a taste for it), it meant that my weight would often shoot up several pounds between riding on a Saturday and turning up for work on the Monday morning.

One Monday, I had been booked to ride for Major Nelson. The horse obviously had a decent chance but I was required to do very light – with my claim, I was due to carry 6st. 7lb. To my horror, I was nine pounds overweight and, to make matters infinitely worse, I was beaten a head. I got a good bollocking from Major Nelson, but worse was to come because he then got on the phone to Frenchie, who really went for me.

This was always likely to be a passing phase, but one event which helped, in that it gave me stability and peace of mind, quite apart from regular nutritious food, was a change of digs.

I had spent eighteen months in my first lodgings in Cheltenham. They were cold and miserable and, because the food was bad, it doubtless encouraged me to seek better, additional grub elsewhere. This meant that I began to eat the wrong food; it also meant that the ten-bob note which Frenchie handed over each week did not go very far.

The chance to move was simply a stroke of luck. Frenchie's daughter was two years older than I and, being of similar age, we had got to know each other reasonably well. I had told her more than once that my digs were bad and, one day, she mentioned that her first husband (they were now divorced) lived next door to a dear old couple called Wilson. Having checked that I would be interested, she went to see them on my behalf and, sure enough, they said they would be happy to have me as a lodger.

The Wilsons, George and Ann, lived in a council house in Prestbury. It may have been nothing grand but, to me, it was special because, for the first time since I had come to England, I felt as if I had a proper home. Right from the start, they made me feel that their home was mine, and the difference it made to me is hard to quantify.

I was approaching eighteen when I moved in with the Wilsons. I had just bought my first car, nothing flash but reliable, and each morning, when I went outside to start the working day, I would find that it was ready to drive away, no matter how bad the weather. When, in the winter, the weather turned nasty and going to Frenchie's yard loomed as a chore without even the lure of the afternoon racing to anticipate, the process was always smoothed by George having tended the car.

The windows would be defrosted and wiped clean, the heater would be on and the engine running. The bodywork would have been given a polish so that, even on dank, dirty days it looked spanking new. And, as a finishing touch, it would be pointing the right way!

Each evening, no matter what time I came home, dinner would be on a tray and on my lap within ten minutes. Good food, too. They were a marvellous couple and I was so lucky that they took to me and my career immediately, for until then they had not had the slightest interest in horseracing.

Before my arrival, I would wager that the Wilsons had never taken a racing newspaper in their lives and that their knowledge of the game was scant at best. Yet within a few weeks of my moving in, George had ordered *The Sporting Life* – and not just for my benefit. He began to study each day's racing programme to see what my prospects were, and in time they both developed an animated interest. I believe they loved it all, because it gave them something new in their lives, and as they became more involved they would both keep reassuring me that I would make it to the top. They had virtually adopted me for their own and, so far as I was concerned, this was fine. They looked after me wonderfully well, and very quickly I developed a deep affection for them both which stretched beyond the landlord-tenant relationship.

The time came when I was in a position to buy a property of my own for the first time, but it did not mean I had any desire to say goodbye to them. By then, we had been together for almost four years and when I asked them to move in with me, in the Prestbury house I had bought quite close to Frenchie's yard, I was genuinely delighted when they agreed.

It was to be a lasting relationship. Although Ann considered my current home in Buckinghamshire just too far for her to move at her age, she still phones me once a week from her daughter's house, where she now lives, and I swear she watches every race I ride on television and must assuredly bore her daughter to death with racing talk.

In all, Ann was my housekeeper for fifteen years, and was with me through some wonderfully successful years. George would love to have shared them but, tragically, he did not live long enough.

Having bought that first house in Prestbury, in the winter of

1973–74, I went to Hong Kong to ride for a few months. George by now was old and frail, but not too ill to be excited by what was happening, and it was arranged that he and Ann would move into the house in December and have it ready for my return in the spring.

On the moving day, George was evidently like a small boy with a new toy. He walked up the path into the house which was to be his new home as well as mine, and instantly dropped dead in the kitchen from a heart attack. I believe he died happy, but he never got to live in the house and he never got to see me achieve the success that, loyally to the point of embarrassment, he had always sworn I would achieve. The following summer, I became champion jockey for the first time, and more than a bit of the title was dedicated to George.

4

DASHING AND CLASHING: The Quest for Speed on Both Road and Track Brings Brushes with Authority

In September 1972, on the day my apprenticeship ended, I was completing the comfortable routine I had followed so many times before. Mrs Nicholson was driving us home from the races and Frenchie was in the passenger seat. I can't honestly remember how my rides had gone that day but I have a vivid recall of the exchange which took place when, as usual, I was dropped off at my Prestbury digs, the Wilsons' house.

Frenchie, as was his habit, threw a farewell over his shoulder and added: 'Don't be late in the morning, boy.' I had no idea whether or not he had forgotten that it was my coming-out day or whether he simply assumed that things would carry on as before, but, with the freedom going to my head, I could not resist replying: 'I don't think I'll be in in the morning, guv'nor.'

Sharply, and gruffly, Frenchie retorted, 'What d'you mean, you won't be in?'

'I finished my apprenticeship today,' I explained, adding the 'guv'nor' which always would come naturally to me where Frenchie was concerned.

There was a pause, an unusually long one for this man, before he said in more conciliatory fashion, 'Well, you might as well come up and ride out every day until the end of the season.'

I smiled. It was what I had hoped and intended to do anyway, so long as the Nicholsons did not throw me out. But it had felt good to say what I did, to establish an independence in my own head, if nowhere else. There was not the slightest thought of upsetting the old man, which in any case was pretty hard, because by now my affection and admiration for him knew few bounds.

I had just been a boy, a basically uneducated boy with a wild vision of what he wanted from life, and I had come to work for a master. The usual way would have been to leave him and move on, once the apprenticeship was over, but I did not do that and neither did I want to. It was a measure of what I felt for the man, and what I knew for a fact he had taught me, that I stayed on and he became my manager. When he fell ill, the illness which led to his shockingly sad death in 1984, Mrs Nicholson took over and it was only when her health, too, prevented her from doing the job, especially the driving, that Terry became my manager. He, like me, had learned a great deal from Frenchie and Diana.

Those final years at Frenchie's stables in Lake Street were the years which fully established me as a jockey with a future, rather than one of the many unfortunate lads who attracts great attention as a talented apprentice and then, through problems of weight, discipline or simply ill-luck, disappears into obscurity.

Frenchie was as determined as I was that this should not happen to me, but even his constant advice and attention could not avert every mishap. The early seventies might have been good years but they were also hairy ones, for all too often I was in trouble with the stewards of the racecourses and what one might call the stewards of the roads, the police.

Twenty years on, I am still not immune from the type of racing incidents which bring suspensions – no jockey is – but there is a subtle difference. In those early years I was sometimes so high on ambition, and will to win, that my riding became irresponsible, even reckless. The same was, to some extent, true of my car driving.

It was a rule of the Nicholsons that none of their boys could have his own car for the first couple of years of his time. When I was finally allowed one, it was nothing very great but when the time came that I could afford something better, the trouble started. I bought a big, new Mercedes and it happened to coincide with the period in which I had begun to drive myself to the races more often than not.

Within a fairly short spell, I picked up two six-month bans for speeding. The worst was still to come. It was around this time that I first started riding in Europe on Sundays, a perk which has long since grown to be a habit. One Sunday I was due in Germany and had a morning flight booked out of Heathrow Airport.

To Be a Champion

For one reason or another I was late setting off from Prestbury and it was obvious I had to put my foot down if I was to catch the plane. There was very little traffic about, the Datsun 260Z felt good and we were soon flying along the A40 out of Cheltenham. A short way past the village of Northleach I noticed in my rear-view mirror that I had unwelcome company – or, at least, would-be company. A police car was chasing at a respectful distance.

At moments such as this, you either give up and come quietly or you pretend not to notice and plough on regardless. With my heart beating a little quicker, I kept my foot on the accelerator and reached Oxford in what may have been a track record time. The police car had been unable to make any impression on my lead but, heading out of Oxford towards London, I got caught at a red light. That was the end of that, or so I thought. The police, however, had other ideas.

Initially, they were unwilling to accept that I was simply someone driving his car too fast. They plainly did not believe it was my car at all. I looked younger than my years and they had marked me down as a joyrider. One of the policemen was decidedly unfriendly, running back from the patrol car and yelling: 'Get out of there.' I did as he commanded and stood self-consciously on the side of the road while they made their suspicions clear.

Although I told them repeatedly that it was my car, they insisted on phoning the licensing office in Swansea to check. Then, perhaps understandably riled by the long chase, they searched every inch of the car and its boot – for what, I have no idea – while I vainly pleaded the case that I had to ride in Germany in a few hours.

Finally, grudgingly, they let me go. They added that I could not expect much leniency from the courts as they would be reporting that they had pursued me at 140 miles per hour and been unable to peg me back! I drove on knowing that my time behind the wheel was strictly borrowed but, with an anxious glance at the car-clock, I weighed up my prospects of catching that plane and knew there was nothing for it. I put my foot down again, and prayed.

I made it to Germany but the court, as I feared, was not prepared to consider that an extenuating circumstance. With my previous record, I could hardly have expected otherwise. They banned me for a year this time and I have seldom driven to the races since Terry came to work for me full-time, the arrangement which still exists happily today.

If, however, I was fortunate to have a ready solution to my driving excesses, the same was not true when it came to race-riding. I picked up my first suspension in 1970, at the age of eighteen, and they did not stop coming. There were times when I felt the stewards were looking for me, and others when I thought certain jockeys were using me as a convenient fall-guy, but in general I could have few complaints. I invariably knew I was guilty, indeed sensed as much as soon as the incident took place, but whatever I did, I did it instinctively, and for the sole purpose of trying to win races.

The problem, of course, was that I was trying too hard. Tiny gaps might fleetingly appear in the heat of a race and I would go for them, without properly assessing (a) whether I was on a horse with the speed to get there, or (b) what grief my manoeuvre might cause other jockeys and horses. There was nothing malicious in my riding and I never set out to hurt another rider. It was simply that I wanted every horse I rode to win and that is not possible even with the good horses I ride nowadays; it was a hopeless obsession on some of the slow creatures I rode twenty years ago.

Most apprentices go through this phase to some degree but I would admit that probably very few take it to the extremes I did. Frenchie ticked me off about it time after time, and not only on the occasions when I had attracted the stewards' attention. He would talk me through my mistakes in great detail but I am afraid it made no difference. Out on the track, I was not the same person who had listened to his words, absorbing the lessons and agreeing to act upon them. I was someone different, someone who had to win. If I was in trouble during a race and I saw a gap appear, I would go for it instinctively, thinking nothing of the risks until it was too late.

They say that Lester was pretty similar in his early days, though I only have other people's word for that. I can believe it, because he, like me, has always been consumed by winning, and he, like me, must have made himself some enemies in the weighing-room over it.

Most senior jockeys treated my uninhibited style with nothing more than light-hearted concern. Joe Mercer, one of the great stylists, nicknamed me 'Polyfilla', because I was always filling the cracks. But there were others, who may primarily have been jealous of the amount of winners I was riding, who became openly hostile; there were even a few who tried to turn my reputation to their advantage, painting me as the villain in pieces where I had played little, if any, part.

In 1970, which, after all, was only my third full season, I would certainly have been champion apprentice but for receiving two seven-day bans. I finished up riding fifty-seven winners, a tally with which I should have been unreservedly delighted but for the fact that Ian Balding's apprentice, Philip Waldron, rode fifty-nine. It had been an intense but friendly duel between us all season. Phil was a good friend and a very good young rider. Later, his career was to epitomise the fact that one bad decision can ruin you; he was going well and took up a retainer to ride all the horses owned by the Esal group, a conglomerate involved, among other things, in bookmaking. Esal went bust in quite unpleasant circumstances and Phil headed to Hong Kong, where he is still riding with some success now. He could, with different allegiances at a crucial time, have become a top rider in Britain and, back in 1970, nothing looked more certain.

The season had begun well for me and, it must be said, quite smoothly. In April, at the same Liverpool meeting at which I had made my debut two years earlier, I rode a double and, to my great pleasure, both were for Frenchie's son, David. In June I won the London Gold Cup at Alexandra Palace, the race in which Alvaro had met his match the previous season. Eleven days later I won again on the same horse, Angarrick, in the William Hill Handicap. This was run at Ayr, the first time I had ridden in Scotland and the first of several forays north of the border which the Nicholsons, my faithful drivers and mentors, were to undertake for me that summer.

Things were going famously, but my come-uppance was in wait. Chepstow is one of the loveliest courses we flat jockeys ride, but on a Friday afternoon late in June its appeal was utterly lost on me. The day began badly and got unspeakably worse.

The opening race was a two-year-old maiden and the frustration of being beaten by a short-head was compounded by the fact that the winner was ridden by Philip Waldron. I had

[43]

another, unplaced ride and then climbed aboard a horse called Juicy Lucy for a six-furlong handicap. I quietly fancied my mount but the hot favourite was Dublin Decision, ridden by David Yates, himself a former champion apprentice.

Two furlongs out I was still in with a squeak but wanted to get my horse over to the rails for a final challenge. In moving across much too sharply, I brought down Dublin Decision. Yates was obviously lucky to get up unscathed and I did not even have the minor satisfaction of winning – I finished second – before the inevitable summons to the Stewards' Room started me on what was to become a familiarly unwelcome ritual. On viewing the evidence of the patrol film I knew I was in hot water and the stewards held the opinion that I was entirely to blame for the mid-race accident. They stood me down for seven days, starting the following Monday, and although I had time to win the Northumberland Plate on the Saturday, it was a chronically impatient young Eddery who kicked his heels into July while potential winners were partnered by other riders and Waldron booted home one or two more of his own.

In time I came to look upon it as a lesson harshly learned, which was phlegmatic if, as it turned out, presumptuous, and as the winners began to flow again as soon as the suspension ended, I just got on with the day-to-day business. But before the season ended I was to experience two more days of wildly extreme emotion.

They came within five days of each other, which meant that I had hardly come down to earth from one when I was buried by the other. The first, which still seems to me today one of my better achievements, was the riding of five winners in an afternoon. These came from my seven rides on the Saturday afternoon card at Haydock Park on August 22nd and the irony is that, while the Nicholsons were driving me up to the Lancashire course that morning, I remember thinking I would do well to come away with just one winner.

I was still only eighteen and this was apparently the first time that an apprentice had ever ridden five on a card. But it was just one of those magical days when everything turns to gold dust. I won two by the minimum short-head and, with four in the bag, went out to ride one for Frenchie, thinking it had no chance. It won easily, and that one gave me more pleasure than anything. I travelled home on Cloud 9, dumbfounded by it all.

The following Thursday, on the seaside track at Brighton, I collected another seven-day ban for 'causing severe interference' on a horse of Major Pope's called Yellow Flash. This was not as blatant a case as that at Chepstow and there were grounds for thinking the stewards had been harsh. But new and stricter guidelines relating to race discipline were in force that year and it is possible they felt that, with my previous record, they were obliged to make an example of me.

This second ban allowed Phil Waldron to take the apprentices' title. It was a season which, for me, ended with slight disappointment and also a certain apprehension, for in October, I lost my weight claim. This is frequently the watershed for a young jockey, for no longer are they saleable to trainers on the basis that they can claim valuable poundage in handicap races. Although I remained an apprentice I was now riding on equal terms with Piggott, Murray, Carson and the other big names of the day.

As it turned out, I need not have worried. Partly, perhaps, through the impression I had made over the preceding two years, but also through the continuing association with Frenchie, which seemed to infuse trainers with confidence, the bookings never let up. Quite the opposite, indeed, for in 1971 I had 655 rides, a figure exceeded by only two jockeys in the country. I also won the apprentice title this time, leaving my old adversary Waldron seven behind when I finished the year with seventy-one winners.

If this was a satisfactory year, that was not least because I had avoided trouble with the stewards. I could not say the same in 1972 but, nonetheless, it was a momentous season, for I won the Ascot Gold Cup and rode in my first Derby.

Both these rides were for a Newmarket trainer named Geoffrey Barling, who retired a year later but, for a brief few seasons, supported me loyally. He was then one of the top trainers in Newmarket, with a lot of good two-year-olds in his yard, and it was a feather in my cap when he phoned Frenchie and said he would like to take me on. For that 1972 season there was an unwritten agreement that Geoffrey should have first claim on me, and it worked very well.

Geoffrey was a large, well-bred and gentle man, known locally as the 'Vicar of Newmarket'. I liked him a lot. He had a huge Bentley, the lap of luxury to me, and as we used to go racing together quite often, I would always look forward to travelling with him in style. The trouble was, I could never keep awake. Geoffrey would sit in front with his chauffeur and I would fall asleep immediately, in the vast and comfortable back seats. Geoffrey was always going on to me about it and, quite rightly, pointing out that I would never learn the routes to racecourses if I insisted on sleeping all the way.

The Derby ride was a huge thrill. We went to Epsom in the Bentley and the atmosphere was everything I had always dreamed of. The race, too, promised to be a dream, if only briefly. It was agreed that I should try to make all the running on Geoffrey's horse, Pentland Firth, and we did so for much of the race. Roberto and Rheingold eventually swept past for their epic battle, finally decided by a mere short-head, but my fellow stayed on to finish third and that was more, much more, than I could realistically have hoped for, from a 30–1 shot.

By then, however, I had fallen foul of the stewards again, and picked up yet another seven-day ban. I could have no complaints whatever, because my 'crime', at Chester, was probably the most blatant and unforgivable thing I have done on any racecourse, and it came about because I got mad with my old idol, Lester Piggott.

We were riding in the May meeting at Chester, where the course is as tight as any in the country and the unwary rider can find himself hopelessly boxed in. The Chester Cup is a stayers' race and, at the final sharp turn into the straight, I still had a chance on a horse named Pirate Glen. The problem was that Lester was immediately on my outside and making life deliberately difficult by allowing his mount to hang into mine, without actually making contact.

I kept trying to ease him out to give me room to challenge the leaders but, out of the corner of that famous mouth, Lester just said: 'You're not coming out.' Finally, my volatile temper blew completely and I resorted to a barging match to get the desired position. I finished a close second but the familiar call was inevitable, and so was the fact that I received no help at all from Lester.

As the film was shown, Lester's voice piped through. 'It's his fault, innit . . . Look at him . . . ' and so it went on. Lester was right, of course. He had taught me a lesson. Nowadays, in similar tight spots and with a rider of his stature keeping me in, I would be a shade more subtle. In 1972, I didn't give a damn.

If Lester played cunningly on my bad reputation, I was soon to encounter an example of something more unscrupulous when, following a particularly rough race at Newbury in June, I was referred to the Jockey Club at Portman Square on the most serious charge of dangerous riding. For once, I was convinced of my innocence, but there was a difference between my own conviction and those of the senior stewards, who were unlikely to be favourably swayed, considering the list of prior offences against my name.

It had been a race of chaotic events in which two horses came down, their jockeys, Brian Taylor and Geoff Baxter, both suffering injuries. Willie Carson was first past the post but no sooner were we back in the weighing-room than an objection was lodged by Geoff Lewis, who rode the runner-up. He accused Willie of hitting his horse across the head.

The stewards naturally inquired into all aspects of the race and there was a queue of jockeys waiting to be interviewed. I was one, after finishing fifth, and the Australian, Ron Hutchinson, was another. To my amazement, the stewards did not even view the film but they listened to Hutchinson, who told them: 'Little Paddy did it, he got Geoff Baxter on the floor.'

I was, frankly, in dread of the appointment at Portman Square. If they had found me guilty I could have been stood down for a long while, my name inevitably tarnished. Frenchie came with me to the hearing and, although he was not there, Ron Hutchinson had sent a letter, again implicating me.

This time, of course, the patrol film of the race was shown, several times, and to my relief it vindicated me completely, showing that my mount had been nowhere near Baxter's horse when he came down. I was cleared of the charge and free to ride at the Royal Asoct meeting where, ironically, I won the Gold Cup in the Stewards' Room!

Erimo Hawk, a thoroughly good stayer of Geoffrey Barling's who also went on to win at Goodwood, was beaten a head by the odds-on favourite, Rock Roi, but that horse had hung badly into mine in the closing stages and the placings were rapidly reversed at the inquiry without us needing to object.

It seems this was a year of irony and coincidence, for Rock Roi was trained by Peter Walwyn, very much the man of the moment, and ridden by his stable jockey, the tough man from Glasgow's Gorbals, Duncan Keith. It was no secret within racing that Duncan had serious weight problems and that, in trying to conquer them, he suffered bouts of ill-health. Finally, late in that 1972 season, he was forced to give up the battle and the most coveted job in flat racing was on the market.

I thought no more about it. I was going well, happy with my lot and just coming out of a successful apprenticeship. It did not occur to me that I would be in the running, and it was the farthest thing from my mind when, out of the blue, Frenchie phoned one Sunday morning and asked me to come up to the house for lunch. I couldn't believe this, because it was the first time he had had me to lunch in my four years at Cheltenham, but I put it down to some unspoken celebration of my passing-out.

I was wrong. After lunch, Frenchie took me through to his lovely old snooker room and, although I had never played in my life, insisted that we should have a game.

It was obvious that he had something to say, but he took some time to say it. Finally, he began by asking: 'If you had the chance, which trainer would you most like to ride for?'

I did not have to think long. 'The way things are, it would have to be Peter Walwyn,' I replied, still not catching on.

'That's funny,' said Frenchie, now quite enjoying himself. 'You've got the job there as from next season.'

Peter had apparently telephoned Frenchie, making the approach in the correct way, and terms had pretty much been agreed. I could barely believe it, but I was about to embark on eight years which I still consider among the happiest of my career.

5

PETER WALWYN: A Valued Association with Some Memorable Moments

In the world of the jockey, reliant as it is on the nature of often fickle owners and trainers, doors can open and close with baffling regularity. But when I became Peter Walwyn's first jockey, I felt immediately that the biggest, stiffest door of all had been thrown open. For the first time since I had set out on this precarious existence, I really believed I could become champion jockey. What I did not anticipate was that it would happen in only my second season with Peter at Lambourn

Perhaps we joined forces at a good time for both of us. My riding career had just begun to take off and Pete, who began training in the early 1960s, was the fastest-rising star in his field. He had more than 100 horses in his yard at Seven Barrows and very few of them were useless. In the first few years that we were together, the quality of the Walwyn horses simply got better and better. He provided the ammunition and I fired the bullets. It was a good team.

From the start, however, it was more than simply a clinical business arrangement. I quickly developed a great liking for Pete and, I like to think, he did for me. We got along well from day one and we remain great friends now. In the early days, at least, he always treated me like his own son.

Now this may not sound quite like the Peter Walwyn of popular racing legend, the tall, intimidating figure whose temper flared frequently and indiscriminately, and far be it from me to dismiss such perceptions of the man. Not for nothing, after all, was he known as Basil for his quite passable likeness to the manic hotelier of *Fawlty Towers*. Pete had a temper, all right, and I was witness to it several times. But in the eight years we were together, he never once lost his temper with me.

He could be at his most irascible around breakfast time, set off, maybe, by a mishap on the gallops, a sick horse or perhaps a slip-up in the secretary's office. I used to ride work for him every Tuesday and Friday and then stop on for breakfast afterwards. Often I would be having a cup of tea in the kitchen with Pete's wife Virginia, known to all as Bonk, and we would be creased up laughing at the sound of Pete ranting and raving in the office down the corridor. Then he would stride in on those enormously long legs, very Basil Fawltyish, bolt his breakfast and hare off again to berate some other poor miscreant.

I might at first have thought I was taking my life in my hands by following him into the office while the mood was upon him but I soon learned differently. Pete really was a classic example of all bark and no bite, and if I sat down with him and began a discussion on, say, the runners for the following day, he would quickly settle down and chat as if nothing had disturbed him at all.

The key to Pete was always his horses. He was not just involved with them, he was consumed by them. I believe he had put all his money into that yard and quite a bit more besides; its success was obviously materially vital to him. But he was never a material man in that starkly financial sense; far more than riches, he sought his contentment from winners. The big ones, of which there were quite a few in the mid-1970s, were certainly sweet but I often thought Pete derived just as much pleasure from winning a maiden race at Salisbury. A winner, no matter the grade or the opposition, made him visibly happy all over but, although I could sense his disappointment when he got beaten, he never publicly showed it.

With this craving for winners gnawing away at him, it would have been easy for Pete to turn on his jockey now and again. The man on top is, after all, a convenient scapegoat whether he has ridden a bad race or not. But he never took the cheap way out; indeed, he never openly blamed me for anything, even on the occasions when I might have deserved a rocket.

The best example of this I can give is with one of the worst, elementary race-riding errors I ever made, one which obliged me to make a hurried and undignified exit from Ripon racecourse one mid-summer evening.

To Be a Champion

I had a couple of rides early in the day at Brighton but Pete had this runner in the last at Ripon which looked a likely winner. She was a decent filly and it was certainly worth my while to get there and ride her. The owners were keen, too, and so a plane was laid on for me to fly between the two courses. My car would then be waiting for me up in Yorkshire.

The travel arrangements worked perfectly. The race went badly wrong. I gave the filly a confident ride, over-confident as it turned out, but she had outclassed her field and came to the front at the furlong pole, still on the bridle and with the race at her mercy.

The Ripon course goes into a dip at this point and, not wishing to give the filly a harder race than was necessary, I eased her down and stopped riding after one reassuring glance over my right shoulder. With the post looming, instinct told me to look the other way too, but it was too late. One had come on my left side, clear of the pack and with the jockey riding flat out. I galvanised myself and my filly for the final strides but the momentum had gone and I was touched off.

My first thought was that there could be a lynching in store for me. She had been a deservedly well-backed horse and I had got her beaten in the most transparently complacent fashion. The punters were not going to take kindly to it. My second thought was that Peter would not take kindly to it, either, but with my personal safety uppermost in my mind, I had to extricate myself from one dilemma at a time. Pete was not at the course; the miners were there in force. Sure enough, my welcome, back in the unsaddling enclosure, was hostile, verging on the menacing. I scuttled back into the weighing-room and changed as quickly as possible. Then, aware that there was a 'welcoming party' waiting for me at the front door, I climbed through the back window and ran to the car park, heaving a long sigh of relief as I nosed the car out into the anonymity of the traffic.

One problem solved, one to come. I pondered on how to tackle Peter and decided it was best done quickly. Better that I should tell him how the horse got beaten than that he should hear it from elsewhere.

Halfway down the M1, I pulled off and telephoned to Seven Barrows. Pete answered the phone, gruff as ever. His phone manner would not, in all honesty, have won him promotion in the Diplomatic Service. Undeterred, I launched into my account. I told it honestly, saying that I had been cruising on the filly but took things too easily and found myself caught napping. Pete listened in silence, then gave his judgement. 'I want bloody winners, that's all there is to it,' he said. Then he put the phone down.

As explosions go, it had been short, sharp and not very shocking. Best of all, it was then obviously forgotten, because when I rode work at Seven Barrows two days later, the subject was never mentioned. It had, though, not entirely been forgotten; Pete is too shrewd and ambitious a man to dismiss entirely such a defeat and he gently chastised me, in his own way, the next time I rode for him. As we stood in the parade ring and the bell sounded for jockeys to mount, Pete turned to me and said: 'Nice horse, this one. Have him handy . . . and don't look round.'

Loyalty was his strongest suit. There must be countless trainers who run down jockeys to their owners. There are many more who will abide totally by the owners' wishes when it comes to riding arrangements, for fear of losing their patronage. Not Peter. Once he had engaged me as first jockey he made it clear to everyone that I would ride their horses unless a clash of meetings prevented it.

Twice he displayed this loyalty to his jockey in circumstances which might have had another trainer compromising principles for expediency. In 1974, I missed the Irish Derby through suspension and Peter booked the French jockey, Yves Saint-Martin, to ride his horse, English Prince. With a variety of emotions from yours truly, the horse won as well as we had hoped he might, whereupon the owners, Mr and Mrs Hue-Williams, told Peter they wanted to keep the same jockey for English Prince's next race, at York. Pete refused. He went further, saying that if they would not agree to me riding the horse, then English Prince would have to be taken away. This was some show of support, because English Prince was just about the best three-year-old of his year. But there was a second occasion when Peter took such loyalty to the extreme.

Daniel Wildenstein, a millionaire whose horses cleaned up many big races around Europe in the early 1970s, then became a prized patron of the Walwyn yard. One of his horses at Seven Barrows was Buckskin, a good stayer, and I rode him in the Ascot

Gold Cup. When he was beaten, Wildenstein claimed that I was 'not man enough' for the horse and said he did not want me riding for him again. Peter's response was to tell him to take his horses away. Wildenstein did exactly that.

The bond between us must have been strong to support such drastic action but, in truth, it was a relationship which worked from the very first. I had already had a few rides for Peter when he offered me the job, but in those closing weeks of the 1972 season we linked up regularly and shared quite a number of winners. By the end of the year it was obvious to me that we were on the same wavelength and that this could prove to be a very special break for me.

We settled into a routine which seemed to suit us both. I was only expected two mornings a week at Seven Barrows but this did not mean that my contact with Peter and the yard was distant. Far from it. Each evening, whether I had been riding horses for him or not, I would phone him to chat about the yard and the imminent runners. It was never a brief conversation, because we shared a passion for the horses and a fascination for the means of planning their victories. Sometimes we would talk for an hour, while suppers went cold, but I don't suppose either of us realised it. We were living out a relationship as close, in its own way, as any courting couple, because his aims were mine and mine were his. We never argued as such, although some competitive debates would often develop, but by the end of our evening call we would always have mapped out some short-term futures and pondered the highs and lows of the day gone by. It must be said that we both enjoyed the calls because, for each of us, the horses were very much more than simply a means to make a living.

Working with such a kindred spirit was a blessing at that time because I was aware that I was not universally popular among the blokes I spent each day with. To be quite honest, there were jockeys who openly resented me, not only because I was getting plenty of good rides and plenty of winners but because my style was altogether too aggressive for them. Looking back, I can at least half see their point.

I was still too pushy, too eager to turn every ride into a winner. It was a good fault, perhaps, if one which was making me a high-risk property. But, young and confident as I was, it really didn't bother me. I got a lot of jocks messing me about during a race, tightening me up and basically challenging me to cause an incident. It was very seldom the senior jockeys who got involved in this, though, because whereas I was at an age and of a disposition where I could not have given a toss if I had fallen during a race, the older guys certainly had a bit more concern for self-preservation. This, inevitably, made them slightly wary of me.

Although others may dispute it, I was also maturing as a rider. The roughest edges were disappearing and I was not quite the desperado of old. To a large extent, this was because I neither needed to be nor could afford to be. My retainer with Peter Walwyn meant I was earning proper money for the first time; I had a string of valuable, talented horses to ride. I would have had to be horribly naive and irresponsible to jeopardise all that for the sake of a blown fuse in mid-race.

My first full season at Seven Barrows was 1973 and I finished up with 119 winners. This was only good enough to place me third in the jockeys' table but, as the names ahead of me were Carson and Piggott, and as I was only just twenty-one, it was a year of eye-opening realisation. I was no longer the promising kid let loose among the big boys. I was now one of them, and I had to survive by their rules and on equal terms.

When the following season began, the bookmakers offered the usual antepost odds on the jockeys' title. Willie was odds-on favourite, followed by Lester. I was an 8–1 chance. In hindsight, that may seem to have been a very generous price but, at the time, I encouraged nobody to take it. Instead, I openly suggested that it was no value at all and that I would have to wait a bit longer yet to break the Carson–Piggott monopoly.

It was to prove a momentous season, though, and not only because of the championship. Off the mark with a winner on the second day of action, I felt as if I was on a relentless rollercoaster. There were a few occasions when it seemed I might fall off but it was a year in which so much went right that the occasional setback could be taken in my stride.

I was not the only new champion in 1974. Peter Walwyn won the trainers' title for the first time and that gave me enormous satisfaction. Together we also took a classic, my first, and we very nearly won two with the same filly, Louis Freedman's Polygamy.

To Be a Champion

Louis was one of my favourite owners, such a nice guy, and we had all been very optimistic that the 1,000 Guineas might come our way. Polygamy had been a very successful two-year-old, winning three times at Newmarket and finishing a good fourth at Longchamp on the day that Lester won the Arc on Rheingold. Naturally, we had the Guineas in mind for her and after she had trounced the opposition at Ascot in her first run of 1974 she was made favourite.

I couldn't argue with that because, from what I had seen, she was the best around. She had her lazy streaks but she lacked nothing in ability, and when it came to Guineas day I was pretty confident.

We got in a little bit of trouble in running, which didn't help, but we still hit the front when I wanted to and although Joe Mercer came upsides on the Queen's filly, Highclere, I would have sworn we were still in front at the post. The photograph told a different tale but I had to study the print before I could really believe we had been beaten and that I was still awaiting that first classic winner.

I did not have to wait long. Polygamy started favourite for the Oaks, too, and this time she did win, and whilst I felt we were slightly unfortunate to get beaten at Newmarket, I also realised the Epsom win had a little luck about it.

Willie was riding Dibidale for Barry Hills and, before the race, they would not hear of defeat. They might well have beaten me, too, because I sensed Willie cruising upsides me a furlong out and thought, 'Oh no, we're going to miss out again.' He really was cantering. What I did not know was that Willie had felt his saddle slipping a couple of furlongs earlier and suddenly, as he looked down, it had gone right under the filly. He did amazingly well, getting his feet out of the irons and riding her bareback, cowboy style. Even in this ungainly pose, Dibidale finished third, close up behind me, but because a leadcloth had slipped out she was disqualified.

At the time I felt that Polygamy was such a game filly that we might have won anyway, but when we went to The Curragh for the Irish Oaks, and Dibidale beat me easily, I had to revise my view. Polygamy never raced again, and if she was a slightly lucky classic winner she had no luck in later life, dying at stud before she could produce. It must have been a terrible blow for Louis

Freedman, who continued to be one of Peter's most loyal patrons for some years.

My other big winner that season came in the Eclipse, at Sandown, and if I say it was unexpected I am guilty of gross understatement. I had taken the ride on a horse called Coup de Feu only because I had nothing else in the race. I also liked his trainer, Duncan Sasse, who was only about my own age and had just set himself up with a few horses at Lambourn. He was really enthusiastic about everything, but I can remember laughing when he tried to convince me that his horse had a decent chance. I had looked up his form and he had been beaten in an apprentice race at Wolverhampton, not quite what is usually needed for one of the toughest all-aged races in the calendar.

Coup de Feu went off at 33–1 and that was not a case of the bookies being over-generous. But I bounced him out, turned into the straight in second place and cantering, and suddenly it dawned on me that Duncan's optimism was not misplaced after all. He simply bolted in and, although he never won another race, he gave Duncan a great start and gave me a surprise bonus.

At this stage, the title battle was in full swing and, although I did not get to ride for him very often, Duncan Sasse was to have a part to play even as the curtain came down on it. He and Coup de Feu also had a walk-on part in one of the most controversial races of this or any other season, for they were promoted from sixth to third place in the first event at Royal Ascot, the Queen Anne Stakes. Their unparalleled elevation was due to the sensational stewards' decision to disqualify the first three horses home. It was the first time in racing history that such action had been taken and, needless to say, I was one of the three.

Greville Starkey and I, together with an Australian named Micky Goreham, were each suspended for four days for 'careless and improper riding' after one of the roughest finishes to a race I have ever been involved in. The three of us were battling it out – Greville riding Confusion, for Denys Smith, on the outside, Goreham in the middle and myself on the rail, riding a big, black horse, name of Gloss. We came together inside the final furlong, Greville leaning in and Goreham's horse shoving him away before coming back to tighten me up against the rail. In one of those moments of mad instinct, I pushed Goreham away with my arm and immediately knew I was for the high jump.

To Be a Champion

All of this must have been transparent from the stands. It was certainly obvious to at least one of the jocks behind us because as we flashed past the post, cursing and swearing at each other and at ourselves, another drama was developing. Willie should have been fourth but he was not sufficiently alive to what had gone on and he dropped his hands before the post, allowing Brian Taylor, on an Italian grey called Brook, to get up on the line. As we pulled up Brian was grinning gleefully, and called across: 'You three will go down – I'll get the race.'

He was right and, in all honesty, so were the stewards. When I went into the inquiry it seemed all too improbable that they would disqualify all three of us, however, and although I was so resigned to my fate that I tried hard not to look at the film, I fully expected one of the others to keep the race.

As Greville had initially been first past the post on the aptly-named Confusion, the newspapers did not have to think too hard for their headlines the following morning. If this was a blow for me, however – and, as it meant I missed the winning ride in the Irish Derby I certainly didn't welcome it – it was one I could quickly overcome. The winners were still flowing, those headlines were generally being kind to me and one newspaper even described me as 'Britain's most eligible bachelor', which was one title for which I had never expected to be in the running.

The other title, the jockeys' championship, was not won without an epic head-to-head, which dominated the closing weeks of the season and attracted interest, I think, even among people who would never normally follow racing at all. The reason is that the protagonists were 'good old Lester', the punters' pal and housewives' favourite, and a young and previously unconsidered whipper-snapper from Ireland. It made for good newspaper copy, good television footage – and they milked it for all it was worth.

Although Willie had been most people's idea of the champion, he had trailed both Lester and I all season and, as we came into the last month or so, the only other jockey with a prayer of catching us was Eddie Hide, who did virtually all his riding in the north and had the pick of a number of their biggest yards up there.

At the end of August I was past 100 winners, for the second successive year, but still six winners behind Lester. Peter's yard had suffered a fleeting attack of equine virus and he had closed down for a week or so, which had slowed the flow of winners, but on the plus side I, or so I kept hearing, was half-a-stone lighter than Lester and able to get on some decent, well-weighted handicappers that he could not ride.

I must say I never quite saw it so rosily. All I could see was the old fella riding pretty much anything he wanted to ride. His network of contacts was immense and, although he would regularly infuriate trainers by keeping them waiting while he weighed up various options for a race, he always got away with it because he was so very good. It was beyond my wildest boyhood dreams to be involved in a championship battle with Lester, and it was a long time before I finally convinced myself that I could win it.

People often asked me what was said between us when we met each day in the weighing-room, and at the end of each meeting when the title scoreboard might have undergone yet another swing. The answer, which seemed to surprise everyone, is very little. We hardly spoke at all.

Lester would usually change in another part of the weighing-room, or even in a separate room, and although he was never openly unfriendly, he never went out of his way to speak to me either. I might get a muttered 'Good morning', or a grudging 'Well done' after a winner, but discussing where we stood in the championship race was anathema to him. At that stage, he was poker-faced and unsmiling; almost, it seemed to me, as if he was playing a part, living up to his image and reputation.

Even though we were now colleagues and rivals, scrapping for a title on equal terms, in my mind I still set Lester on a pedestal. He was the greatest, so far as I was concerned, and I still closely studied his riding to the point of copying some of his moves and tactics. Because of this, because he was a legend and I was a young pretender, I did not think it was my place to start a conversation with him. I waited for him to make the move and, I suppose, I waited at least five years.

Lester has never been above a little psychology to help his cause and, during those weeks, he would remain totally deadpan and tell anyone who asked – including newspaper and television reporters – that he would beat me. I preferred to be gently non-committal and it was only as we entered the final week of the season that I began to think even Lester, who could do almost anything, now had his work cut out.

He had kept coming at me, with doubles and trebles, each time I had nudged a few winners ahead. But with one day's racing left, I had a lead of four. Haydock traditionally staged the final meeting in those days, and as I anxiously scanned the declarations I saw that Lester had five fancied rides. It occurred to me, irrationally but inevitably, that I had ridden five winners at Haydock two years earlier. If I could do it, then so could Lester.

It was horrible weather, I remember. Driving rain and heavy ground. Terry, who by now was driving me, steered through the wet roads around Manchester and we arrived to what was by now a familiar army of TV cameras and microphones. I tried to say the right things, tried to look relaxed, but in fact it was not until Lester's second ride of the day, when we both finished unplaced, that I accepted I had done it.

Lester finished the day without a winner and I rode the last winner of the season, one for my pal Duncan Sasse. Again, it had an appropriate name – Talk of the Town.

6

GRUNDY AND BUSTINO: A King George VI and Queen Elizabeth Diamond Stakes, still known as 'The Race of the Century'

A jockey is invariably remembered more for the great horse or horses he rode than for the number of winners. And so, although there must be people who can readily recall that in 1974 I became the youngest champion since the great Sir Gordon Richards half a century earlier, there are many more who will always associate me with 1975 and Grundy.

I am not sure that Grundy is the best horse I have ridden but I am pretty certain he won the greatest race I am ever likely to take part in. Ascot's King George VI and Queen Elizabeth Diamond Stakes, run on a steamily hot July day, will never be forgotten by most of those lucky enough to be present, plus many more watching on television. It will also never be forgotten by me or, I suspect, by Joe Mercer, who rode Bustino in that heart-stopping finish with Grundy which features pictorially in so many racing books and even rated a book to itself, the title of which was *The Race of the Century*, and I would not argue with that.

Like most top flat horses, Grundy had achieved a great deal in a relatively short space of time. Jumping horses can race for years, picking up their prizes along the way and attracting the affection and following of the racing public because they become an anticipated part of the annual routine. Very few flat horses can do that, simply because the breeding side of the sport demands that their active racing days are limited. Most of the best, the élite, will have only two seasons of racing, and Grundy was no exception. But in those two years he managed to achieve a rare affinity with his public. They loved his style, they loved his boundless courage; most of all, at least in the case of the habitual gamblers, they loved him because he usually won!

Grundy came into Peter Walwyn's yard in Lambourn after being bought at the Newmarket Yearling Sales. A bloodstock agent named Keith Freeman purchased him for £11,000, which seems an absolute bargain at today's inflated prices, and he went into training in the ownership of the Italian businessman, Dr Carlo Vittadini.

Matt McCormack, who, at the time, was Pete's assistant head lad, looked after Grundy and rode him most days and, although I had heard some of the lads around the yard speaking of this new horse with the white flashes on his head and the blond flash in his tail, it was not until I rode him on a work morning that I paid much attention. Even then, on the first morning I ever sat on him, Grundy struck me as potentially a bit special. In this instance, I was not wrong.

To back up my opinion, I elected to ride Grundy ahead of another very highly-rated two-year-old in our yard, No Alimony, when Pete ran them both in the same Ascot six-furlong race on July 26th, 1974. It was a great race for the stable as we finished first and second, but Grundy had won pretty much as he liked. He was impressive, all right, but I could hardly have imagined then that, twelve months on to the very day, he would be back at Ascot winning a King George.

He was entitled to run green on his first racecourse appearance, yet at Ascot, and throughout his unbeaten two-year-old career, he was an easy horse to ride, because he was tough and he had a turn of foot. You can ask for little more. He won his second race, at Kempton, with ridiculous ease, took the Champagne Stakes at Doncaster in September by a cosy half-length and then headed for the traditional end-of-season championship race for the year's best juveniles, the Dewhurst Stakes at Newmarket.

The Irish thought they had a pretty good contender in Steel Heart, trained by Dermot Weld. This horse had apparently cost a lot of money, at least £50,000 more than Grundy, but money does not always buy talent and I knew it would take something out of the top drawer to stop us. In the event, it was virtually a no-contest, Grundy taking up the running at the two-furlong pole and drawing away on the rise to win unchallenged by six lengths.

Now the excitement in our yard really was mounting. Grundy went off to winter quarters the clear favourite for the 1975 2,000 Guineas. Both Peter and I thought he merited the position, too, and his three-year-old programme was really something to dream about during my winter in Hong Kong. There are years when you finish a season believing you have only a very moderate crop of three-year-olds for the following campaign and they come out and surprise you; equally, there are years when you buzz with anticipation over a particular horse but he never lives up to your expectations. With Grundy, he was to exceed all our hopes and expectations, though not without an alarm or two along the way.

My private hopes for the horse can best be measured by the fact that I named a dog after him! Soon after the Dewhurst in 1974, I bought an Afghan pup. I had no idea what to call him but, Grundy being on my mind a fair bit at the time, I thought that was as good a name as any. Sadly, because I love having dogs around, I could not keep Grundy. He was a great big ignorant dog, very agile, but no fence I could build was big enough to keep him in my garden. I had no proper chance to train him, as I was away riding so often, and dear old Ann, my landlady, couldn't control him. When the neighbours started complaining I knew he had to go and, as there was a young lad down the road who had grown very fond of the dog, I gave Grundy to him to look after.

The other Grundy, the one with the flashy blond tail, wintered well and looked a million dollars when I first saw him at Seven Barrows the following spring. Pete thought so, too, and when we discussed plans for the horse it was agreed he would be aimed for the Guineas trial at Ascot, early in April. Then something happened which not only forced us to revise that plan but might, tragically, have cost us the best horse either Peter or I had ever been associated with.

It was a Tuesday morning in mid-March, when the racing public was far more concerned with the jumping festival at Cheltenham, my home town, than with what were essentially pretty fluid arrangements for the upcoming flat season. At least they were, until news travelled quickly up from Lambourn that Grundy had met with an accident. This was real news; for us, it threatened to be the worst possible news.

The accident was a freak, the sort of freak which can occur in any yard, however well disciplined. I was there to see it and it made my heart drop into my stomach, I can tell you. What it did for poor old Pete, with the owners to report to and the public to answer to, heaven knows.

What happened was quite simple. As the string pulled out for first lot on this work morning, we were filing along the covered ride when a horse called Corby, no slowcoach himself, lashed out and kicked Grundy in the centre of his face. Immediately, blood spurted out. In a moment such as this, the worst scenario usually springs to mind first, and the worst scenario was that a blow of that intensity could end Grundy's racing career. Simple as that. It might have caused all manner of internal damage, notably to his sinuses and his breathing systems, and if a horse cannot breathe properly, he won't run as fast as he otherwise would.

That morning, we thought we had lost him, but, once the shock had passed, Pete just sensibly gave him a few days' complete rest, then began trotting again. He bled once, after a canter, but with time running out before the Guineas a plan had to be made. He could not go there without a prep race and so Peter declared him for the Greenham at Newbury, a race he admits to hating for its tradition of destroying reputations.

It did nothing for Grundy's reputation, because despite starting odds-on, he was beaten into second place. It is always a blow when such a high-class horses loses his unbeaten record, but this was not a defeat which worried me greatly. The last thing I wanted was to give him too hard a race, after his training setback, and on pretty soft ground which did not suit him I eventually gave him a very easy one. He was beaten by a very fit horse, ridden by Lester, but even in the immediate post-mortem I swore that this was a result which could never be repeated.

We had another scare in the unsaddling enclosure when more blood came out of Grundy's nose as he blew hard from his exertions and, momentarily, it seemed that our careful approach had been wasted and we would not, after all, get him back for the classics. But it seemed that breaking then had cleared his system; he never bled again and a few harrowing weeks were over with a relatively happy ending.

What we most needed after all this anxiety was a trouble-free Guineas. What we got was pandemonium. This was the year of the stable-lads' pay dispute, a plea of poverty with which I felt great sympathy. They did deserve more money, they had right on their side . . . but in disrupting Guineas day with a demonstration on Newmarket Heath they may have lost more support than they gained. Whatever the strength of their cause and their feelings, they were compromising the most basic principle of their job by endangering horses. It goes without saying that they were also putting jockeys at risk. Because of their action the 2,000 Guineas was a totally unsatisfactory classic; indirectly, I suspect they may have cost Grundy victory.

The lads brought their action to a crescendo during the preliminaries of the Guineas, spreading across the course in a human shield to try to prevent the horses going down to the start. I decided discretion was the better part of valour and cantered Grundy on a circuitous route across the heath, rather than going straight down the course. The lads left me alone. Other jockeys were more confrontational, some of them quite incensed, and at a signal from one rider, a whole group of them charged the human barrier like police-horses breaking up a riot. Willie Carson went flat out at them but some of the braver lads stood their ground and pulled him off the horse. It was an ugly scene, the like of which I never wish to see on a British racecourse again, and it made a farce of one of the calendar's most important races.

I had already got Grundy installed when a decision was taken to abandon the stalls and start the race by flag. The demonstrators had been cleared off the track but the stewards were obviously fearful of further disruption and got the race away as quickly as possible, though significantly, as far as Grundy was concerned, over a trip now just short of a mile. It may only have been thirty yards or so, but that may well have made the difference in this race.

I hit the front with a quarter of a mile to run and felt confident, but Bolkonski, a 33–1 shot trained by Henry Cecil, came to take if off me. Grundy, though, was staying on well again at the finish. The margin at the line was half a length and in another five strides we would have won.

It is, of course, impossible to be dogmatic about the difference the flag start made, because the race might have panned out differently from the stalls. Similarly, there was no gain in making excuses about the fact that Grundy had got in a lather over the

My mother Josephine and my father Jimmy on their wedding day.

My first trip back to Ireland as an apprentice, in 1969, to ride for Paddy Prendergast.

My grandfather Jack Moylan (left) with Vincent O'Brien at Leopardstown in the early 1940s.

Seamus McGrath (left) the trainer whose early instruction was invaluable to me as an ambitious youngster.

Frenchie Nicholson at the Playboy Club, London, with a line-up of the former apprentices who went through his 'academy'. (Back row, left to right:) M. Dickenson, D. Nicholson, G. Dale, I. Johnson, B. Scott, G. Shoemark, B. Davies, K. Barnfield, K. Davies, K. Williams, (Front/middle row:) P. Cook, M. Morris, A. Murray, S. Spendlove, Diana Nicholson, W. Wharton, Frenchie Nicholson, F. Messer, J. Farrel, me, R. Fox, C. Leonard, W. Swinburn.

My first classic winner Polygamy (left) gets up to win the Oaks Stakes at Epsom, 1974; and is led in with Peter Walwyn (right).

A typical breakfast at Seven Barrows in 1978 sees me receive instructions for the day from Peter Walwyn. (From left to right:) Pete's wife Virginia, me, Jamie Douglas-Hume and Pete.

posite Grundy and
stino in 'The Race
the Century'; the
art-stopping finish
the King George VI
d Queen Elizabeth
amond Stakes,
cot 1975.

ght Grundy is led in
Dr Vittadini and a
iling Peter Walwyn
ght) after his
forgettable triumph.

e Arc, 1980. Detroit
), who always ran
th his tongue
nging out, gets up to
n from Argument,
ree Troikas and
-Mana-Mou (8),
ngchamp, 1980.

The crowds at the 1982 Epsom Derby cheer on Golden Fleece as he passes the post three lengths ahead of Touching Wood.

Vincent O'Brien (left) and Robert Sangster, the legendary trainer and owner partnership who gave me so many successful rides.

A foretaste of things to come: an early trip to England in 1983 where I form the beginnings of a fruitful relationship with owner Prince Khalid Abdullah (left), Grant Pritchard-Gordon and trainer Guy Harwood.

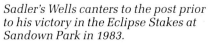

Willie Carson (right) and I catch up on each other's news.

Sadler's Wells canters to the post prior to his victory in the Eclipse Stakes at Sandown Park in 1983.

Dick Hern (corner left) watches El Gran Senor take the Dewhurst Stakes at Newmarket from the favourite Rainbow Quest in 1982.

Jeremy Tree (right) and his team with Rainbow Quest await the outcome of my objection after the Prix de l'Arc de Triomphe in 1985.

demonstrators, because that was doubtless true of other runners as well. In the final reckoning it was just another near-miss but, disappointed as we all were, I now felt very confident that Grundy would get the mile and a half of the Derby course.

This had been a major concern, because Grundy was by Great Nephew, who did not get more than ten furlongs. But the way he had stayed on up the rising ground in the Guineas convinced me and, although some of the horse's connections remained dubious, his next race convinced them, too. Grundy went to The Curragh for the Irish Guineas and won it in great style. Mark Anthony, the horse which beat us in the Greenham, was well beaten in third but more important was the style of our win on what is a very tough course. He won on the bridle and could clearly have gone much farther. We were now bound for the Derby.

Considering the dramas to befall us in his earlier runs, the Derby was a breeze. It all went perfectly to plan, Grundy handling Epsom very easily and coming home an emphatic winner by three lengths. I cannot recall a moment of concern throughout the race, as we kept well clear of the barging which habitually occurs down the hill. From halfway, although I could not see us being beaten – having hit the front pretty much when I would have chosen to – I still had that dreadful feeling that something would come and take it off me on the line. Yet I always felt Grundy was the best horse in the race and he could not have proved it more positively.

There are many vivid memories from winning the Derby for the first time, like pulling up with a huge grin and having the other jocks shake your hand, like being summoned to the Royal Box to discuss the race with the Queen, and like waking up the next morning and having the full enormity of it finally sink in. But my most lasting memory is of walking back towards the winners' enclosure and seeing Pete racing to meet us, triumphantly emotional. It was a great, great day for both of us and I could not have wished to share it with a better man.

What do you do when you have won the Derby? How do you feel? The questions are among the more obvious and persistent that I face from time to time, yet I have no profound answer. I honestly believe that, on the day it actually happens, the event washes over you, only to leave its mark the following morning. In my case, Terry drove me home as usual; we might have had a glass or two of champagne with dinner, and then I followed my usual routine. Certainly, it was not a late night of revelry.

And then, when the realisation strikes home that you have won the most famous of all the world's flat races, what else can you do but start dreaming of the next conquest? This was easy; at least, the concept was. Having proved himself the best three-year-old in Europe, Grundy now had to take on older horses, and that meant the King George.

I had only ridden in the race once before, and then I finished last, but as the day approached and the field took shape I assessed all the potential dangers and found it hard to believe that Grundy could be beaten by any of them . . . with one exception.

Bustino had won the previous season's St Leger, so his staying power was not in doubt. Neither was his speed, judging by the fact that he had broken Ascot's one and a half mile course record in the Coronation Cup, his only run of the 1975 season. He was to be ridden, as usual, by Joe Mercer, whose career had begun five years before I was born; and his trainer was the redoubtable Dick Hern. It all added up to the fact that here was an opponent to be reckoned with.

As one would expect, Dick Hern had done his homework thoroughly. He plainly believed that the way to beat Grundy was to stretch his stamina beyond previous limits and, in pursuit of that, he was leaving nothing to chance. Bustino himself could go a fair clip, and sustain it over a trip, but the Hern yard decided they would additionally run not one, but two, pacemakers. All three horses were in the same ownership, the Beaverbrook family, and they were to ensure the most demanding pace I have ever known in a race of that distance.

If the '75 Derby still endures in my memory it is for the unparalleled occasion that the race always provides. But in terms of pure racing excitement I am not sure it is possible to beat that blissfully summery day at Ascot. The measure of its greatness as a sporting event is that people still discuss it and recall it in words and pictures, almost two decades after the event.

Naturally, we were well aware of the intentions of the Bustino camp and quietly confident that they could be overcome. But when I talked over the race in advance with Pete, our priority was plainly to keep Bustino within range at all times. The first pacemaker would obviously set off at a killing speed and then give way to the second; they did not matter, so long as I could keep the real danger in my sights.

At first, all went according to expectation. Frankie Durr burst out of the stalls on the first Hern horse, then, like a runner in a relay race, handed on the baton to Eric Eldin on a horse called Kinglet. That one had had enough half a mile from home and it was there that Joe took it up on Bustino. The vast crowd packing the Ascot stands must have been waiting for me to pounce on the favourite but, as we turned into the straight, Joe had a four-length lead and, although not panicking, I knew I had a real race on.

I got to Bustino a furlong out and at that point I had no doubt Grundy would go on and win tidily. I had underestimated Bustino. He came at me again, tigerishly refusing to give in, and I had to throw everything at Grundy to hold my wafer-thin advantage. At one point inside that final furlong I think Joe just got his horse's nose in front again, but my chap was so tough, so brave, that he kept answering every question I posed him.

At the line there was a neck in it. Two strides past the line, Grundy had gone. The poor bugger just stopped. He had no more to give. So totally exhausted was he that he literally could not walk back to the winners' enclosure without being chased in by his lad. What a horse, running himself to a standstill to prove that he was undeniably the best around.

Both Bustino and Grundy had beaten the course record by more than two and a half seconds, a phenomenal achievement, and as we came back, ponderously but triumphantly, to unsaddle, the noise and fervour of the crowd was simply unbelievable. I may not be the most emotional of sportsmen, but the welcome brought a lump even to my throat.

There was more emotion to come with Grundy, but no more success. It would have seemed at the time a ridiculous notion to entertain, but neither he nor Bustino ever won another race. Bustino, indeed, never set foot on a racecourse again and Grundy's one later run was, in hindsight, a palpable mistake. He went to York for the Benson and Hedges with his jockey and trainer believing him as good as ever. But the spark had gone and he trailed in a tragic fourth, beaten by three horses he had earlier trounced by up to twenty lengths. The race of the century had taken its toll – a severe toll – on the two battlers involved.

I had not knocked him around at York and I think I knew then that he would not race again. Peter still hankered after running him in the Champion Stakes but when I rode him in a piece of work the week before the race I had to report that it was hopeless. He simply wasn't the same horse any more.

He had been sold, for a million pounds, prior to winning the Irish Derby. After the Ascot win he might have been worth three times that; after York, who knows? But it seemed he must still be a bargain for his new, breeding owners and, when I wistfully saw him off from the Seven Barrows yard for the last time, I consoled myself with the thought that there would be some very exciting progeny coming along, and that I would hopefully get to ride some of them.

It was not to be. Brilliance on the racecourse does not guarantee efficiency in the paddocks and the sad truth is that Grundy was a complete failure at stud. His buyers will have been devastated, understandably so. As for me, I still have the memories that nobody can ever take away.

7

THE HONG KONG EXPERIENCE:
A Winter's Tale

They say life is all about meeting the right people at the right time and, in my experience, that is certainly true of racing. I consider myself fortunate to have encountered the 'right people' at opportune times during my career and if many of them are well-known names, at least one is certainly not. But it was a chance meeting on a racecourse, in the summer of 1972, with a lovely man named John Brown, that took care of my close-season employment for the next eight winters.

The winters had not been a dilemma for me until then, more of a frustration, in fact. During my time with Frenchie, we continued riding out three lots right through the winter, just as usual and, if anything, the yard was livelier in those months because Frenchie's jumping horses were all in serious training. But by the end of the 1972 season I was no longer an apprentice and I now had to consider how best to make a few bob between the months of November and March.

John Brown solved the problem. He had been in English racing for years, many of them as an assistant trainer, before taking the plunge and setting himself up in Hong Kong. He had become very successful out there with some good owners and a full yard of potential winners, and he now wanted an English jockey to come out and ride for him. In fact, he wanted me.

I knew nothing about Hong Kong as a place, much less its racing, and I had never considered the possibility of going there to ride. But, being young, single and ambitious, it took me virtually no time at all to conclude that it was a very attractive offer. It was an exciting place, or so I was told by those who had been there, it was regular money and the job came complete with a flat to live in. I reasoned that if I took an intense dislike to the place I simply would not go back the next year. But I did go back, not just the following winter but for six more, too. I still go each year now, not to ride but just for a few days' holiday in which I can catch up with some of the many good friends I made in my time there.

Everything you hear about the vibrancy of Hong Kong is true, and much more besides. It is a teeming, frantic place in which life constantly seems to be moving above the speed limit. Everywhere is crammed with busy-looking people, to the point where you wonder how there can possibly be enough homes for them all. The streets are clogged with traffic; the bay separating Hong Kong island from Kowloon is furiously dotted with small craft, ferries and cruise liners. All day, and all night too, there is noise and action through the city streets. Hong Kong never sleeps, or so it seemed to me when I made my wide-eyed debut on the island that November.

Beginning a routine I was to follow each winter, I flew out the day after our flat season ended and I was riding in Hong Kong within the week. I stayed right through to the beginning of the following March, when it was time to come back and begin riding all the good young horses which Peter Walwyn was now putting my way. At Christmas there was a ten-day break from racing and I quickly got into the habit of spending the festive season in Penang, or some other coastal hotspot, smugly reflecting on the dank, dark days I would otherwise have been enduring back in Gloucestershire. I was very soon mighty glad that I had met up with John Brown, and I never had reason to regret it.

At that time, the only racecourse in Hong Kong was Happy Valley, which is perched just off the main streets of the city centre. My flat was conveniently placed next to the course, the view out of my window looking over the five-furlong start, but even this proximity to my workplace did not quite prepare me for the uncivilised hours kept by Hong Kong trainers.

The Happy Valley track is, for some reason, only open for exercising horses until eight o'clock each morning, so the trainers based there used to compete for the short time available by getting their strings out earlier and earlier. When I first reported to work for John Brown I was startled to be told that I was expected to start riding work at 4.30 a.m.! Over the course of that first winter I niggled away at John to revise his work times to something a little less ungodly and gradually, because we had hit it off together and were having our fair share of success, he moved to a more tolerable 6 a.m.

Each work morning I would ride the horses that were due to run that week and it was an education watching them appear at the track as if they had materialised from the hills . . . which is exactly what they had done. All the horses were stabled in the hills which loom over the course and they were led down the streets to the track each morning, wearing soft boots so that they wouldn't make so much noise and disturb those residents who actually did go to sleep sometimes.

There was racing every Wednesday night and Saturday afternoon and the furthest thing from the Jockey Club's minds was any concern over crowd figures. Their problem was one of space. Happy Valley has an enormous grandstand, the length of the straight on many a course and capable of holding about 70,000 people. But on Saturdays, when the first race would usually be off at 2 p.m., there would be a red light flashing at the entrances to indicate a full house, some three hours earlier than the start.

I had never experienced anything like this before, and I have still never seen such spectator passion for the sport anywhere in the world, but I was quickly disabused of any romantic notion that the crowds came in such vast numbers owing to a love of the thoroughbred, or even because they thought there might be some good jockeys to watch. They came to gamble, and with an intensity of purpose and a lack of inhibition that would alarm even the most regular and hardened of British racegoers.

Horseracing remains the only legal gambling outlet in Hong Kong and, as the Chinese were apparently bred to gamble, horseracing has become rather more than a sporting hobby to many thousands of them. They back their selections with quite frightening conviction, born of many hours' study of the form and the familiar punters' belief that his conclusions cannot possibly be wrong.

There is a very visual indicator of the betting at Happy Valley. It is a massive electronic screen, erected in centre-course, which flashes up the number of Hong Kong dollars invested on each horse in the following race, with a running aggregate of win and place bets at the foot of the screen. To watch this screen operate is to be hypnotised by money, for several million dollars is wagered on each race at Happy Valley and nobody is in any doubt about which horses the cash is down on minutes before the stalls fly open.

There are no rails or ring bookmakers here – indeed, Britain is one of the very few places where they do exist – and the hundreds of brightly-lit Tote windows attract a constant stream of excitable little men clutching fistfuls of banknotes. Where all the ready cash comes from I haven't a clue, yet to spend a night observing the punting at Happy Valley is to come away with the firm impression that the entire population of Hong Kong has money to burn.

Things have become slightly less chaotic in recent years since the introduction of off-course bookmakers. When I began going to Hong Kong, the only legal betting was done at the course, which partly accounted for the fact that the place was always sardine-jammed so many hours before racing. Now, there are betting shops all over the island, where the trade is every bit as frenzied on a racing day.

Towards the end of my eight-year stint, the Hong Kong Jockey Club opened its second course, the spectacular Sha Tin, built on reclaimed land on the Chinese mainland of Kowloon. The facilities are stunning, a match for any racecourse in the world, but it is a fair distance out of the city even for those who live on the Kowloon side, and there were those who feared the Jockey Club might have a white elephant on their hands. Not a bit of it. Sha Tin was an overnight success, as it plainly deserved to be, and if anything it seemed to strengthen the locals' obsession with racing. Huge silver screens were built at each course for the beaming of live racing between the two. The outcome of this was staggering. If Sha Tin was staging a Saturday afternoon card, they would have a full house of 70,000 there and the Happy Valley track would also be full up with people punting from the silver screen. It also goes without saying that there was never much breathing space in any of the country's betting shops. The fearless gamblers would not be denied and nothing is more certain than that, at the end of the race-day, most of them would go home and have a private bet on a game of mahjong.

The Jockey Club's initiative in funding an apprentices' school for young Chinese jockeys has eventually paid dividends and anyone who goes racing in Hong Kong now will see that local riders are in the majority. The advent of Sha Tin also created more competition, through a greater number of training centres, and the substantial prize-money increased. The Hong Kong Derby is now worth around £200,000, and each week there are decent events with purses which are the envy of many courses in Britain.

Ownership regulations were also adjusted to meet the changing times. Prior to this, owners had no say in what horse ran in their name, a situation that would not be tolerated by many in our country. Prospective owners would apply to the Jockey Club, who first investigated their means and standing. If these were acceptable, the would-be owner went into a ballot for the season's horses in training and, if he was lucky enough to be allocated one, he was stuck with it, whether it was brilliant or useless. Anyone selling his horse, either privately or at the sales, was disqualified from owning another.

This apparently bizarre system was largely influenced by the absence of any breeding in Hong Kong. All their horses are imported, many from England, New Zealand and Australia, and although the relaxed regulations now allow prospective owners to buy their own animals, strict definitions still apply to what they are allowed to purchase. Each horse must be a winner and have earned a certain amount of prize-money. This prevents the very real possibility of a rich Chinaman coming to the yearling sales in England, paying a million pounds or so for a beautifully-bred animal which could become a Generous or Dancing Brave, then taking him home and having him gelded before running him into the ground around Happy Valley. Too much of that, and the bloodstock industry would be in ruins!

My good fortune was that John Brown trained some of the best horses in Hong Kong and that he had a generally decent bunch of owners. I was never asked to do anything unscrupulous during my years there, possibly because it was realised by all that it simply would not have been worth my while even if I had felt inclined. I had far too much to risk with my 'day job' back home, taking off as it was.

And so it was a very agreeable lifestyle, the early mornings apart. I would ride a few winners most weeks, work for the day would be over very early when there was no racing and I was able to enjoy a pretty full social life in a part of the world where there is absolutely no shortage of things to do.

Hong Kong is a man's place and I am glad I was able to go there when I did. I never did take to the food, too much of it appearing on the plate raw for my simple tastes, but at least this helped keep my weight in check during the long winter months. I met some great people and, as I was young, free and single, it was certainly the right time to be there.

All that was about to change for me. In the early 1970s, while riding out at Newmarket for Harry Wragg, I had met a blonde-haired girl called Carolyn. She turned out to be the daughter of Joe Mercer's elder brother, Manny, who was tragically killed in a fall at Ascot in 1959. Carolyn was beginning to ride in lady amateur races and I liked her, fancied her if you prefer, right from the start.

We began to go out together in 1974 and, four years later, immediately after the end of the 1978 flat season, we were married. This alone made 1978 an outstanding year of memories for me, although it must be said that in racing terms it was close to being a disaster.

8

LEAVING SEVEN BARROWS: A Reluctant Break with Peter Walwyn

I was sitting pretty, of course, which is the time you are always most prone to a fall. A young man could hardly have asked for more, or so I felt. I had a great job with Peter Walwyn, I was champion jockey, I had a lovely lady who was soon to become my wife, a housekeeper who fussed over me like a mother and a lifestyle in which I was utterly comfortable, no matter how hectic it may have seemed from the outside. It was perfect, so something had to go wrong. The rules of life dictate as much.

By the end of 1977 I had been champion four years in succession and I was still only twenty-five years old. It had been a spectacular rise, certainly when I look back upon it, but at the time it just seemed a natural, very agreeable progression. The teachings of the Nicholsons, a subject on which I may be repetitively emphatic, had been of huge benefit, enabling me to handle whatever pressures, real or imaginary, accompanied the new-found fame. I suppose many a young sportsman who has achieved so much so young has taken the other side of the hill even quicker than the ascent but in most cases I put that down to poor guidance, something from which I had never suffered.

The sadness of those mid-seventies, to me, was the termination of my long and happy association with the Nicholsons. Frenchie passed away in 1974, but he had been in poor health for some time previously and, after a lengthy spell in hospital, had been confined to a wheelchair at home, where Diana devotedly tended him. Somehow, she managed to continue making my riding arrangements, and even driving me to meetings on the odd occasion, until one midwinter day when the snow was thick on the ground outside their Prestbury home.

Typical of the lady, for throughout the time I knew her she thought no job beyond or beneath her, she set to with a stiff brush to sweep the drive clear of snow. It was, however, so cold that, no sooner had she cleared the surface snow away, than the ground behind her would become icy. When she reached the end of the drive, and the end of a job few women of her age would even have attempted, she turned to walk back to the house, slipped and fell heavily. Unable to move, she lay on the iced-over concrete, in sub-zero temperatures, for more than two hours. Back in the house Frenchie was sleeping, oblivious and, anyway, helpless in his wheelchair. It was not until someone passed by and saw the shivering body on the drive and quickly summoned help that Diana was rescued. She might easily have died there and then; as it was, she had broken her hip and was admitted for a longish stay in hospital.

I visited her there as soon as I could and was shocked by how weak she appeared. Frenchie was on his last legs and I feared the same might be true of Mrs Nicholson. She is a very tough lady, however, and she bravely pulled through, but it was plain to both of us that she could no longer go on acting as my manager. From that day on, Terry Ellis took on the job and applied the lessons he had learned from Frenchie and Diana in the previous four years when, largely due to my brushes with the police, he had invariably been driving me to the racing.

The first time I had met Terry was only a few years earlier when he and my sister Olive, having got together in Germany, came back to England to get married. They set up home in Southend and Terry took a job selling cars. He was not especially settled in that line, though, and when I asked him if he could drive me the arrangement soon fitted snugly into place. He quickly got to know most of the trainers I rode for, simply by meeting them at the races day after day, so when he came to take over from Mrs Nicholson he was not just a disembodied voice on the end of a phone line. The trainers knew him and liked him and the transition was remarkably smooth.

Over the years, Terry has grown into the job, mastering the formbook and applying it to the task of obtaining the best possible winning chances for me. Our system is straightforward: when I have ridden a horse once I will tell him whether or not I think it is worth riding again. This, he will file away, along with any additional knowledge I may have gleaned from a race, such as having spotted a horse who was obviously on the upgrade and might be worth trying to get on the next time it ran. While he is at the races each day he buzzes around speaking to my regular trainers and trying to piece together their plans for the next week. The jigsaw is then completed on the telephone and he presents me with a book of rides each day.

This, then, was the situation in 1978 as the fresh season began. Terry and I could have been excused for thinking we had got this job down to a fine art. We had enjoyed four great years and, in 1977, I had ridden 176 winners, the best score of my career. Peter Walwyn's high-powered yard at Seven Barrows was churning out so many winners, and occupying so much of my riding time, that the good outside rides Terry booked were just slotted in like cherries on the cake. There seemed no good reason why any of this should change, but then you can never account for the onset of the dreaded equine virus.

It hit Big Pete's stable in 1978 and it hit hard. Just when he began to hope that the effects had been shaken off and normal business might be resumed, the virus struck again, still more savagely, in 1979. From being the country's number one trainer, regularly firing in upwards of 100 winners a year, Peter Walwyn tailed off to nothing, the miserable dribble of winners drawing constant attention to his downfall. The racing press was sympathetic, and rightly so. Mostly, they liked Pete, even if some of the journalists had been verbally assaulted by him on occasions when they had picked an untimely moment to telephone with a mundane inquiry. They understood that this was an instance of a man, who had been able to do no wrong for some years, suddenly sinking in a swamp and utterly helpless to do anything to save himself.

The virus was not confined to Seven Barrows. During those seasons it insinuated itself into a number of other yards in the Lambourn area and there, too, the winners pretty much dried up. But nowhere was it more devastating than at the Walwyn base, for no yard had farther to fall. There had been an aura of invincibility about the place during the mid-1970s and each time I stepped into the yard I sensed the vibrant mood, the expectation of success. When the virus hit, the mood was very different, a mixture of frustration, depression and fear.

A trainer can only do so much to combat the virus. He can isolate horses as soon as they show the symptoms. He can even shut down the yard as an exercise in damage-limitation and, it must be said, as a public relations gesture, because there is no point in betting-shop punters still backing the formidable Walwyn team when the horses simply cannot win. Pete did all this and more, but no trainer can shut down indefinitely. You simply have to keep fighting, keep training those horses who still appear to be healthy, and hope that the bug will move off. Sometimes the virus will lift in a matter of weeks and the stricken yard can resume full operations with confidence. At Seven Barrows it lasted for two full seasons and the effects were a disaster for a very fine trainer and a very good friend.

Pete's gallops at Seven Barrows are some of the best in the country and they had played an appreciable part in the success of the preceding years, helping him to get his horses fitter than his rivals could manage and to know exactly when they were peaking. Now, though, the gallops merely mocked him. They mocked me, too, because, week after week, I would ride work, as I had done each year, and I would jump off a horse and report quite honestly that he had impressed me. The horse would go to the races, if not with confidence – because that was an emotion of the past – then with genuine reason for optimism that here was one who remained in good health. But, time after time, the horses would flop at the races, finding nothing under pressure, and invariably the obvious fears were realised when they got home and quickly deteriorated.

Although he never took it out on me, I could see that the problem was getting to Pete very badly, and who could blame him? It is no exaggeration to say that this was a crisis in his fortunes. To run a yard of that calibre with virtually no winners costs a fortune anyway, but the sadly predictable consequence is that the thing snowballs because owners react by running away.

There were many decent people with horses at Seven Barrows and a lot of them stayed loyal for a considerable time. Finally, money talked, as it always will. If I put myself in the position of an owner, paying upwards of £200 a week to have, maybe, each of half a dozen horses trained, then there would come a time when I literally could not afford to keep them in a yard with no imminent prospects of producing a winner, no matter how much

To Be a Champion

I may like and respect the poor trainer.

Stavros Niarchos, who must have been one of the richest men involved in British racing at the time, was a patron of Pete's and had the exciting two-year-old, Nureyev, at the yard. Pete hoped and believed that this colt was still OK but Niarchos did not want to take the risk. He sent Nureyev to François Boutin in France and, three weeks later, he won a Group Three event at Deauville by eight lengths. I refuse to believe that a new trainer could have improved the horse in that brief time, so he obviously had been free of the virus and all Pete's careful preparation of the horse had gone to someone else's credit. It seemed cruel, but it was the sort of thing that could happen all too regularly to a yard grinding to virtual standstill.

There must have been times when Pete felt betrayed by everyone and everything around him, when the whole saga seemed a sick conspiracy. I never asked him, then or later, how close he came to packing it in, but it is a fact that he never did recapture the great days of the mid-seventies.

By the time the virus did lift from the yard, the horses there were no longer of the same quality. Through no fault of his own, he had been demoted in the minds of the big owners so that whereas, before, they would have offered him first pick of each year's crop of two-year-olds, he was not getting third pick, even from the owners who still sent him anything at all. Carlo Vittadini, Louis Freedman and Lord Howard de Walden, all major owners at the Walwyn yard during the good years, had transferred most of their patronage to Henry Cecil, blows from which Pete never really recovered.

In recent years Hamdan al-Maktoum has sustained Pete, sending him some nice horses, though still not the best-bred of any year. During the 1980s he would average about forty winners a year and, although many trainers would be delighted by such a return, P. Walwyn was accustomed to rather grander figures.

When the virus was at its worst I felt dreadfully sorry for Pete. But I did not emerge completely unscathed myself. A retainer with a big stable is a great help to a jockey while the yard is going well, but it becomes a millstone if the yard has a bad patch. I still had to ride all the Walwyn horses, but I was going racing every day resigned to the fact that they would not win. The upshot was that I could not sustain a challenge for the jockeys' championship and, after four years of vainly pursuing me, Willie Carson took the title from me in 1978 by a wide margin of thirty-four winners. The following year Joe Mercer, who was first jockey to Henry Cecil at the time, became champion for the first and only time; I dropped to third with my lowest tally of winners since 1973.

The fact that I was still managing to ride more than 100 winners a year during this period shows how well I was served by outside trainers. It put an extra emphasis on the booking of rides and meant that Terry and I had to get things right, because with the Walwyn yard contributing so little, the outside rides had to keep winning if I was not going to finish tailed off in the championship.

A great variety of trainers booked me but two who used me a lot, and still do today, are Neville Callaghan and Barry Hills. Both are intense men, utterly committed to the job, but in terms of personality, especially at the races, they could hardly be more different.

Barry started training pretty young and has made a tremendous success of it. After a spell at Manton, for Robert Sangster, he is now back at his original base in Lambourn, South Bank, and turning out as many winners as ever. In the late 1970s he was flying high in the First Division, with a decent yard of horses, and I always found him a pleasure to ride for. He manages to look impassive after a race, usually quietly smoking a cigar and saying very little, win or lose. The same cannot be said of Neville. Both men had very good seasons in 1978, Barry training eighty-six winners to finish second in the trainers' table and Neville turning out forty from his Newmarket yard. It is fair to say that Neville was much the more animated when he greeted a winner, but it was when he confronted a loser, particularly an unexpected one, that his volatile nature came bubbling to the surface.

When he felt he had a decent horse, or simply one good enough to win a seller, Neville would get very hyped up at the races. He has mellowed in the past years but in the early days woe betide any jockey who got beaten on one he fancied! But any outburst was quickly over and forgotten. I was lucky enough to get to know the man behind the trainer and to like him as a friend.

In our predominantly happy relationship, we only ever had one small row which was really a result of crossed wires and schedules. He phoned asking me to ride a couple for him at some Scottish course. He said they would win but I already had rides at

To Be a Champion

Leicester which was much more convenient, so I told him I could not consider going so far north unless the owners were willing to pay some expenses for me to fly up. I suppose I should have been flattered that the short sharp retort which made my telephone ear ache stemmed from his disappointment and value of my ability. However it must have been two years before the hatchet was buried and I began to ride for him again. He has had the occasional high-class horse, perhaps none better than Stanford, upon whom I won the Gimcrack Stakes at York in 1978, but he has never managed to attract the really big owners.

I judge as I find, however, and a trainer always gets good marks from me if he allows me to ride the race I want. Barry Hills is the sort who can get quite fussy before a race, but if I am riding for him he will give no firm orders at all, probably because he thinks I take no notice anyway. He would be right, because it is my firm belief that the job of the jockey becomes impossible if he is tied down with too many instructions. A trainer cannot know in advance how any race is going to be run so he should have faith in the jockey he has chosen for the job.

The first time I ride any horse, I will expect the trainer to tell me about his temperament, his action, whether he pulls or causes problems at the stalls, if he stays well or if he has a turn of foot. All these things are fundamental knowledge, essential to have in the brain. But I will not need the information repeated if I ride the horse again and I will never want to be told where I should be at any particular point of a race. That part is down to me.

If the connections absolutely insist that their horse is ridden in a certain way, despite my opposition, I might feel I have to go along with them. More often than not, the plan gets the horse beaten, because no one other than the jockey can take decisions which influence a race. Often, I simply ignore instructions I believe to be wrong and ride my own race anyway, well aware that if I then get beaten there will not be too many welcoming smiles when I come back to unsaddle.

There were 130 times for welcoming smiles during the 1980 season but, once again, the title eluded me. This time, I finished behind both Willie and Lester and, although it could by no stretch of the imagination be called a lean season for me, it was to be the last of an era. In late summer I had a phone call from Ireland which began an exciting new chapter of my life.

9

OVER TO IRELAND: Vincent O'Brien, the Master of Magnificent Ballydoyle

Vincent O'Brien was sixty-three years old and had achieved everything that horseracing has to offer, but that did not make the job of riding as his first jockey any more resistible. It was, perhaps, the one offer no right-minded jockey could refuse.

The phone call which came through to my home in Witney one September evening in 1980 set off a merry-go-round among jockeys. Lester Piggott, for so many years attached to O'Brien's all-conquering Irish yard, came home and joined up with Henry Cecil, a retainer which was to help make him champion jockey for the first time in ten years. Joe Mercer left Cecil's Newmarket yard and took a retainer at Lambourn with Peter Walwyn, the job I vacated with regrets, but no doubts, in order to ride for a racing legend.

To anyone involved in racing, a study of Vincent's big-race successes is enough to make the hair on one's neck stand on end. His record is awe-inspiring. Before turning full-time to the flat, he had dominated British and Irish jump racing, winning the major events with a facility that no trainer, before or since, could approach. The Grand National, Gold Cup and Champion Hurdle were each won three years in succession, and in the big novices' hurdle at the Cheltenham festival, which in those days was split into two divisions and named the Gloucestershire Hurdle, ten of his twelve runners were successful over an eight-year period. The two 'failures' both finished second!

He won his first Derby in 1962 and then, in ten seasons starting from 1968, he took the Epsom classic four times with horses whose names have become part of our everyday language – Sir Ivor, Nijinsky, Roberto and The Minstrel.

To Be a Champion

Lester rode all four and there were many good reasons for believing he would end his riding career at the great Ballydoyle yard, for why on earth should he want to go elsewhere? Lester Piggott in the late 1970s, however, was a law unto himself. He could do exactly as he chose because he was Lester, a jockey apart. Hardly anyone would challenge him but, at the O'Brien yard, he was dealing with some very rich and powerful people and, come 1980, they decided it was time for a change of rider. Exactly what Lester had done to upset them I am not sure but it was certainly Vincent's decision to end their long-standing agreement and offer the job to me.

He asked me if I could find the time to fly across and talk to him at his home in Cashel. Could I find the time? I went the following Sunday afternoon and, by the time I came away in the evening I was mentally if not physically committed to him.

I may not be a man who is easily impressed but Ballydoyle stunned me. Vincent had lived there for almost thirty years when I paid my first visit and the house, large, rambling and dignified, with tasteful extensions on the back, fitted him like a glove. The yard and the gallops, which we walked around later, would alone have convinced me that I was doing the right thing, because not only was every conceivable facility on hand but the design was innovative and very clearly efficient. Already, I began to look forward to work mornings; already, I was subconsciously riding the beautifully bred animals we were inspecting.

There had been no intention on my part to seek a new job, despite the trials and tribulations of Peter Walwyn's yard over the previous three years. I was still comfortable in that job, I still got along famously with Big Pete and that, I am sure, is the way things would have stayed if the O'Brien approach had not been made, because there was not one riding job in England which would have had anything like the same attraction. However, the O'Brien job would mean being part of a unique place and of riding some of the best-bred horses anywhere in Europe. And there was the undeniable appeal of a quite staggering pay rise.

By the end of my eight years with Peter Walwyn, my retainer was good – not a huge sum, but I thought a fair one. The O'Brien offer was an annual retainer worth five times more, plus all expenses. In addition, I would be entitled to a share, at stud, in one horse of my own choosing each year. This last perk alone was potentially worth more money than I had previously been able to earn in any one year. Combined with the retainer, and the near certainty of some big purses for winning major races, it was a package which could turn me into a tolerably wealthy man. I could not turn it down.

If all this makes it sound a straightforward decision, however, it overlooks one compelling factor. I still had to talk it over with my existing employer, and that was one conversation I could have done without. Peter had supported me, even in the bad times, and I like to think we had been good for each other. If the years of the virus had caused inevitable strain and notes of discord, we had never had a serious argument in eight years. If Frenchie Nicholson gave me the chance to reach the top, Peter Walwyn made sure I got there. I had a lot to thank him for and now it would seem to some that I was kicking him while he was down, an interpretation I would have given much to avoid.

Apart from Carolyn, Pete was the first person I told about the offer. I owed him that, at least. He never was very adept at disguising his feelings and I could tell immediately that he was both shocked and upset. He asked me to defer any definite decision until he had spoken to his owners, and I agreed. To give him his due, he came back to me in a matter of days with an offer which all but matched the terms Vincent O'Brien had put to me. Considering what he had been through, and the owners he had lost, this was a sterling effort and the irony, as I understand it, is that a good part of the funding for the increase came from Stavros Niarchos, who was also heavily involved in the O'Brien empire.

It was no good. My heart might still have belonged at the Walwyn yard but everything in my head pointed me across to Ballydoyle for what was sure to be a completely different experience. Pete eventually accepted that there was nothing more he could do to make me change my mind. To my relief and pleasure, we remained good friends and although Joe Mercer took over my job, I still rode the odd one for him and continue to do so today. He is a great guy.

The contract I soon had to sign was between Vincent and myself. No other names were included on the document. It was commonly believed, however, that Robert Sangster was behind the deal and the press – not just the racing specialists but every paper in Fleet Street – had a field day guessing the amounts of money involved. The departure of Piggott was, in itself, very big news, but, oddly enough, I was never conscious of having an additional burden through replacing the great man. If the job involved any kind of burden it came from the fact that every horse I rode for Vincent was worth at least a million pounds.

The trend in training then, as now, is for the major players to have ever-larger strings. Vincent went against that trend in a quite striking way. During my five years at Ballydoyle, we never had more than forty-two in training. Of these, two would always be fillies and the rest colts. All would be bred in the pink, expensively bought and, in many cases, destined to go to stud for quite astronomical fees. This was not just an emphasis on quality, it was an obsession with it. Not every horse that came through the yard could be good enough to win a Derby, of course, and those that did not match up to Vincent's standards did not take up valuable space any longer than was necessary to prove their shortcomings.

Most of the horses were owned in partnership and, at that time, Robert Sangster owned at least a share in virtually all of them. He and John Magnier, a leading Irish stud owner and breeder, had joined forces in 1974 to form what became known simply as 'The Syndicate'. They had enjoyed some wonderful years of success with Vincent, and Robert, for whom I had ridden some winners over the years, was unstinting in his rating of O'Brien as the greatest living trainer. The three of us were all champions in our own right and, for me, this new partnership had endless possibilities.

If there was any question of a need for me to make an impression on Robert, which I don't think there was, I did not exactly get off on the right footing when he asked me to ride his filly, Detroit, in the Prix Vermeille at Longchamp that autumn. Detroit was not an O'Brien horse, being trained in France by Olivier Douieb, but the Sangster connection made it an important ride for me and the Vermeille was a significant race, traditionally the final trial for the Prix de l'Arc de Triomphe.

Detroit was a rapidly improving filly and had won her last three races on the bounce. She should certainly have won the Vermeille, too, but I made the mistake of allowing myself to get boxed in on the Longchamp straight. There was no way out other than by knocking a couple of horses out of the way, which would not only have lost me the race anyway but also earned me a holiday. I sat tight, utterly frustrated, and Detroit went past the winning post still on the bridle behind a horse of Ian Balding's called Mrs Penny. I still have a vivid recall of that race now, but two things prevented it from being an absolute disaster. Firstly it was obvious to all the disappointed connections that Detroit had not had a hard race and that, given a clear run, she would have won with something to spare, so they immediately determined to send her back to Longchamp a fortnight later for the Arc. Secondly, despite getting the filly beaten, I kept the ride.

I was still learning about racing in France at the time, for it was not until the O'Brien job was under way that I began to go there every Sunday. But I had already learned to be wary of the French stewards, and their notorious strictness was in the forefront of my mind during that infuriating Vermeille. My chances of riding again that season would have been minimal if I had barged my way out, because you are in trouble if you so much as come off the straight on the Paris tracks. Many is the time, in succeeding years, when I have finished a race which contained no obvious interference, only for the hooter to sound, announcing a stewards' inquiry. Some hapless jockey, and more than once it has been me, will find himself summoned to explain why he failed to keep his horse straight and, quite naturally, will plead his innocence. The next thing he will know is that, having returned to the weighing-room, he will be approached by a little guy with a thin smile and given an envelope, which contains the unwelcome news of a few days off.

You get away with nothing in France and, partly for that reason, it is essential to keep out of trouble. Longchamp presents particular problems. The Arc course sets off uphill but, once you have climbed up the back straight, the downhill stretch is all on the turn. Once you reach the foot of the hill and complete the turn into the straight, your horse already has a momentum from freewheeling down the slope and if you ask him for his effort immediately, you can hit the front way too soon. It is possible, often desirable, to come from off the pace and to wait as long as possible on Arc day at Longchamp. Where you certainly do not want to be is in midfield and on the rail because, with a big field, your chances of an untroubled run are negligible and, against quality horses, being checked once is tantamount to conceding the race.

To Be a Champion

All of this was in my mind when I arrived in Longchamp on the first Sunday in October. So, too, was the matter of pace. French jockeys often dawdle for a mile and turn every race into a sprint over the last few furlongs. This can be deceptive, however, because French horses are, in general, trained to get home, no matter the pace. English trainers frequently believe they can take a decent stayer to Paris, set a smart gallop, but the French still come to win the race. Having decided where you want to sit in a race it is important to keep to that plan whatever the early pace, because it is a safe bet that the ones in front will not stop very quickly.

My plan on Detroit was the one I have usually liked to follow at Longchamp, sitting near the rear of the field, moving up on the final downhill turn and then challenging on the outside once into the straight. It was a big field and I wriggled my way out slowly and methodically before delivering my run. Detroit responded well; the race was won.

This was a fantastic boost in starting the new job and there was another to come before the end of the season. Although, officially, my retainer at Ballydoyle did not come into operation until 1981, Vincent introduced me to some of the two-year-olds and I was able to take the ride on Storm Bird in the Dewhurst Stakes at Newmarket in late October. Bought at the Keeneland Yearling Sales for £1 million the previous year, Storm Bird was by Northern Dancer and a close relation of two O'Brien Derby winners, Nijinsky and The Minstrel. He was a seriously good horse and, when he impressively won the Dewhurst, his fifth consecutive win as a two-year-old, he was installed as winter favourite for the 2,000 Guineas, with the very real prospect that he could go on and occupy a similar position in the Derby market.

It was a severe setback to Vincent and to Robert Sangster, whose syndicate owned Storm Bird, that none of this came to fruition. The horse did not even run, either in the Guineas or the Derby. Early in 1981, while Vincent was away on holiday, Ballydoyle's security system sprang a leak and whoever it was who broke into the yard cut off Storm Bird's mane and tail. I have no idea if the motive for this bizarre act was political, religious or simply malicious – what is certain is that it cannot have been financial.

[87]

Storm Bird did not at first appear to have suffered lasting damage to anything except his dignity but, when we worked him in preparation for the Guineas, there was none of the sparkle he had shown as a two-year-old. He missed that race while Vincent tried to prepare him for the Derby, but another disappointing piece of work convinced us all that it would be a waste of time.

He only ever ran once more, at Longchamp that September. This was to have been his prep race for the Arc and he went off a short-priced favourite. We took up the running on schedule but when I pressed the button there was no petrol in the tank. He finished seventh and Vincent, who normally showed no visible emotion after a race, was transparently bewildered and upset. For Robert Sangster, who was also at Longchamp that day, the disappointment was now not a financial blow, however. A couple of months earlier, The Syndicate had sold Storm Bird to an American oil tycoon named Robert Heffner for a mind-boggling £24 million. This was his first race for the new owner and he would never see another racecourse; instead he was syndicated for £30 million and became a very successful stallion.

Considering that he failed to win a race as a three-year-old, these sums of money were beyond my comprehension, but perhaps the Storm Bird saga was the catalyst for my sharpened interest in the stud book, when before I had never looked farther than the form book. Breeding had never interested me because it was not my province; I would know the sire of any good horse I came to ride but nothing beyond that. Riding for Vincent, I quickly saw that this had to change because in all the world of thoroughbred racing there was probably no greater student of breeding, and no man of greater knowledge, than M. V. O'Brien.

When I stayed with Vincent at Ballydoyle, I would take myself off to one of the studies on quiet evenings and, for the first time in my life, pore over the type of books that, previously, I had been happy to leave to the bloodstock agents. I found that it was not such an uninteresting area of racing after all and, by regularly doing my homework with the studbook and the sales catalogues, I developed enough knowledge to be able to discuss pedigrees with Vincent. This was apparently what he expected of his jockey and, if it was an aspect of the job I had never intended pursuing, I know it has stood me in good stead in the years that have followed.

10

GOLDEN FLEECE: Possibly the Best I have Ridden

I won the Derby in my second year with Vincent O'Brien, on what may just have been the best horse I have ever ridden. I also picked up many of the major Irish prizes on O'Brien horses and grew accustomed to the phenomenon of virtually everything I rode for the yard being sent off favourite. In those days, Vincent could have run a donkey and it would still have started 3–1 on.

Simply being part of the Ballydoyle operation, and observing the great man at work, was an education for me. I had reached the stage of feeling on equal terms with almost everyone in the racing game, but Vincent O'Brien was somehow different. Immaculate in appearance, meticulous in his work, he was a very smart guy in every sense and I think it was natural for anyone coming into his circle to feel slightly in awe of him.

He was, doubtless still is, a very quiet and private man, so much so that I found it very difficult to assess his thoughts and impressions after a race. He was much the same, whether we had just won a moderate maiden race at Naas or lost the Derby on the favourite. Unfailingly, he was gracious and unemotional in public and if he let off steam in private, then I never got to hear about it. It is quite an achievement to remain equable when each of your horses could be valued at a fortune, but then I suppose Vincent had had plenty of practice. He did, after all, start training nine years before I was born!

If our relationship was based entirely on business, rather than embracing a friendship such as I enjoyed with Peter Walwyn, it was nonetheless a harmonious one and I never had any cause to complain that Vincent made life difficult for me. Quite the opposite, indeed, for he made adjustments in order to accommodate *my* schedule, rather than vice-versa.

I joined him fully aware that it meant giving up any ambition to be champion jockey in Britain; that just wasn't on, as even Lester Piggott could verify. But having said that, I still topped 100 winners in Britain in all but one of the five seasons at Ballydoyle. The one year I missed out was 1982 when I consciously turned my priorities to winning the Irish championship for the first and only time.

A pattern of work evolved which seemed to suit both Vincent and myself. I would go to Ballydoyle ten days before the start of each season, stay for perhaps a week and ride every horse in the yard at least once. In this way I was at least able to acquaint myself with them and draw some early impressions about the forwardness of the two-year-olds and the improvement, or otherwise, made by the older horses.

The layout of the stables and gallops made this intensive riding work quite simple. There was no question of the horses having a lengthy, time-consuming walk from stable-yard to heath, as at Newmarket, or to downs, as at Lambourn. At Ballydoyle everything was to hand, and the clever design made my job easy. I would jump on each horse in the big, spacious stable-barn, walk him down an all-weather track, then turn and canter up the grass gallop, turn left again on to the all-weather, then back into the barn and jump on another one. It was an early indication, to me, that Vincent O'Brien had achieved his eminence by more than simply having good horses. His training brain was sharper than the rest, too.

Once the season started, I would ride in Ireland every Saturday, when racing is usually either at The Curragh or Leopardstown, and Vincent usually brought another half-dozen horses to the course to work after racing. This arrangement was a huge help to me as it meant I did not often need to make another trip to Ireland in midweek. Occasionally, I would be required to ride at Phoenix Park, which Vincent and his syndicate had recently bought and were naturally trying to promote, and if a major race, like the Derby, was imminent, and a racecourse gallop was thought to be too public, then I would go and ride the prospective runner in his midweek work at Ballydoyle. Otherwise, I was free to ride in England from Monday to Friday, which was not only important in keeping the winners ticking over but also in retaining training contacts which otherwise would have passed to another jockey.

Saturday was a busy day, and a long one. I caught the morning flight out of Heathrow to Dublin and then it was usually a taxi-ride to the course. I also had an arrangement to ride, whenever possible, for John Oxx, another very able Irish trainer, so with two good stables supplying rides I regularly had a full book of six or seven and there would not be many who went to the starting stalls without a squeak of a chance. I was not often a man for the once-a-week punter to follow, however, unless he especially liked betting at odds-on.

By the time I had finished riding work on the course it was usually past six o'clock, which meant a quick change and a dash for the eight o'clock flight back to Heathrow. Airports being what they are, there was habitually some kind of delay so it was sometimes not much before midnight when I arrived back, all thoughts of a nice dinner regretfully abandoned. After a couple of years of this routine I mentioned it to Vincent and, typically, he arranged for a private plane to fly me to and from Oxford each Saturday. This made a big difference: it meant I actually managed to eat something most Saturday evenings!

My weekends were now fully international: Ireland on Saturdays and France every Sunday. During those great Ballydoyle years, Vincent sent horses every week for a crack at the good French prizes and, although people in other jobs might raise their eyebrows if I sound enthusiastic about adding a seventh working day to each week, the French trips were something I looked forward to, and still do today when my commitments for Prince Khalid Abdullah take me there even more frequently.

Most of the decent French tracks are central to Paris – Longchamp, Chantilly, Maisons-Laffitte and Saint-Cloud – but there were also occasional trips to Evry, in the provinces, and the annual month, much beloved of the European socialites, at Deauville. One of the main reasons why I never found riding there a chore is that the tracks are so good. In England, we have some very good courses, such as Ascot and York, but we also have to suffer a lot of bad ones, largely because there are far too many of them and they cannot all make money. In France, the top jocks will seldom go outside the tracks I have mentioned, with every one of them on a par with the best in England.

I have been very lucky to find myself wholly accepted by the French jockeys and I have never had a problem with them, though I still cannot speak the language; so I must admit to being lazy in this respect after going there almost every week for more than a decade. No doubt I would make more effort if I went to France to ride for an entire season but the laziness in me is encouraged because everyone in French racing seems to speak English and, even in the Paris restaurants, I have never had trouble making myself understood. It is probably an unattractive side of being English-speaking that we tend to expect everyone else to make efforts to understand us, rather than vice versa, but I am not alone in my guilt.

Vincent himself would only go to France on the big days, not least because, for all his consummate professionalism as a trainer, he was also a devoted family man. Whether he had flown across or not, though, it soon became a habit to phone him each Monday evening, when we would talk about how the horses had run that weekend and our prospects for the Saturday ahead. We would often be on the phone for a very long time, analysing races in some detail, and while the conversation was racing I always found Vincent a very easy man to talk to.

It is probably true to say that, because he concentrated all his efforts on relatively few horses, compared to the big English yards, he knew each one better, but he would forever be seeking new knowledge and picking my brains for what might have seemed the most trivial of details. This, of course, helped make him the peerless trainer he was, but it was not all brainwork and planning. He also had an indefinable gift for dealing with horses and, although we had any number with leg problems during my years there, most of them were kept sound, an achievement which is the very art of successful training.

Despite his heavy involvement in the yard, I saw little of Robert Sangster, other than in the parade ring on big-race days. He never made the mistake of trying to interfere with the part of the business which must essentially be a trainer-jockey relationship and that remains the case now, although as he has horses spread among many different British trainers he understandably wants the best man available on board when they are fancied. I like Robert a lot and admire him for his tenacity within racing. I know he had plenty of money behind him when he came into ownership, but Robert has ridden out the bad times and retained his enthusiasm when many others of similar means have fallen by the wayside through lack of success or lack of genuine interest. He is one of racing's great survivors and, although the advent of the oil-rich Arabs in the mid-eighties stripped him of the champion owner title and caused him to rethink his strategies, he is back with a vengeance now and, in 1991, had some of his best horses for many a year. A naturally sociable man, he would often throw parties of legendary length and style after a big race, which weight and commitments always prevented me from attending. But I did, more than once, go to his home on the Isle of Man for a party and I can confirm that he throws a very good one!

One of the bonuses of my new job was that I got to ride regularly, and win regularly, on those Irish courses that had so frustrated me when I was a boy at Seamus McGrath's, waiting for any sort of chance. Being an Irishman coming home, as it were, also gained me instant public acceptance and the crowds took to me warmly. Cash Asmussen, the French-based American who took on the job after me, had no such luck.

Whether it was his personality or his riding that riled the Irish punters, Cash could do very little right in their eyes. He was still riding a lot of winners, both for Vincent and for John Oxx, whose rides I had happily passed on to him, but whenever he got beaten on one of the 'talking horses' that Ballydoyle seems to create, there were some nasty scenes in the unsaddling area. I have no idea how Cash got along with Vincent but, the way things were going, it came as no real surprise when they mutually agreed to terminate his contract a year early. I felt sorry for Cash. He does yap on a bit, and his brash, American style may not suit everyone, but I like the guy and I believe he can ride. He had certainly done nothing to attract the treatment he got from the Irish crowds.

For Cash, of course, riding in Ireland was a new and foreign experience but, even for me, the sense of belonging had diminished with the years. I had lived in England for the adult half of my twenty-eight-year-old life when I joined Vincent and although I remain a proud Irishman, Ireland no longer felt like home. Perhaps it would have been different if my family had still been there in force, but apart from two sisters and a clan of aunts and uncles, all my close relatives had come to England – most of the brothers to seek a route into racing.

My Mum and Dad were both in England but, sadly, no longer together. Jimmy had come across to work for the trainer, Gordon Smyth, in the Sussex town of Lewes. It was a case of full circle, really, because his racing days had begun in the south of England. He came over when barely into his teens and spent seven years working for Atty Persse in Hampshire, days, he would always say, which made my apprenticeship seem soft. But he had made his name back in Ireland, and a good name it was too, even if his riding style made the stewards wince a few times too often. He had given up the game when I came to England, and taken over the running of a pub in Kildare. For Jimmy, who always liked a drink anyway, this was the start of a slippery slope and, when he got out and went back to England, it was to work as an ordinary lad again.

That lasted a few years but, when Gordon Smyth cut back in 1975, Jimmy was out of a job, and there he stayed. He never worked again in his life and, in the years of idleness, he drank heavily. My mother got to the point where she couldn't take it any more and I bought her a house in Newmarket. I saw a fair bit of Jimmy and sometimes he could be a bloody nuisance, but he was still my father and I still tried to look after him as best I could.

His interest in racing had pretty much gone altogether, aside from loyally following my career, and because he had no work to keep him out of the pubs he literally drank and smoked himself into an early grave. He died at the age of sixty-four and, for a man who had spent the majority of his life fit, active and outdoors, it was criminally young to go.

In those early 1980s, then, my links with Ireland were tenuous, which may explain why I felt no inclination to spend more time there than was necessary. There were also my own domestic circumstances to consider. I was a married man now and Carolyn saw little enough of me during the season. Being bred into racing, and involved in a certain amount of race-riding herself, she naturally accepted this without a problem; she had married me knowing the score. But in 1982, our first daughter Nichola was born, an extra incentive for me to get home as early and as often as possible.

This, though, was 1981, my first year at Ballydoyle. A year in racing which I remember for my first, rich experience of the O'Brien horses. For me, it was the year of King's Lake, Achieved and Woodstream; for everyone in racing it was the year of Shergar.

He was a quite fantastic horse, no doubt about it. He just kept slaughtering whatever opposition he encountered, winning by so far it was ridiculous. Wally Swinburn, who was only a boy of nineteen, had the incredible experience of winning his first Derby, pulling up, by ten lengths. He got suspended during Royal Ascot and Lester jumped in to ride Shergar to victory in the Irish Derby, but Wally was back on board for the King George at Ascot and Shergar won impressively again.

Michael Stoute, his trainer, had wanted to run him in the Arc but this never materialised. Michael ran him in the St Leger first and the horse was clearly over the top, finishing only fourth. Fortunately for his connections he had by then already been syndicated to go to the Aga Khan's stud in Ireland and, as the world now knows, it was there, at Ballymany, that Shergar was kidnapped.

All manner of theories have been expounded as to why he was taken and what subsequently happened to him. My own views are quite clear. He must have been snatched for political motives and, tragically, killed by his captors. Those who say he could have been taken overseas for breeding purposes are talking nonsense. A big stallion like Shergar needs a great deal of experienced care and attention; any idea that he might have been surreptitiously housed in some rustic little stable and illicit trysts with unknown mares arranged is just too ridiculous for words.

How they got the horse is simple enough. It seems they just drove into the stud, loaded Shergar into a box – the one part of the operation for which they must have had the help of people used to handling horses – and then drove away again. The furore was naturally enormous, for this horse was one of those who enter the consciousness of the whole nation, and it may well be that, within a few days, the kidnappers realised they had taken on more than they had bargained for and, rather than risk being identified if they gave the horse back, they put him down.

I fervently hope they didn't torture the poor creature, for he had never done anything in his life but give pleasure to people. It was a great sadness for the bloodstock business, because we never got to see the progeny of this exceptional horse down the years, and it was a saga which did nothing for the public image of horseracing. When a real, blatant case of skulduggery afflicts the game, it only fuels the imagination of those who like to believe that nothing in racing is quite as it seems.

If I had nothing quite as good as Shergar to ride in 1981, I still sat on some very exciting horses. In England, I won the Benson and Hedges Gold Cup at York on Beldale Flutter, for Michael Jarvis. In Ireland, Vincent introduced some lovely two-year-olds. There was a colt called Achieved, who won all his three starts, including a raid on Doncaster for the Champagne Stakes, and a filly called Woodstream, who won four out of four, including the Cheveley Park at Newmarket.

This was also the year when I had a couple of memorable scraps with Greville Starkey as King's Lake, from the O'Brien yard, took on Guy Harwood's To-Agori-Mou. This was an Anglo-Irish battle of some passion and, when it went to a return match, the interest was tremendous.

To-Agori-Mou had won the English Guineas, giving Guy his first classic. He was a decent colt, there was no doubt about that – I had a good view of him in the Guineas as I finished third on Bel Bolide for Khalid Abdullah, a foretaste of things to come. But at Ballydoyle we thought King's Lake was pretty useful, too, and when Guy decided to send his horse over to The Curragh for the Irish Guineas, Vincent unhesitatingly decided we should take him on.

King's Lake won by a neck, but it was a finish full of incident and the local stewards reversed the result, awarding the race to To-Agori-Mou. Vincent felt strongly enough about the decision to appeal to the Irish Turf Club, who controversially overruled The Curragh stewards and gave the race back to us. It was a prolonged process of sorting out a winner and it is true to say that not everybody thought justice had finally been done, so when the horses were scheduled to meet again in the St James's Palace Stakes, on the opening day of Royal Ascot, feelings ran pretty high. The punters, too, had latched on to the saga and there were not many voices raised in support of the Irish invader that day.

One of the racing yearbooks, looking back on the atmosphere that day, likened it to 'a seaside clash between mods and rockers'. It was certainly an unusual feeling for the Royal meeting, but the crowd got their money's worth as the two principals did, indeed, fight out a close finish and, this time, To-Agori-Mou held off my challenge to win by a neck. As he passed the post Greville raised his fingers in what may have been a victory sign to the crowd or could have been something more unpleasant directed at me. The press made a lot of it, photographs and all, and it was indicative of a very highly-charged occasion, but soon forgotten by both of us.

As the season ended, Achieved came out on top in the official ratings of Irish two-year-olds but, just behind him, was another O'Brien colt who had run only once. His name was Golden Fleece. Bought for around half a million pounds at Keeneland, where Vincent did so much of his shopping for yearlings, Golden Fleece won a single two-year-old outing, a maiden race at Leopardstown, with some conviction. He gave me a good feel but, on that evidence alone, I could not have nominated him as a future star.

It was when he ran for the first time at three that we realised he was a horse of unusual ability, albeit one with idiosyncrasies to test a trainer's initiative and a jockey's skill. The first of his problems was that he showed an aversion to the starting stalls. He was a big, rather awkward horse and the stalls plainly made him claustrophobic, so we made sure that he was the last to be put in. He then made sure he was the first out the other side!

It was a mile-and-a-quarter race at The Curragh and there were a lot of runners. Ideally, I would like to have held him up, got him settled and then assessed just how much toe he had in a finish. Golden Fleece was having none of it. He burst away like a five-furlong sprinter and, hard as I tried, there was nothing I could do to hold him. Coming into the straight, he was still pulling for his head, but I just about had him under control. Usually, at this point of a race, the air is thick with the sound of horses' hooves and jockeys' curses, but now I had the weird sensation of pure silence around me. I chanced a look over my shoulder and the others were all so far behind I could not believe it. I was able to start pulling up from the two-furlong marker and he still won by ten lengths.

Impressive though this may have looked from the stands, it gave me more concern than confidence. There seemed no doubt that Golden Fleece would be our Derby horse but, as I jumped off him, I said to Vincent that something would have to be done to give him a chance of settling because he could not expect to win in that style against Group One horses. He had got away with it this time, I added, because the rest in the race weren't in the same league.

For his next race, back at Leopardstown for the Derby trial, Golden Fleece was spoiled. Vincent ran two pacemakers, whose job it was to set such a strong gallop over a mile that the big horse would consent to settle for being towed along. It was a logical tactic but it failed because the pacemakers were not good enough. They simply could not go at the necessary pace and, although I managed to hang on to Golden Fleece for about half a mile, he then ran away with me again. He was, however, so good that he still won, and beat another good horse of Robert Sangster's called Assert, trained by Vincent's son, David, in his first season with a licence. David operated quite independently from his father, as future years were to prove, and Assert was fancied for the Derby. So now we knew where we stood with at least one of the dangers; the main danger that I could envisage, however, was that Golden Fleece's foibles would not suit the unique Epsom course at all.

The great Vincent O'Brien racing brain tackled this dilemma in the days leading up to the race and decided that the pacemaker ploy would be abandoned. Instead, Golden Fleece travelled over to Epsom on the Sunday, three days before the race, and on the Monday and Tuesday mornings I drove down there to give him a spin. Under Vincent's instructions, we walked the horse up the course to the point where the Derby stalls would be placed, let him pick around for a moment or two, and then hacked him to the seven-furlong pole. It was a sensible attempt to get him accustomed to the surroundings he would confront before the race but, as he was so headstrong, I still remained fearful that the combination of a lot of runners and an awful lot of noise would make him behave at his worst.

Before the Derby, Vincent and I had gone through the field, discussing each opponent. This was common practice for him. But he never was a man to burden me with detailed instructions and I recall that he said virtually nothing as we waited in the parade ring at Epsom that day. What was there to say? We had laid our plans and we thought we might well have the best horse in the field. We had no idea, though, how the horse himself was going to react, and by that stage there was nothing to be gained by debating the possibilities any further. We stood with our private thoughts, hoping and praying. What transpired out there on the track, though, was something neither of us could have anticipated, because when Golden Fleece came out of the stalls, he switched off completely.

I had braced myself for the usual explosion of energy beneath me when the stalls flew open, prepared to try for all I was worth to tuck him in behind some horses for as long as possible. Instead, nothing. He had gone to sleep, just as if he was out for a quiet hack at Ballydoyle. Unexpected though this was, I did not intend to look the proverbial gift horse in the mouth. He seemed remarkably relaxed, but I still feared that he would take off with me the moment I moved on him. So I decided to let him idle along for as much of the race as I could, banking on the prospect of getting a good run through in the straight.

I was last at the top of the hill, and last all the way down. It flashed through my mind that the guv'nor, up in the stands, must have been wondering what on earth I was doing and I later heard that this was visibly the case; even the famous impassive face was betraying an unusual amount of anxiety.

As we reached the foot of the hill and began the swing into the straight I surveyed the scene in front of me. There was a wall of horses, all right, but none of them were going anywhere. I felt my fellow could take that pack any time, so I eased him gently to the wide outside and, heart in mouth, asked him the question. Within two strides, I had the spectacular answer. He went past most of the field with breathtaking speed and I was able to take a pull two furlongs out, before asking him again. The track had not suited him at all, but still he won by three lengths in the fastest time for the race since electronic timing had come in, back in 1964.

It was an extravagant victory and a performance which persuaded some pretty good judges, Lester Piggott among them, that Golden Fleece might have been the best of all Vincent's Derby winners. There are not many greater tributes one can pay a racehorse than that. I remain convinced, though, that the secret of his victory lay in taking him on to the track each day that week.

He had never switched off at all in any of his previous races and I believe it must have been the familiarity which relaxed him.

Sadly, we never got to know if it had reformed him for good, nor did we have the chance to truly assess his quality. The Derby was his last race. Within days of Epsom he was showing signs of a bug. Vincent is adamant that he could have had the bug on him in the Derby, but I find that difficult to take; I doubt if he could possibly have found such a dramatic turn of foot if he had already been sickening. It is true that he coughed a couple of times on the morning before the race and that this caused understandable concern, but he did not cough again for some days afterwards.

Golden Fleece was retired to Robert Sangster's Coolmore Stud but, there too, his career was cruelly cut short. Eighteen months later, he died of cancer. I shall always remember him as a freakish horse. He was not the nicest to ride because he was a typical Nijinsky, with a mind of his own, and would have you off as soon as look at you . . . but for a seventeen-hand animal he had a decisive, race-winning kick, off any pace. He was good, very good, and he might have gone on to true greatness.

11

JUMP JOCKEYS: My Admiration for the National Hunt Boys and My Brother Michael

There are any number of reasons for being grateful that I was drawn naturally to riding on the flat, rather than over jumps, but that does nothing to diminish my admiration for the National Hunt boys. Quite the reverse, in fact, for it is these very reasons which drum home the fact that, in general, the lifestyle of the summer game is infinitely more comfortable.

The financial potential is far greater for those who make the grade, largely because flat racing is more international and, of course, has the fat chequebooks and acquisitive spirits of the bloodstock industry in tow. Despite the occasional dreadful fall, at high speed and under an army of flying hooves, the flat is unlikely to break your bones with the same unnerving regularity that jumpers endure. And then there is the factor of seasons: we race from March to early November, packing up just when the nights have really drawn in and the first thick frosts are forecast, while the jump jockeys not only have to ride in the worst of winter weather, they also have to drive many thousands of miles in it, returning home each night long after dark.

It never really entered my head to ride jumping, despite the Irish passion for it, despite the fact that Frenchie Nicholson was predominantly a National Hunt man and despite the un- paralleled training achievements, in the major jumping events, of Vincent O'Brien. By the time I went to Ballydoyle, of course, the die was cast and there would have been no turning back even if I had had a secret inclination to; yet I have always continued to marvel from afar at the fortitude of jump jockeys, a view poignantly hardened by a crisis in our own family.

My elder brother Michael had no choice in the racing game. If he wanted to ride, it had to be over jumps, for he was far too heavy to contemplate a career on the flat. When we were young, I doubted whether he would ride at all, because he was never quite as obsessed by it as I was. But, being physically strong and mentally tough, he was, perhaps, ideally suited to the demands of National Hunt.

Starting out in the game at about the same time as me, he went to the north of England and began riding for that experienced trainer Denys Smith. Things were going well for Michael until, late in 1972, a promising career ended tragically. He was riding in a 'chase at Newcastle. Approaching the last, with the race still there to be won, Michael's horse was carried ever wider by another runner and he ended up crashing through the wing of the fence. His right leg, which took the full force of the impact, was badly broken but that, initially, was all I knew.

He had been admitted to Newcastle Infirmary and, with the flat season just drawing to a close, I drove up there as soon as I heard how serious a fall it had been. My parents, alerted by the hospital, also made tracks there, but I was the first of the family to reach Newcastle and so, at the young age of twenty, a dreadful decision fell to me.

The specialist attending Michael called me into his room and told me the worst. The leg was shattered beyond hope of repair. There was a very real and frightening risk of gangrene unless he performed an amputation.

He took me into the curtained-off area where Michael was lying, unconscious, and I almost vomited at the sight of his injuries. I don't think I am especially squeamish but what I saw would have turned my stomach at any time, let alone when the victim was the brother with whom I had grown up.

I was asked to give my permission for surgery and I did so in a daze, knowing it was the only possible decision but horrified at the enormity of it. I was not just writing off Michael's career when I signed my name on the consent form, I was sanctioning the loss of a limb. When my parents arrived I hardly knew how to tell them but, on hearing the dire alternatives from the surgeon, they were, thankfully, in no doubt that I had done right.

To my knowledge, Michael was never told that it was his kid brother Patrick who gave the go-ahead and I can only imagine how difficult he found coming to terms with the fact that he had woken up with his world turned upside down. He had begun the day as a young, fit and reasonably successful jockey. He ended it with his leg missing below the knee, necessitating not only a long and painful period of rehabilitation, of learning how to walk all over again, but also an essential reappraisal of his entire future.

He coped with the trauma indomitably and was helped through it all by a particular nurse. Her part in his recovery, both physical and mental, cannot be overstated because, when it was over, Michael married his nurse and they still live, very happily, in Newcastle, the place where it all happened.

Michael had an artificial limb fitted and, to my amazement, he was soon so adjusted to it that, on visits down south, he would chase us at a good running speed. He was not long in driving his car again and, far from being soured against the sport which had done this to him, he found a job on the periphery of racing, selling horse-feeds to trainers. He travels the country in his work and I have heard from many a trainer just how good at it he has become. Apparently, he begs, badgers and bullies all the trainers in Newmarket until they take some of his products!

A few years after the accident, Michael was in my area and came to stay. He was unfamiliar with the country roads around my home and, in overtaking another car on the brow of a hill, he had a head-on collision with a truck. It was the sort of accident which invariably maims if not kills those involved and, when the police arrived, the signs were not good. They found Michael slumped across the steering wheel, dazed and contorted. Far worse, they found his right leg lying outside the disfigured car. 'Poor bugger,' you can hear them saying, 'the impact was so great it must have torn off his leg . . . '

This time, though, he had been lucky. The artificial leg had come adrift, but that could easily be strapped on again and, aside from a few minor bruises, Michael was astonishingly unscathed. A great escape it may have been but, after what had befallen him earlier, I think he deserved it.

Time was when we flat jockeys spent a fair amount of time with our jumping colleagues. There was a three-day mixed meeting at Newbury in late October and then, in the spring, came the Liverpool fixture, famous for the Grand National but nowadays exclusively jumping. When I started riding, though, each of the three days had some flat racing, too, and I think the riders from both codes enjoyed it as something a little different, a chance to witness life on the other side and to catch up on a few friendships.

I used to stay out at Southport, in a hotel peopled by many of the jumping fellows, and it was always a great gas. Johnny Haine, Jeff King, Terry Biddlecombe and company certainly knew how to enjoy themselves. With them, there was always a sense of living for today and never mind tomorrow; in the ultra-professional world I inhabit now, it would not do to behave in such a cavalier way and, even then, neither my weight nor my constitution could have coped with too many Liverpool weeks in a year. Once in a while, though, it was an enjoyable release from the accustomed routine and, although I can appreciate the fact that it might be administratively easier to keep flat and jumping separate, I regret the ending of the mixed meetings.

It does not matter that one group of jockeys jump obstacles and the other does not, or that our sizes and styles are necessarily different. We are all in the game together and I believe that contact between us can only be healthy. In business terms, we encounter many of the same problems, on and off the course, and so discussion is useful; in social terms, I certainly feel I am now missing out on some very diverting company.

Peter Scudamore, for instance, is a man for whom I have the utmost respect. For the past few years we have generally been champion jockey in our respective parts of racing and we have both achieved something extremely rare in riding more than 200 winners during a season. We have any amount of things in common and the man in the street quite possibly imagines that we live in each other's pockets. The fact is, I hardly know him at all. Richard Dunwoody, another highly successful jump jockey and Peter's closest challenger more often than not, is even more of a stranger. I have met him only once, at a very rare dinner to which both flat and jumping jockeys were invited.

All of this is a real pity. It means that I know no more of the top National Hunt jockeys of the day than what I might hear from other people in racing, which surely cannot be right. Scudamore has, along with his main retaining trainer, Martin Pipe, expanded the logical boundaries of expectation within his profession, and done it so often that it cannot be coincidence. I would love to know more about what makes him tick, but the modern programme does not allow it.

If Cheltenham is the mecca for all jumping folk, there were times when it had a pretty strong pull on me, too. Living there for as many years as I did, and working my apprenticeship within a jumping stable, could hardly do other than develop my interest in National Hunt racing. Even today, I follow the Nicholson runners – now trained by Frenchie's son David; but in years gone by I never missed attending the three-day festival at Prestbury Park during March, when the high quality of every race is matched by what we Irish would call 'the crack'.

For anyone who lives in Cheltenham, life undergoes a dramatic transformation during that annual week in early spring. What, for fifty-one weeks of the year, is an attractive, understated town, suddenly becomes a crowded, animated and utterly single-minded place in which racing is the sole topic of conversation among the thousands who invade from Ireland and all points closer. Many of them appear to need no sleep for the duration of their stay and not a few are seldom seen without a glass in one hand and a copy of *The Sporting Life* in the other. On their faces, invariably, is that conspiratorial smile of people who are enjoying the best week of the year to the full and, more than likely, think they have a sure thing for the second race tomorrow.

I used to love the week myself. Still do, really, although in recent years I have tended to confine my watching to the comfort of an armchair at home. This is partly because the television coverage is so good, but largely because I appreciate that I would no longer be able to go, as once I did, just for the famed crack. Like it or not, my face is now too well known. Imagine the scene: it is a week before the start of another new flat season but talk of Guineas favourites and Derby contenders has quite properly been shelved for the annual jumping festival. Into the general free-for-all of the Cottage Rake bar – a meeting and drinking area of the members' stand which was named after Vincent O'Brien's triple Gold Cup winner – comes the current champion flat jockey with a few friends. They watch the racing, they drink two or three sociable glasses of wine . . . and what happens? Inevitably, there are those who have had rather more than three glasses and who, speaking through alcohol, launch into the man, taunting him and provoking him. There are others who may not be drunk at all but who, for reasons best known to themselves, believe that a top sportsman should not be seen drinking in a racecourse bar.

So now I never go. Just once, in recent years, have I been to the festival, but then it was because I had been invited to spend the afternoon in a private box and knew that I could relax there without fear of harassment.

It is not just Cheltenham I avoid. For many years now, I have not set foot in a racecourse bar at the end of a working day, and it has reached the stage when I do not even think of doing so. Most of the other leading flat jockeys are the same and, sad reflection though it may be on the general standard of behaviour in bars, it is undoubtedly in our interests to avoid them. At the end of a racing day, any bar on the course will contain punters who have burned holes in their pockets and are looking for a convenient scapegoat on which to vent their bitterness. What better scapegoat than the man who may have ridden the beaten favourite on which they had planted their last fifty quid?

The overriding fear is that it might not stop at verbal abuse, but it would be sufficient, if it did, to justify my avoiding these places. In truth, they do not attract me anyway. Quite apart from the fact that many of those in England are shabby, uninviting rooms, badly stocked and staffed, going in there would, for me, be like anyone entering a bar immediately after work to have his day's efforts dissected. I don't need that, not on the good days and definitely not on the bad ones.

I would always rather get away from the racecourse, which is the equivalent of an office to me, and seek the company of my own family or friends for the evening.

I am not a hermit, though, and when my weight and my schedule allow it, I will happily go out to a pub or restaurant. I am aware that I am never immune from those who want to be provocative or malicious, not even in a restaurant of my own choice and in my own locality. There is always the chance of some big-mouth trying to impress his friends by decrying my performance on a horse I have ridden in a TV race he happened to see. Sometimes, when this happens, what is said is hurtful enough to touch a nerve and, while nine times out of ten I can ignore it, I have occasionally got up and walked out on an evening to avoid making a scene. Once or twice, no more, I have allowed the provoker to win and said something back, but I know *I* can never win that way.

What does now seem elementary to me is the folly of any high-profile sportsman putting himself in a position where he can be a target. If it arises on neutral territory, and for no foreseeable reason, then fair enough, but going somewhere socially has to be a selective process for those in the public eye. There can be no sorrier example of this, in recent times, than the England footballer Paul Gascoigne.

It was one thing for him to suffer a serious knee injury in the FA Cup Final. It was quite another to inflict one upon himself during a visit to a Newcastle nightclub where, it goes without saying, he was part-hero, part-villain, recognised by everyone and a focus of attention which might not exclusively have been idolatory.

Gascoigne may not have asked for the overplayed image he has attracted, the endless newspaper mentions and the scrutiny of every aspect of his life. But neither was he strong enough to control it nor his management good enough to prevent it all getting out of hand.

Jockeys, even at the very peak of their powers, thankfully escape the full volume of attention which feasted itself upon Gascoigne. But we are still widely recognised and regularly abused, and I would no sooner enter a potentially hostile social environment than I would get off a favourite in the Derby. The effect could be very similar.

12

EL GRAN SENOR: Success and Disaster in Our Partnership

Of the twenty Derbys in which I have ridden, I might have set off in six or seven thinking I had a decent chance if things went to plan. In only one, however, did I come out of the stalls convinced that I was going to win. It was in 1984 and, aware as I was of all the dangers that come with confidence, I found it hard to envisage defeat. Two minutes and forty-nine seconds later, the unthinkable happened. El Gran Senor was touched off by a short-head and I had suffered the greatest disappointment of my life in racing. It remains that way today.

During those early years at Ballydoyle, I sat on so many top quality colts that it might have been easy to fall into the trap of complacency. There was certainly a sense of the bottomless well about the place, a feeling that if one gold nugget failed to make the standard required, it was only a matter of reaching down to pull out another. None of this, however, had any bearing on my assessment of El Gran Senor.

Oh, we had enjoyed plenty of prior successes in my time with Vincent. Each week, at The Curragh or Leopardstown, seemed to throw up another likely lad for the classics. Although Storm Bird had ultimately deflated us in 1981, Golden Fleece had won the 1982 Derby and there was a time in 1983 when we seemed spoiled for choice. The Leopardstown Derby trial, which Golden Fleece had won twelve months earlier, this time went to Salmon Leap. The 2,000 Guineas at Newmarket was won by Lomond. Both were Sangster–O'Brien horses, yet we had another whom we regarded as better than either of these. His name was Caerleon and he would certainly have represented the stable at Epsom but for a minor training setback. Instead he won the French Derby at

Chantilly and then raided York to pick up the Benson and Hedges Gold Cup.

That same year we won the Eclipse Stakes at Sandown, with Solford, and our minds were already being diverted towards the 1984 classics by a pair of promising two-year-olds, Sadler's Wells and El Gran Senor. Sadler's Wells was to become an outstanding three-year-old and I must take nothing away from him. Apart from that same Leopardstown Derby trial, he won the Irish Guineas and the Eclipse and finished runner-up in both the French Derby and the King George. He was a very good horse – but El Gran Senor was better.

As a two-year-old, El Gran Senor was unbeaten in his four races, culminating in a defeat of the highly-regarded Rainbow Quest in Newmarket's Dewhurst Stakes. He was 7–4 favourite that day, which seems an ungenerous price in a ten-runner field for a traditionally competitive and instructive two-year-old event. But it reflected the reputation he had already made during three facile victories in Ireland, and it fairly reflected the high opinion in which I and everyone else at Ballydoyle already held him. It was worth recalling that his time, in the Dewhurst, was the fastest for many years, a full nine seconds quicker than that recorded by Grundy nine years earlier. And he was not exactly slow!

The imponderables are always there when you have an exciting two-year-old. Will he train on? Will he avoid sickness, injury and all the other unanticipated training setbacks? And, the greatest of all the annual teasers, will he stay a mile and beyond? There are, of course, any number of good races to be won at a mile but, when you start out with a good horse in his three-year-old season, the Derby is never far away from your mind. It is the ultimate; anything else is a settlement.

In aiming a horse for the Derby, a trainer will invariably increase his trip only gradually. Many times, he will not be convinced that his horse stays, and he cannot be convinced that he will handle the idiosyncrasies of the Epsom course. All he can confidently assess, in advance of the race, is how much speed and class his colt possesses, and in the case of El Gran Senor, he had it to burn.

His first run as a three-year-old was more a relief than a revelation. It eased any fears we may have had about him making the transition from juvenile to maturity and confirmed everything we had hoped about his ability. The Gladness Stakes at The Curragh may not have been much of a benchmark for the Derby, being run over only seven furlongs, but El Gran Senor won it so smoothly and impressively that I came away from Dublin that evening smugly certain that I had just ridden a horse who would never be beaten over a mile. In that, I was quite correct.

The O'Brien stable won both the English and Irish Guineas that year but I still had no doubt that El Gran Senor was a better horse than Sadler's Wells. At Newmarket, my horse beat Chief Singer and Lear Fan to take the 2,000 Guineas; Lear Fan had already won the Craven, and Chief Singer, although he did not stay, was a top-class miler who also went on to become the leading sprinter in Europe. So El Gran Senor had speed to spare. But would he stay?

In my heart, I felt he would not truly get a mile and a half, but that did not deter me from believing he could win at Epsom. I have never been so sure of anything in this game. Experience has taught me not to go into a race, any race, thinking it is merely a question of steering to collect, and only a fool would be over-confident in the Derby. But what I did know was that El Gran Senor had the ability to win this or any other Derby if I rode him correctly and if the race went to plan.

He was a bit like Dancing Brave, in a subsequent year, in being a smashing little horse who would fly to the front as if the others were standing still, but find nothing extra once he was there. In hindsight I would say El Gran Senor was one of the best horses ever trained at ten furlongs but that he never genuinely got twelve.

As the Derby meeting arrived, however, we just sat back and hoped and laid our private plans, while the annual Derby hype reached its pitch and the media chanted their personal fancies ever more loudly. Many of the pundits fancied El Gran Senor, which was hardly surprising. I think he had been favourite for every race he had run and, up to then, he had won them all. There was, to the general public, something mystical about the partnership of Sangster and O'Brien, something which suggested a virtual invincibility, and as the race came ever closer, the feeling grew that it would take something very special to stop us winning.

There were seventeen runners and some obvious dangers among them. One that I discounted was Secreto. His form just did not seem to match up to the race. I could not believe he would trouble us but I was to some extent aware of the potential for irony. Secreto was trained by David O'Brien, Vincent's Harrow-educated son, now in his third year by himself and doing very nicely. He was to be ridden by Christy Roche from Tipperary, who has ridden a fair bit for Vincent over the years. The ownership was also significant, for if Secreto had been in the name of Robert Sangster, David O'Brien's major patron, he would not have taken us on. But he was owned, instead, by a Mr Miglietti, a Greek businessman, so he took his place among the outsiders of the field.

Although it is only natural, especially prior to the Derby, to study the strength of the opposition, I had so much faith in my own mount that it seemed almost irrelevant to spend much time on it. Nevertheless, formalities were met and I discussed the race-plan in some detail with Vincent. Robert Sangster, although understandably excited by what seemed an exceptional Derby horse, left all such planning to his trainer and jockey, and all credit to him for that.

Our tactics were to be quite simple. Over a mile and a half, we agreed that the horse needed holding up for as late a run as possible. This was my job and, to this day, I believe that I was unlucky, rather than unprofessional, in being unable to carry it off to perfection.

Settling him was no problem. This was no headstrong Golden Fleece type we were dealing with. El Gran Senor was the easiest horse in the world to ride. He would always respond to orders, doing exactly what I wanted whether we were going a hack canter or a real good gallop. There was no danger of being run away with on this horse, because you had only to say 'Whoah, boy' to him and he would stop in a few strides. So I tucked him in and watched the horses in front, and the longer the race continued the more confident I became that, with the speed of El Gran Senor, I could take them all whenever I wanted. It was just a question of biding my time, because I had no intention of being in front until well inside the final furlong.

The thing which got us beaten was that the others were not

good enough. This may sound a hopelessly Irish statement, so let me explain. What I needed was to be led into the last furlong and the final, demanding climb to the finishing post. If I only took it up fifty yards from the line, that would be fine, because I was convinced that when I pressed the button on this horse, it would be all over in a matter of strides. But all the horses in front of me were beaten, their runs finished, even before the furlong pole. When a horse called Claude Monet gave up the ghost, I glided past him without any effort and I was exactly where I had not wanted to be – in front too soon.

He was so vastly superior to the others that he was running all over them despite my trying to cover him up. I had ridden exactly the race I planned to ride but, with nothing to lead him, the hill found him out. He simply did not see out the final furlong and Secreto, whose jockey had been hard at work a long way out, just got up.

It was a huge blow to me, I don't mind admitting. Never, before or since that day, has any defeat had such an effect on me. To lose any Derby by a short-head is a galling experience but for it to happen when yours was the class horse of the field, beyond any shadow of doubt, well, that was something I found quite devastating. At the time it had no bearing on the fact that Vincent had been beaten by his son. It was a great story for the papers, of course, but I honestly hardly gave it a thought. We had lost; that was what mattered.

It came as no surprise to me that the papers, once they had explored the human interest angle of the O'Brien family, turned their attentions to me in pretty uncomplimentary fashion. It was a controversial race and a controversial way to be beaten. I was prepared to believe that people would talk about that Derby for years to come, and I would have been right, but it upset me that the heavy-handed criticism which came my way was basically misguided.

The headlines and the press comments which hurt were those which said I had lost the race because I had not kicked on sooner. It might have been easy to make such a judgement from the stands but, having ridden El Gran Senor in all his races, and spent a lot of my waking hours and some of my sleeping ones pondering his strengths and weaknesses, I know it was wrong. If I could have the race all over again, I would wait longer, cover him up still more snugly, so that Secreto might have come past me sooner but I would still have had my horse's short, sharp run to deliver.

I am an admirer of the British racing press as it is today and I like to think I have a good relationship with the reporters. Men like Geoff Lester of *The Sporting Life* and George Ennor of the *Racing Post* will not simply guess at what might have happened during a race, they will ask the people involved. Day after day, they come to me for my verdict, on both winners and losers, and I will not shrug them off and send them away. If they ask the questions, I will tell them the story. But on that miserable June day at Epsom, nobody asked me. Whether or not the reporters assumed I would be unapproachable in defeat, they just ignored me and wrote it as they had seen it rather than as I knew it had been.

A jockey may not always be infallible in his judgements or his opinions and it is the right of any journalist to put his own interpretation on a sporting event. I would have thought, however, that the version of the man riding the horse has a place in any story, if only for the sake of balance and authenticity.

I have been lucky in my career, not too frequently falling foul of the press. Sometimes, when I have earned a suspension, I have attracted criticism and not resented it a bit, but this was different. They turned what was already the greatest disappointment of my riding life into a personal failure by suggesting – in some cases insisting – that El Gran Senor would have got the trip perfectly well and would have won the race if I had made more use of him.

Such arguments raged for weeks afterwards, and the theory that the horse did indeed stay the mile and a half was pushed still more vigorously by its supporters when, in his next race, El Gran Senor won the Irish Derby at The Curragh. Again, I read the race in a different way and, for my money, the Irish Derby confirmed the view that my horse was very much better when not being asked to race two furlongs beyond his optimum trip. In a true-run race over twelve furlongs, he did not get home and it was critically to our advantage that the race at The Curragh was not truly run at all. If it had been, I am doubtful if our horse would have won.

In the aftermath of Epsom the criticism which came my way, loudly from the media and, unheard, from losing punters, in no way reflected the reaction of the horse's connections. Rumours always abound of trainer, owner and jockey falling out when a favourite has been so contentiously beaten and I know many people have wondered if Vincent O'Brien blamed me, either in public or private. The truth is that he did not. He knew the horse as well as I did and his natural disappointment, slightly assuaged by the pleasure of triumph for his own son, produced no recriminations in my direction. Another trainer, a less dignified man, might have reacted unrealistically at such an emotive time but Vincent, impassive as ever, totally accepted my verdict on the running of the race and told me that he agreed. Robert Sangster was equally supportive and the upshot was that when we went to The Curragh we remained faithful to the original riding plan and determined to take it to extremes if necessary.

This time the race was run to suit me. There were only eight runners and they all seemed intent on a cat-and-mouse game, which played straight into my hands. They were travelling at such a poor pace that I was able to sit happily in behind them all, knowing that when, eventually, the heat was turned on, they would be unable to match my fellow's turn of foot.

Rainbow Quest was the obvious danger, but he was pulling hard over the first half-mile, so hard that his jockey, Steve Cauthen, finally let him run because he would never have got home if he had continued to fight him. So the pace perceptibly quickened and I was still quite content to wait behind Steve. I waited, and then waited again. We were little more than fifty yards from the post when I asked El Gran Senor to quicken, and took it off Rainbow Quest.

It was compensation of sorts, but it did not make up for losing the English Derby and it certainly did not change my view of the horse, or the way he had to be ridden. Years later, I still feel the same way.

If the Derby of 1984 was a bitter setback, it was just the start of a week I would love to forget but never will, the sort of week which seems designed to act as a reminder that, no matter how well things have been going, the equalisers are always just around the corner in racing.

When Terry drove me to Epsom on the Thursday I was still digesting the hammering I had taken in the morning papers and did not feel in the sunniest of moods. Although the Oaks is run on the Saturday, the Epsom meeting tails off badly on days two and three, the standard of the supporting races falling way below what might be expected of a classic programme. I had some pretty ordinary rides on that Thursday and was not expecting anything to brighten the gloom. Neither, however, was I expecting anyone or anything to make it worse.

I had taken a ride for a small trainer I hardly knew. He did not stay in the game long and I cannot even recall his name now, which is probably just as well. His runner was any price on the books, at least 20–1, I think, and it was quickly obvious that he did not act on the track at all. Many horses are completely nonplussed by Epsom and this was one of them. He came down the hill awkwardly and as we completed the descent and turned into the straight I was still out with the washing. This was not a useless animal, though, and once we were back on the level and heading for home he began to run for me. He flew, in fact, and under some pretty strong driving I got him into the race and he was only beaten a head.

I walked him back imagining, in my innocence, that the trainer and connections would surely be delighted to have come so close at Epsom and to have had such a decent run from their horse. How wrong can you be? This little trainer, whose opinion on anything I would never have sought, stood in the unsaddling enclosure and slagged me off in front of anyone prepared to listen. Naturally enough, this included quite a number of journalists and, Eddery being the week's popular scapegoat, the next day's headlines were predictable. There were quotes from the trainer everywhere, claiming that I had ridden a badly judged race, and for the second successive day I was painted as the villain of the piece.

It struck me as ironical that Vincent O'Brien had remained supportively silent after a furiously controversial Derby in which many observers thought I had got things wrong, but that a day later some completely undistinguished trainer had publicly abused me for almost winning on a horse which had no right to be involved in the finish . . .

The week had an appropriate ending. On the Saturday I rode Out of Shot in the Oaks and picked up a seven-day suspension for careless riding. As I came out of the weighing-room after the last I expected Terry to be waiting with the car engine running for our usual quick getaway but instead he was standing by the winners' enclosure looking as glum as I felt. He told me he had lost the car keys! So, to cap a perfect week, we had to discover the difficulty of getting a taxi on Epsom Downs on the Saturday evening after the Oaks. I can tell you, it is neither easy nor cheap!

13

RACING IN FRANCE: The Unexpected in the Arc de Triomphe

Winning the Prix de l'Arc de Triomphe is, in its way, every bit as big a thrill as winning the Derby. It is Paris in the autumn, it is glamour and drama, it is the meeting of the best horses in Europe. Any jockey would give a lot to win the Arc once; Steve Cauthen and Willie Carson are just two who never have. And yet, in the years from 1985 to 1987, I won the race three times in succession. Even now, it makes my head spin to reflect on it, because of all the things that have happened to me in racing, I consider this the most remarkable. Since the race was first run, more than seventy years ago, no other jockey has won it three consecutive years and it would not surprise me if nobody ever does.

I won the race for three different trainers, three very different men, each of whom has given me a great many winners over the years – Jeremy Tree and Guy Harwood in England and André Fabre on my Sunday outings to France. All three races have their story attached but the saga of my success in the Arc actually dates back to 1984, the year I will always remember more than anything for El Gran Senor's Derby defeat.

It had its consolations, as most years do, and some of the best were provided by the victories of that other Sangster–O'Brien three-year-old, Sadler's Wells. After he had won the Eclipse Stakes, a ten-furlong event at Sandown Park, Vincent began to think of him as an Arc horse. Subsequently, however, Sadler's Wells ran in the King George at Ascot and could only finish second, admittedly behind the previous season's Derby winner, Teenoso. Now, Vincent was undecided, and while I waited for him to make up his mind, I rode, and won on, Rainbow Quest in the Great Voltigeur, a one and a half mile race at York.

Rainbow Quest was entitled to win that day as his starting price of evens would suggest, but Jeremy Tree, who trained him, had already marked down the Arc as his end-of-season target and, on the basis that I would keep the ride if available, I rode him again in a racecourse gallop at Newbury, about a fortnight before the big day at Longchamp.

He worked fantastically well. I had not ridden him in many of his three-year-old races, usually because Vincent ran something against him, and the ease with which El Gran Senor had picked him off at The Curragh did not encourage me to think that here was an Arc contender, But the Newbury gallop completely changed my mind. I got off him and told Jeremy that he not only felt in good enough form to run in the Arc but that he would probably win it.

From that day on, I prayed that I would be available for the ride but, after a good deal of thought, Vincent elected to run Sadler's Wells. It was not a decision I could disagree with, and nor would it have occurred to me to ask to be released in order to ride Rainbow Quest. It was a fact, however, that Sadler's Wells had never won at anything beyond ten furlongs, and he was destined never to do so. Like El Gran Senor, he did not stay the extra two furlongs in a true-run race, which the Arc invariably is.

So it was a disappointment to me, but not a surprise, when Sadler's Wells finished in the pack at Longchamp, not seeing out the trip. The surprise came in the running of Rainbow Quest. Tony Murray came in for the ride and, on the Sunday morning, I would have nominated him as the luckiest man in Paris. Yet he ran terribly, finishing nearly last, and my initial reaction was one of disbelief. I did not think I had suddenly become a hopeless judge of a horse and he had certainly given me a hell of a good feel that day at Newbury.

In retrospect, he must purely have been suffering from the familiar effects of a hard season. Although he did not run at Epsom he had been kept very busy and had also done plenty of travelling, running in both the French and the Irish Derbys after the Guineas, then coming home for the King George and the Voltigeur. He had finished up by winning nothing, but he had been very consistent and a great credit to his trainer, who assured me that he would be back in the yard for a four-year-old career.

I looked forward to that, and not least because of the trainer.

To Be a Champion

For some years, I had been on a second retainer with Jeremy and I always found him a pleasure to work for, both in the planning of my schedule and on race-days. He was a very organised trainer, who always knew precisely which horses he would be running, when and where, some days in advance. This meant that one phone call a week to him would enable me to map out a skeleton programme for my week, into which the outside rides could be slotted. If only every trainer could be so positive, life for the jockeys would be a whole lot easier but, sadly, many of them dither until it is too late, and a jockey either has to turn down the ride or, if he really wants it, to get off another for which he has already been booked.

Jeremy never ran anything unless he thought it had a winning chance, which was another great factor in his favour. Naturally, the young horses sometimes needed educating and he could not be sure how far forward they were, but he never ran anything just for the sake of going to the races. For a retained rider, this is very good news, because it means that his rides for the stable will all have a chance and that he is free to seek freelance mounts more often than he would be if his contract demanded he rode a lot of no-hopers.

There was a mistaken impression within racing that Jeremy Tree was a mellow, sanguine man, immune to the visible emotions of many another trainer. It was not true. As I came to know him better I realised that there was a lot going on beneath the contented smile. He was very far from being as laid-back about racing as most people seemed to imagine and, although the majority would probably never have noticed it, I could always sense in the unsaddling enclosure when he had got fired up about a race.

He adored having a nice horse in the yard and would get extremely nervous before that horse ran. There would be plenty of emotion during a race, too, even if he did not display it in the transparent style of a Neville Callaghan. Jeremy was a completely different sort of individual, but he cared passionately about his horses, all the same.

A confirmed bachelor, Jeremy lives in great style at Beckhampton, near Marlborough. It is an elegant, old-fashioned lifestyle, which would not suit me but seems to fit Jeremy like a glove. He has beautiful food, cooked to perfection and served with ceremony and dignity by his butler. I found all this rather amusing, but it did not prevent me taking up every breakfast invitation Jeremy put my way on work mornings – the breakfasts were among the best I have ever eaten. Jeremy has been retired for a couple of years now but he still lives in the house and, if I go to ride work for his successor, Roger Charlton, I still go to breakfast with Jeremy! He will go out to watch the horses work, maybe on a Saturday morning, for the sake of interest but he never interferes with Roger's training methods, and nor did I ever imagine that he would. He is a real gentleman, but also a lot of fun to be with; I enjoy his company now as much as ever and still speak to him regularly on the phone. Looking back over all the winners we had together, I would have to say that the 1985 Arc topped the lot.

I think Jeremy always had one eye on the Arc that year and he wanted to keep Rainbow Quest as fresh as possible, no easy matter for a race which comes seven months after the start of the British flat season. I knew the horse was at least as good as ever, and possibly better, when I won the Coronation Cup on him at the Epsom Derby meeting. He might not have beaten much in a seven-runner field but he did the job impressively enough.

Following that, he was placed in both the Eclipse and the King George, behind Pebbles and Petoski respectively, but as these races fell on Saturdays when I was required in Ireland, I did not ride him either time. In fact, as I gratefully accepted the chance, second time around, to partner Rainbow Quest in the Arc, I realised that I had never been beaten on him.

Arc day is special, and has become more so in the past few years with the steady increase of British racegoers being flown over to Paris by a variety of travel companies, but most notably by Ian Fry's innovative outfit, Horse Racing Abroad. There are times, on the morning of the race, when it seems there are more British folk than French in town, and on the odd occasion when I have stayed on either the Saturday or Sunday night, I can confirm that the impression prevails in the hotels and restaurants, too. People go to enjoy themselves, to eat and drink well, in addition to enjoying the racing, and there is the inevitable sense of invasion, of trying to beat the French on their own soil. For all this jingoism, however, the behaviour is invariably good, indeed immaculate compared to football followers overseas, and I like to think this is because those who travel there do so because they are genuine racing fans, not just would-be hooligans spoiling for a public scrap. I have been aware of the British contingent each year at Longchamp and it is good to know there are people up in the stands rooting for you. If this reached its zenith a year later, with Dancing Brave, I could still see and hear plenty of support for Rainbow Quest when I cantered him down to post with the other fourteen starters.

Glance across to the stands from the mile-and-a-half start at Longchamp on Arc day and there is a sight to stir the blood, those mighty buildings full to overflowing, Paris chic rubbing shoulders with streetwise Cockneys and tweed-clad chaps from the Cotswolds. It is one of the few truly international gatherings, off course and on, in a sport which can sometimes be thought insular. It is a day when the winner feels he has struck a blow for his country as well as for himself.

Rainbow Quest was in very good shape. No question, this time, of him having had enough for the year; Jeremy's careful training programme had seen to that. But it was difficult to be wholly confident when among the opposition stood the French horse Sagace who, a year earlier, had provided a second successive Arc win for trainer Patrick Biancone and owner Daniel Wildenstein. He was a star and, although now five, his form suggested he would be as difficult to defeat as ever. But, as we circled at the start prior to loading up, I noticed that Sagace was wearing heavy bandages. Fleetingly, I felt encouraged, because this was almost certainly an indication of a patched-up problem. Then I put the thought out of my mind. We were going into the stalls and I focused my mind on the race I intended to ride.

Often, there are upwards of twenty runners in the Arc and traffic congestion can be a major consideration if you elect to come from off the pace. With fifteen, the risk of being stopped was not so great. I got the run I wanted and, as we really began to race, I challenged on the outside of the horse I most feared. Sagace was still galloping bravely but then, for no apparent reason, he fell away to his left and gave me a bump, momentarily checking the stride of my horse. Twice more he came across, the contact not as great as on the first occasion but still technical interference.

Sagace did not stop. He battled on gamely, holding Rainbow

Quest in a memorable finish. But Rainbow Quest had been good enough to put him under maximum pressure, perhaps exposing the chink in his fitness that those bandages were meant to camouflage. Whatever the problem Sagace had had, it seemed odds-on that it accounted for him going left when the pressure was on.

I did not think it odds-on, however, that the stewards would think the interference deliberate, which almost certainly it had not been, and neither was I completely confident that they would conclude that it had affected the result. To do so would be to take the Arc off a French horse and give it to an English one; strict though the Paris stewards are, this was quite an undertaking.

The hooter, indicating a stewards' inquiry, had sounded as we walked back to the winners' enclosure but I am not sure whether Jeremy had heard it. He loved Rainbow Quest, he loved Paris, and the look on his face as I dismounted told me that, beaten or not, he had just enjoyed one of the great racing moments of his thirty-odd years in the game. He had trained some great horses, like John Cherry, Known Fact and Sharpo, he had won the Guineas and the Oaks twice each and many other big races besides, but I had seldom seen him as happy as he was that day. His horse had only finished second but he was plainly proud beyond words. I was loath to spoil such a joyful scene, but this was, after all, the Arc, and I was not accepting defeat just yet.

'I am going to object,' I said, receiving by way of return one of Jeremy's quizzical, old-fashioned looks. The objection lodged, I waited quietly to enter the judges' chambers, while outside, the course was abuzz with argument and speculation. There are no course bookmakers in France, the Paris-Mutuel operating a Tote-style monopoly, but if there had been I imagine the betting on the outcome of the inquiry would have been close. I thought I had a good chance of getting the race but, on foreign soil, I could not be confident.

There are people in racing, and Jeremy might be one of them, who are slightly squeamish about objecting, particulary if an inquiry has already been called. I have no such scruples. If you believe you have the high ground in any incident, you must make the most of it, and by lodging an objection you are going on the offensive, demonstrating your belief that an injustice has been done. This does not mean there are never times when a jockey misuses the system; some objections are so obviously fatuous that the jockey involved quite rightly sacrifices the deposit he has to put down, a system designed to discourage all but the most genuine objectors. I was plenty genuine enough at Longchamp that day but I was well aware of the rarity of an objection, let alone a revised result, in a race of the Arc's stature.

I was called in. The stewards, who thankfully speak pretty good English in general, said that they accepted I had been bumped by the winner but that it did not appear to have been serious. I replied that the first barge, accidental or not, had been quite hard enough for my horse to lose his action and that, in my opinion, it could have cost us the race. They played the head-on film through again, made a few notes and then sent me back outside to await the verdict.

Jeremy strolled in to see me in that deceptively nonchalant way of his. I think he was still high on the emotion of having come so close; I know he thought we had no chance of getting the race. As we stood together in the corridor, Robin Gray, the British journalist and racecourse commentator, rushed up and shouted to us that the stewards had upheld the objection. By now, even I was sceptical. I didn't believe him. He excitedly pointed to the TV screens above our head which, glory be, were flashing up the revised placings. I had won my second Arc.

For Jeremy, it was a first Arc triumph and, at approaching sixty years old, few trainers deserved it more. He was reduced to silence by the moment, but then he threw his arms around me in a great bearhug before turning to sprint out of the door in search of his owner. I was delighted for him as much as I was for myself, but in the ownership of Rainbow Quest there was also great significance. He ran in those familiar green and pink colours of Prince Khalid Abdullah. I had ridden some of the Prince's horses for five years, through his staunch patronage of Jeremy's yard, but in the twelve months which followed Rainbow Quest's Arc, we were to forge a much closer and more lasting link as my career entered another new phase.

14

DANCING BRAVE: The Story Behind Our Association

A year to the day after Rainbow Quest's controversial win, I once more stood in that corridor outside the Longchamp weighing-room. This time, I was not nervously awaiting a stewards' decision, because the Arc was still to be run, and the trainer with me was not the comfortable, avuncular J. Tree but the lean, greying and transparently tense Guy Harwood.

There were, undeniably, reasons for us both to feel tense, yet while Guy was showing all the symptoms, I felt remarkably calm considering the fact that, within a couple of hours, 10,000 Brits on the racecourse and millions more watching on television at home would be fervently hoping and even expecting me to win the Arc on the horse the nation had taken to its heart, Dancing Brave.

The brilliance of Dancing Brave needs no greater emphasis than this: people went racing specifically to watch him. It is an accolade awarded to very few horses and, when it is, it indicates a very special talent, not just for winning races but for doing so in style. Dancing Brave was a wonderful horse and I was delighted to be riding him but, it has to be said, not everyone was delighted for me.

Greville Starkey was Guy's stable jockey and had been for a number of years. Under normal circumstances he would have been on board Dancing Brave in the Arc. Indeed, if the trainer had been given his way, I am sure Greville would have ridden the horse. But in June of that year, just before the Epsom Derby, Prince Khalid had approached me with an offer to become his retained jockey. I had not immediately said yes, and discussions were continuing right up to the Arc, but the Prince rightly believed I would eventually agree and he personally wanted me to ride Dancing Brave.

It was a sensitive issue, out of which the newspapers had made great capital, and although I had done nothing to jock Greville off, such as approaching the owner or trainer direct, there was a lot of sympathy for the man who, on Lester Piggott's retirement in 1985, had become the elder statesman of the weighing-room.

Guy Harwood is intensely loyal to his jockeys and may very well have felt uncomfortable with the situation. Add this to his habitual state of edginess before a race and the strain showing on the face of the man who stood before me at Longchamp that afternoon becomes easier to appreciate. He had come to me while I was changing and asked if he could have a private word. We found a place as private as any amid the organised chaos of Arc day and Guy asked: 'How are you going to ride this horse?'

It would not have been an unusual question coming from any trainer. From Guy, it was another predictable sign of his tension. For a man who has achieved great success, first in the motor trade and then in the business of training, he is a remarkably nervy character, never more so than when he is preparing a horse for a big race. A jockey must grow accustomed to spending a lot of time talking on the phone to trainers but Guy's calls can come at any hour. He has rung me, at home, at six in the morning and he has rung at past midnight. I am convinced he never sleeps at all when he is really excited by a horse.

Guy is a great one for debating race tactics with his jockey and he can take it to unusual extremes. He wants to know exactly where you will be and what you are going to do. It is, I am sure, not meant unpleasantly; it is just a sign of the man's obsessional involvement. So I was not at all surprised when he came to ask how I intended to ride Dancing Brave, although I am sure my answer surprised him.

'I am going to wait,' I said simply. 'Really?' said Guy, his eyebrows shooting upwards quite noticeably. 'Yes, and I'll be the very last to challenge, you'll see,' I assured him. He said nothing more, nothing at all, but just shook his head and walked out, leaving me in little doubt that he felt such tactics a risk and that I would be in trouble with him if they failed.

None of this was designed to decrease any real or imagined pressure on me for what was certain to be a race subjected to tremendous scrutiny back home, yet I cannot say I was worried by it. I felt the buzz that always comes before riding a good horse in a major race, and I could hardly be unaware of the great sense of anticipation among the record number of British racegoers who had travelled across for the weekend. But I knew I had the confidence of the owner, which meant a lot, and I also knew in my heart that the tactics I had outlined to Guy were right for the horse.

I had ridden Dancing Brave in the King George at Ascot, on that occasion because Greville was injured. It was the first time I had sat on him, but Guy said nothing to me by way of a warning not to come too soon. We cruised into the straight and I felt he could go and win exactly when I chose, so I asked him to quicken, and quicken he did, in dramatic fashion. He shot to the front and it seemed to me inevitable that he would go on and win by ten lengths. Instead, he did absolutely nothing in front and we only managed to beat Shardari a length after I had given my horse a smack.

After the race, I said nothing to Guy, because we had won, but a week or so later I did express my views to him and said that, if ever I rode him again, I would hold him up much longer. So far as that season was concerned, though, I did not expect to ride Dancing Brave again and, as his stud value was rocketing, neither did I expect him to be kept in training. The call to partner him in the Arc was as much a boost to me as, I am afraid, it must have been a blow to Greville who, in my view, was justified in believing he had never done anything wrong on the horse.

Dancing Brave had not been introduced to a racecourse until less than a month from the end of his two-year-old season. He ran twice in what remained of that campaign and won both events, at Sandown and Newmarket, at odds-on. Each of the two races was over a mile, so Guy was apparently already confident that the horse would stay despite question marks arising from his breeding, in which speed was the great influence.

His first race as a three-year-old was the Craven Stakes at Newmarket which he won without fuss, and the obvious next stop was the 2,000 Guineas. Sent off favourite again, he beat Green Desert by a cosy three lengths, once more showing terrific speed. The doubt remained over his ability to stay the extra half-mile but Greville never seemed in any doubt and the public latched on to the horse with gusto, making him a 2–1 favourite.

Dancing Brave will be remembered almost as much, I suspect, for failing to win the Derby as for winning the Arc and, in some minds, Greville Starkey's epitaph will be that he was responsible for losing the Derby. In the aftermath of his half-length defeat at the hands of Shahrastani, ridden by Wally Swinburn, poor Greville came in for some furious and unforgiving criticism. I am convinced this was unfair and that Greville was not to blame for getting the horse beaten.

Just as I did later in the season, Greville rode Dancing Brave with a concern for getting the trip. If he had ridden him closer to the pace, as many paddock pundits vociferously advised him he should have done, there would have been a real danger that he would not get home and that his greatest asset, that short but spectacular burst of speed, would be blunted.

Ironically, I believe that the reason for Dancing Brave's defeat had much more to do with the second Harwood runner, a horse called Allez Milord. He, too, had completed his two-year-old season with a facile win at Newmarket, and although not in the Abdullah colours, he was certainly not sent to Epsom just to give the owners a nice day out. Guy booked Cash Asmussen to ride him and he was thought to have a realistic each-way chance.

The trouble came, as it so often does at Epsom, when the field swept down Tattenham Hill and into the straight. Greville had settled Dancing Brave at the back of the field, just as I would have done, and although he stealthily crept past a couple of no-hopers down the hill, most of the field remained in front of him as they made the turn.

Greville pulled to the outside and got his horse running but, almost simultaneously, Cash tried a similar manoeuvre on Allez Milord. Greville had to check his run and go even wider than he had planned. It cost him the race. At Epsom, you just can't afford to get stopped when you make your challenge because those in front will get away from you on the hill. Wally had got first run and he made the most of it. The fact that Dancing Brave was eating up the ground in the last two furlongs, and that he finally failed by only half a length, confirmed to my mind that he was the best horse in the field and would have won but for that mishap with his own stable companion.

Despite being roundly pilloried, Greville kept the ride when

Dancing Brave went to Sandown for his next run and, knowing Guy, I should not think there was ever any doubt in his mind about it. Over the ten furlongs of the Eclipse Stakes, a trip which was probably his ideal, he soundly trounced Triptych and half a dozen others. But if Greville felt a bit better for that there was more heartache awaiting him. Unfit for the King George at Ascot, he had to watch on television while I won on the horse and, coincidentally, strengthened my convictions about the correctness of the tactics in the Derby.

The press and the racing public had by now begun to talk animatedly of the Arc as the natural conclusion to the horse's season but, as yet, there was no talk of a jockey change. My own negotiations about the job with the Prince were continuing, but much as I would have given for the chance to keep the ride on Dancing Brave, it was not mentioned.

Guy's training of the horse was spot-on. He gave him a break after the King George in order to freshen him up, but then, crucially I felt, ran him at Goodwood three weeks before the Arc. It did not matter that the opposition was so negligible that the bookies did not even form a market, the important thing was to have the prep race and prove, to everybody's satisfaction, that the sparkle was still there.

This, I believe, was where the connections of Generous went awry, five years later. A similarly exceptional horse, Generous had carried all before him and was a justifiably short price to bring home the spoils from Longchamp. But he went there without a recent run and with only an inconclusive racecourse gallop at Newbury to work on. I say it was inconclusive because, to my surprise, Generous was ridden at Newbury by his work-rider, one of trainer Paul Cole's lads, rather than by his big-race jockey Alan Munro, who illogically partnered something else in the gallop. Neither Paul nor Alan could see anything wrong with this arrangement, yet the race-rider was the only one who could have accurately assessed whether the horse was still at his best, simply because he was the only one who could recognise the feel he got from him when he was winning the Derby and the King George. The work-rider knows how the horse feels in the morning but he has no idea how he feels in the afternoon, when it really matters. It is all hypothesis now, of course, but if things had been done differently, and preferably with a prep race, it might have become apparent that the sparkle had gone out of Generous (he was later found to have a low blood count) and he could have been retired to stud without suffering such a deflating defeat in Paris.

Dancing Brave won as easily as he should have done at Goodwood, with G. Starkey in the plate. It was only then, with the days ticking away before the Arc, that Prince Khalid informed Guy that he would like me to have the ride at Longchamp. All sorts of theories were publicly aired as to why he had taken such a step, from the gentle option of my personal record in the Arc to the more brutal opinion that Greville was paying the harshest penalty for failing to win the Derby.

I was never told the real thinking behind it and I did not ask. For me, it was enough to have the ride. I was delighted. I had to look at it that way because this is a tough game in which all of us, now and again, suffer from the preferences of different owners for certain jockeys. I would have felt aggrieved in Greville's position but I could not let it bother me that he had been jocked off. It was not my doing and, another year, I might be the sufferer. The owner pays the bills and, in the final reckoning, he makes the decisions.

It promised to be an outstandingly good Arc and I think it was. There were seven Group One winners in the field and, 300 yards from the post, they were virtually in line across the track. I am told that the race was one of the great sporting spectacles of the 1980s and that the British contingent in the vast crowd almost raised the roof. I am also told that many feared I had left my challenge too late and that, up in the area reserved for owners and trainers, Guy Harwood was among those tearing out their hair. All this is hearsay, for I was so intent on the job at hand that I neither heard nor saw anything else. What I do know for certain is that Dancing Brave won the Arc in the style of one of the greatest horses I have either ridden, seen or dreamed about.

The French challenge was led by Bering, who had won all four of his starts that season, including the French Derby. I always thought he would be the biggest danger even though the Aga Khan's four runners included Shahrastani, who had beaten Dancing Brave in the Epsom Derby. So long as I was not checked in my run through, I did not believe he could beat me again.

The pace was fast, as we had thought it would be, and both

Gary Moore, who rode Bering, and I were quite happy to be tugged around in the rear. Just as I had promised Guy outside the weighing-room, I was the last to challenge. Into the straight, and Shardari, on whom Greville had picked up a spare ride, hit the front. Briefly, he must have had fond illusions of a fairy-tale win. But then Bering came sweeping past him with what must have looked the decisive thrust. Only then did I ask Dancing Brave for everything. Halfway up the straight we had still been as near last as first but with that surge of speed beloved by his followers, Dancing Brave cut them all down and put the race rapidly beyond recall.

I remember there being an explosion of noise when I walked Dancing Brave back into the parade ring, where the winner unsaddles, and I remember some very happy faces all around me. I remember little of what was said, but I can recall telling the press that Dancing Brave had to be the best horse I had ever ridden.

It was not quite the end of his career, because Prince Khalid then agreed that he should go to Santa Anita in California the following month for the Breeders' Cup Turf. Some of his fans went too, their following as loyal as that of true football supporters and just as noisy, but this time there were no celebrations. Fourth place was the best we could manage, whereupon this great, great horse was retired to the owner's Newmarket stud; his first crop ran as two-year-olds in 1991 but if he ever produces another as good as himself, I hope I am still around to ride him.

By complete contrast to the hype and expectation which surrounded Dancing Brave's victory, the last of my three consecutive Arcs passed almost without comment. The reason is that I rode a French-trained horse and that he started at 20–1. But for me, even if Trempolino's year could never quite compare with the one before, I was still not surprised by his win, only by his starting price.

He was trained by André Fabre, who had rapidly achieved pre-eminence among French trainers. His origins were in the game's other code, for he had been a very good steeplechase jockey, but after setting up as a trainer in the provinces and doing well, he took the plunge, moved to Paris and just kept on winning races.

By sheer weight of success, he attracted the top owners and his two principal patrons in a yard which today extends close to 400 horses are Sheikh Mohammed and Prince Khalid.

Trempolino, however, was owned by neither of these dominant Arab figures and nor did I have any obligation to ride him. But, after winning on him in the Prix Niel, I told André that I would not want to ride anything else in the Arc. He had been that impressive.

I've had the good fortune to ride some really successful horses for André over the past five years. In 1991 when Toulon went off favourite in the St Leger, André had enough confidence in the horse's form to stay at home. I won the classic race for him and fulfilled his expectations. He is a seriously good trainer and it is absolutely no fluke that he keeps churning out winners. He gets his horses right for the job. Toulon and Trempolino were no exception! I hold him in highest regard.

Oddly enough, it was the St Leger, in 1987, which made me believe my horse was a good deal better than his price would suggest. I had ridden Mountain Kingdom in the Leger, a decent horse at his best but no world-beater, yet a furlong from home I had come to take on the short-priced favourite, Reference Point, looking as if I might win. Reference Point held on well enough in the end and was obviously a very good horse, but after the Derby and the King George, which he had won, plus the Eclipse, in which he was second, the season had taken its toll. I reasoned that he was over the top in the Leger and I knew for a fact that Trempolino was in a higher league than Mountain Kingdom. So, as the bookies still made Reference Point odds-on for the Arc, I was very hopeful that I was on the right horse. I said as much to Terry, adding that I thought Trempolino would have won the Leger doing handsprings. I think he shot off to the nearest bookmaker's!

The race was run at breakneck speed again, and once more I sat at the back, biding my time. Cash Asmussen and I were last and last but one on the final turn but we both flew home from there. Cash finished second on Tony Bin, who was to go on and win the race the next year when, to my great regret, Trempolino had long since retired.

He did run once more, taking the now customary route to America in November and being unlucky, due to traffic problems, not to win the Breeders' Cup. But the horse by then had new owners and they were intent that he should go straight to stud.

Since my time with Vincent O'Brien I have a much greater appreciation of the breeding side and I fully understand the actions of owners in packing up certain horses after their three-year-old career. But there are times when this seems to happen out of custom and expectation rather than because it is the best course to take. It has reached the stage where a trainer and owner are heartily applauded for keeping a horse in training because it is so unusual, and that, I think, is sad.

With Trempolino, I am convinced it was a misguided decision. There are so many valuable races around now for the older horse, not just in Britain and Europe but all around the racing world, and I was so struck by Trempolino's ability that I honestly thought he could clean up. André had done a great job with him because he had not always been an easy horse to ride or, I assume, to train, and he lost one race at Deauville through pulling too hard for his own good.

André managed to settle him so that it was no longer troublesome to switch him off during a race, and the speed of his improvement that autumn was quite dramatic. He set a new record time for the Arc, only a year after Dancing Brave had done the same, and because he was such a late improver at three, he simply had to be better at four. A tiny horse, by Sharpen Up, he had class, stamina and a turn of foot. A jockey can ask for little else and to say I was frustrated by the owners' decision is putting it mildly.

15

PRINCE KHALID ABDULLAH: A World of Opportunity

Nobody lightly walks away from a job as first jockey to Vincent O'Brien. Nobody in his right mind, anyway. During the years I was with him at Ballydoyle, the job meant good money, guaranteed success and a lifestyle of civilised hours and treatment. There is no one in the whole world of racing for whom I have greater respect than Vincent, nor have I ever met any trainer whose methods could be compared favourably to his. And yet, during the summer of 1986, I was actively negotiating my release from his employment.

I could put forward a few reasons for this apparently illogical state of affairs, but much the most influential was that I felt the time had come to once again drop anchor in England.

I was into my sixth year of a split identity and, while dividing my energies between England and Ireland did have its benefits, it also had drawbacks which, as time passed, I had begun to feel more acutely. The O'Brien job meant, of course, that I could hardly ever ride in England on a Saturday, the major racing day of the week. This not only came expensive in terms of missed winners, but also asked a big question of the loyalty of trainers who might put me up regularly around the midweek gaff meetings only to find that I was consistently unavailable for the prestige weekend races.

It meant trying to be all things to all men, even more so than is demanded of any freelance jockey. It also meant that, each March, I had to mentally write off all prospect of being champion jockey when the English season ended. It just wasn't on. It meant a lot of travelling, tiring weekends during which I would habitually ride both in Ireland and in France. There was no point in complaining about any of this, firstly because I had gone into it with my eyes wide open, secondly because I was being paid generously for it and thirdly because I was still riding plenty of winners, even if they were widely diversified.

But I did hanker after the buzz of chasing the title, which once had been so familiar to me. I also hankered after a slightly more home-based routine. So when Khalid Abdullah decided he would like me to be his retained jockey, I was ripe for the picking.

It was never going to be a straightforward transition, though. Whether I liked it or not, I had become a high profile property in the racing business and I was proposing to trade one high profile employer for another. Whatever I did, however I approached the dilemma, feathers were certain to be ruffled.

The Prince had made his initial approach quite early in the 1986 season, far too early for my judgement to be in any way influenced by Dancing Brave. The factors I considered were the relative stability that such a job would give me, in terms of an English base; the quality of horses; and, inevitably, the money.

Stability meant a lot. I had a young family, two girls of an age at which every day sees changes. I did not pretend, even to myself, that a new job would mean being able to spend a great deal more time with them during the season, but it was a step in the right direction.

As for the horses, Rainbow Quest and Dancing Brave were only two examples of the Abdullah strength. In terms both of numbers and ability, it was building all the time. Vincent, by contrast, seemed no longer to have quite such a formidable team. These things do run in phases and no trainer, whatever his skills in the breeding paddocks and the sales ring, has an immunity to the occasional declines. It was noticeable, nonetheless. In 1985 Vincent had lost the title of champion trainer in Ireland for only the second time in ten years, and his number of winners had dropped from forty-two to twenty-one. In 1986, it was to be still starker – the same number of winners, but little or nothing in prestigious events and only ninth place in the trainers' table. There were reasons for it: the bloodstock market was in depression, men like Robert Sangster were feeling the pinch . . . and the Arabs had arrived on the British and Irish racing scene in considerable force.

From that day to this, there has been no shortage of racing

people anxious to knock the Arab influence and to argue that they exert a wholly unhealthy domination, discouraging and eventually eliminating many of the smaller, less affluent British owners. It is an argument which cannot be dismissed out of hand and there were times when I had considerable sympathy with it, but I have come around to the view that British flat racing would be in a far more precarious state than it already is without the support of certain prominent Arabs.

It is certainly true that the Maktoum family, and Prince Khalid, brought such unprecedented resources to the game that the sale price of yearlings was pushed up, probably unrealistically. But the trend had already been instigated, both by the O'Brien–Sangster syndicate and by some American trainers, such as the legendary D. Wayne Lukas, whose mega-rich owners allowed him to raid Keeneland with what amounted to an open and endless chequebook. The inflationary prices, which undoubtedly ruled many would-be players out of the game, were partly, but not entirely, the fault of the Arabs.

As the years have passed, it has also become very clear that racing is much more, to the leading Arab owners, than a new toy to discard when the novelty wears off. They are serious, even passionate about the sport; indeed, to call it a sport where they are concerned is a misnomer. Although I would hopefully be offending none of them by saying that they do not need the money, they run their racing operations as they would run any other business, and I have learned from personal experience that this means they run them very efficiently indeed.

The business angle does not, however, mean that they put nothing back. They sponsor races, usually for very large sums, and on a day-to-day basis they put their money back into racing simply by employing so many people. With all the lads needed in yards around the country to cope with their vast numbers of horses in training, all the staff on their studs and their racing managers and secretaries, the Arabs employ, directly or indirectly, a tremendous number of people who, within the prevailing economic climate, might otherwise be inflating the numbers of unemployed. Racing has come to rely on the Arab investment and, minor consideration though it was when measured against the risk of lives being lost, the onset of the Gulf War, and its attendant threat to the resources of men like the

Maktoums, threatened the livelihood of many people employed in our game.

Back in 1986, however, the Arabs were getting stronger and the others were getting weaker and the chance to ride full-time for Prince Khalid, who had been giving me winners both in England and in France since the start of the 1980s, was more than tempting. Frankly, it was irresistible. He was offering a staggering sum of money, or so it seemed to me, and for the second time in my career I was being made aware that someone valued my services far more highly than I could ever have envisaged. It was an exciting offer, an exciting time, but also, as I have hinted, an uncomfortable time. There had been no falling out with Vincent, nor was there going to be, and I did not relish the prospect of telling him that I wanted to leave, especially considering the contractual complication that I was signed on to ride for him in 1987, too.

I knew, beyond question, that there would be things about the Ballydoyle experience that I would miss. Not least among them was the week we spent, each spring, working and assessing that year's horses. This was annually a rewarding week in terms of anticipating the season ahead (all over Britain and Ireland, thousands of races are being won in the minds of jockeys and trainers during those dreamers' days), but it was also a remarkably civilised week.

Usually, I would stay at the Cashel Palace Hotel, a couple of miles from the yard and a treat in itself. Whereas, with every other yard I know, riding work would involve reporting for duty some time between 6 a.m. and 7.30 a.m., Vincent had his own timetable, and I fully approved of it. All year round, the first lot would pull out at 9 a.m., which meant I had no need to get up before eight o'clock and allowed me to have breakfast, usually at Vincent's house, even before starting work. This was a rare privilege but Vincent could do it because his was a private training establishment. He had his own gallops, everything was self-contained and he saw no point in the day starting any earlier.

There were many times when I marvelled at the man, usually after I had ridden a winner. Sometimes, in looking at a horse prior to a race, I seriously doubted whether he was right, but I should have known better. Vincent never ran anything unless he was certain it was spot-on, and he was very seldom wrong.

The facilities helped, of course. Ballydoyle is on a par with Manton, the English yard with which, ironically, Robert Sangster is now most closely involved, and Vincent's great gift was in making the very best use of everything available to him. There is no point in having the best gallops in Europe and the best accommodation for horses if they are not properly utilised. Vincent was, no doubt still is, a perfectionist.

I sometimes felt that he must spend every evening with the stud-book for company. The intricacies of breeding, and matchings of stallion and mare, fascinated him as much as anyone I have known, but he did not allow it just to interest him. Like everything else, he wanted to conquer it and to be the best. And so the man who, years before I knew him, came to Cheltenham each year and took home all the best of Britain's jumping prizes, who later made the Derby his personal property and who refined training to an art form, turned himself into an encyclopaedia of bloodstock and put his knowledge to the best purpose.

What drives him on now, in his mid-seventies and with few fresh fields left for him to conquer, I cannot imagine, but he is still training to the same high standard. I had always thought that his son David, responsible for Secreto's Derby win, would eventually take over from Vincent, but it was not to be. In 1988, at the age of thirty-two, David gave up training and, to my knowledge, got out of racing completely. I found this hard to believe, because on the few occasions when I had ridden for him and we had returned from the races together, he would head purposefully back to his yard and his horses at eight or nine o'clock at night. He appeared to love the game, and surely he could not have emerged more cleanly from his father's shadow than by beating him a short-head in the Epsom Derby? He was independent enough in having his own yard, but he had the use of Vincent's matchless gallops. It seemed an ideal set-up to me and I was stunned when I heard he had packed up . . . but then I have never professed to psychoanalyse, and whatever has sustained Vincent's appetite all these years obviously failed to affect his son in quite the same way.

These, then, were the background thoughts jostling for attention in my mind as I came to terms with the desire for my own fresh fields. I had no doubt at all that I wanted to accept

Prince Khalid's offer. I had plenty of doubts about how I was going to extricate myself from the Ballydoyle contract.

Vincent was very good about it. He had been very good about everything, from the day I first went to see him almost six years earlier, and even then, with a jockey able to do little to sugar the pill and saying bluntly that he no longer wished to work for him, he was the perfect gentleman. When the story eventually emerged in the press, I imagine many people leaped to the conclusion that there must have been bad blood between us and that the acrimony inevitably flowed in those final days. It did not. There was never any argument on the matter. I put my cards on the table and Vincent put his; he was prepared to let me go, provided a replacement jockey could be engaged who was acceptable both to him and to the major owners. There lay the crux. The major owner in the yard was still Robert Sangster. Stavros Niarchos and Danny Schwartz, who between them had owned or part-owned many of the horses when I joined Vincent, had pulled out, but Sangster remained, his position among owners no longer pre-eminent, either in Britain or in Ireland, due to the influx of Arab money. It was easy to appreciate that he would not be wildly happy about his jockey abdicating, with a year of his contract to run, in order to join up with one of the aforesaid Arabs.

The issue dragged on, as it had to. There was no easy solution because jockeys of the calibre required were not readily available. To be frank, the O'Brien job was also not quite the compelling attraction it had been six years earlier. All in all, I had begun to resign myself to the extra year, and to think of what chance there might be of keeping Prince Khalid's job open, when Cash Asmussen came to the rescue.

Cash, the eloquent American who had gone to France, charmed the pants off everyone and had ridden countless big winners, fancied a new challenge. For my purposes, he had been sent from heaven because he had the talent, temperament and record to fit the job requirements at Ballydoyle. He went to see Vincent and the transaction was agreed. The fact that it was later to end in sadness, with Cash receiving a bafflingly rough ride from the Irish public and leaving, by mutual consent, a year early, simply could not have been foreseen, but nor was it my concern. Free to take up a new position, I completed my 1986 commitments in Ireland, without notable success, and prepared to begin the next chapter.

It did not end without regrets and certainly it did not end without memories. How could it? I had ridden for a man who lived up to his image in every way and I had ridden horses who invariably lived up to their fine breeding and fancy prices.

Looking back, there were so many good moments, so many invigorating times. As to the best horse to come out of Ballydoyle during my time, it would have to be between the one which won the Derby, Golden Fleece, and the one which didn't, El Gran Senor. There is no doubt in my mind that both qualify for the overused adjective 'great', but quite how great they might have been is difficult to gauge, their racing careers being so frustratingly short. If anything, I may just side with Golden Fleece. I remember, on the night of his Derby win, arriving home and taking a congratulatory phone call from my mother. I told her that what she had just seen was nothing to what was to come, and I believed it. The horse had improved rapidly with every run and Epsom had been only the fourth race of his life. I believed that every major prize the racing world had to offer could be within his scope over the coming couple of years. But, as history relates, he had already run his last race.

The news of my new appointment was made public shortly after Dancing Brave's Arc win and may, I suppose, have hastened the retirement of Greville Starkey. Although Prince Khalid spread his favours fairly widely, and had horses with Jeremy Tree and Barry Hills among others, his main trainer in England was, and still is, Guy Harwood. This was not at all to Greville's advantage. Having already had his nose put out of joint through being jocked off Dancing Brave, he now had to face the prospect of many of the best rides in his yard coming to me. He did go on riding for a couple of years but it was no great surprise to anyone when he called it a day.

Much has been made, in the media and elsewhere, of a rivalry between Greville and me. The assumption is perhaps a natural one after the Dancing Brave episode but students of jockey form dated it back farther than this and cited the infamous scraps between King's Lake and To-Agori-Mou in 1981. We met four times, each horse finishing in front of the other twice, and the margin between us was never more than a neck. The duels became acrimonious, firstly because the Irish Turf Club upheld our appeal over losing the Guineas in the Stewards' Room and secondly because Greville, who could always tend towards the theatrical, got rather carried away. I did not personally take offence at the V-sign he gave me at the end of our Ascot race, but it was as unnecessary as the remarks he offered to Vincent's wife in the winner's enclosure afterwards – something to the effect that, if we wanted to take on his horse yet again, the same thing would happen. It simply built up a good and protracted contest between two very decent horses into something personal. I bore no grudges but I was not sure about Greville and, although we never fell out, I did have the feeling he resented me and the success I was achieving. Greville was a very fine rider, and a very amusing man to boot. But he never became champion jockey during a very long career. That may have rankled.

I was fortunate in that my new job involved riding for trainers I already knew well. It also meant that I was not exclusively tied down to any one of them and this, too, I appreciated. At heart, maybe, I have always been a freelance.

As for Prince Khalid, I found the man a delight to deal with. He is as much a gentleman as Vincent O'Brien and runs just as tight a ship. His racing manager is Grant Pritchard-Gordon, brother of the Newmarket trainer Gavin, and the operations base is an office in Knightsbridge, very close to Harrods. There, Grant spends much of each day on the telephone to Prince Khalid's many trainers, in England, France and America. He will speak to them all at least once a day during the season, checking on the progress of the horses and preparing reports to relate to the Prince. He will also speak every day to Terry or to myself, often both, and it is greatly to our benefit that Grant compiles a list of the probable runners from each trainer, five days in advance. This allows us to prepare an outline of where we will be going and which races are available for us to seek spare rides. Things can always change at short notice in racing, with horses having an injury setback or the weather altering the going, but some guide to forward planning is imperative.

Grant will also attend many race meetings, whether Prince Khalid is present or not, and all things considered, I think he has a pretty hard job, because when things go wrong, the buck stops with him.

I will occasionally telephone the Prince personally if I think the time is right to discuss a certain horse, and he is never less than charming. In all the years I have ridden for him, there has never been one cross word between us. I know for a fact that he has verbally supported me if, occasionally, it has been felt that I made an error in a race. On such occasions, I will be the first to say I rode a bad race if I believe that to be the case, and I think the Prince appreciates the lack of bluff and bluster.

Despite the number of years we have been associated, I would not pretend to know him well. Of his duties at home in Saudi Arabia I know only that he is not far removed from the royal throne. Of his movements in England, I know that he loves his London residence and spends most of his time there, that he visits his Juddmonte Stud, near Henley-on-Thames, at weekends, and that he will occasionally stay in another of his properties in Newmarket.

He is undoubtedly incalculably rich; I am breaking no confidences and surprising nobody in saying that. But like many of the remarkably wealthy Arabs, he is subtle with his affluence, never brash. Most important of all, I have found him the ideal employer, in terms of success-rate, appreciation and my own peace of mind. Long may it continue.

16

LESTER: The One and Only

If I was asked what event I associate with the month of October 1987, I might reply that I won the Arc for the third consecutive year, on Trempolino. I might also recall being locked in a prolonged duel for the championship with Steve Cauthen. But what I remember most vividly about that month is my utter disbelief when the great idol of my lifetime, Lester Piggott, was sent to prison.

There was racing at Doncaster when the news came through and it left me completely speechless, just shaking my head and wondering at the enormity of what had happened. You see, I did not pretend to understand the intricacies of whatever financial malpractices were alleged and I have no clear idea whether the man in the dock was a victim of wretched advice or his own bloody-mindedness, though I suspect a bit of both may have been involved. The shock did not come from the crime, for details of that had been chronicled all too fully. It came from the realisation that Lester was, after all, a mere mortal, subject to the same punishments as the rest of us. Until sentence was passed, I would never have believed that he would be sent down; even now, I find it hard to take it in.

Lester had always seemed so much a man apart, if not actually immune from life's millstones then at least possessing a unique ability to shrug them off, stone-faced as ever. And now he was in jail. My mind flashed back to Blackrock and boyhood and I knew then, as I always have done, that for all the aid of being born into a racing environment, for all the help given by my father and by Bill Williamson, it was Lester Piggott who had been the greatest influence in mapping out my life in my mind. It was he I always yearned to emulate.

Although Lester's background is as English as mine was Irish, there are some striking parallels in our lives. He started young, even younger than I was to do, riding his first winner at the age of twelve. Like me, Lester started out working for his father but, whereas mine was assistant to Seamus McGrath, Lester's father Keith was a licensed trainer, apparently a good one. Lester was his apprentice, but he had the same capacity as the young Eddery for seeing the winning post and not minding overmuch what was in his way.

In 1954, the year of my second birthday and Lester's nineteenth, he experienced the two extremes of fortune in a matter of weeks, and on the same horse. Never Say Die gave him the first of his nine Derbys (so far!), but when he rode the horse again at Royal Ascot he found himself on the worst of all stewards' reports, a dangerous riding charge. The Jockey Club suspended him for the rest of the season, noting that 'in spite of continuous warnings he continues to show complete disregard for the Rules of Racing and the safety of other jockeys'. It must have been a crushing blow for him, especially as it came with the ruling that, in order to regain the licence to ride, he must be attached to a yard other than his father's.

And so Lester was launched into the big, bad world, joining a Newmarket trainer called Jack Jarvis for a time, but really beginning to achieve the enduring stardom which has been with him ever since he was signed, as stable jockey, by the great Sir Noel Murless. Together, they won both the Oaks and the Derby in 1957 and they were still winning the classics as a team in the early 1960s which, I suppose, is when the Piggott magic began to hypnotise me, via the wonders of television, each Saturday afternoon.

He very quickly became a hero to me. He seemed different from all the other jocks I watched, not only because he tended to win more races but also in style, balance and flair. The famous sight of Lester's perpendicular rear may have been a curiosity but it was by no means a handicap. The Long Fellow was very obviously long, too long by most assessments of a jockey's optimum size, yet he rode perilously short and still had the gift of communication with his horses, something no amount of coaching can produce.

Some parts of his riding were undoubtedly self-made, however, and it was one of these, his whip style, which I set out to copy when my own race-riding days began. I have always believed it is foolish to try to imitate any other rider, as it often leads to a distortion of whatever personal talents you may have, but there are things to be learned from watching the best, and there are none better than Lester. His method with the stick has, in the past, attracted criticism for being heavy-handed, but its remarkable effectiveness is self-evident. He mastered the whip totally, urging every available effort from his horse while retaining perfect poise in that precarious balancing act of his.

I have never seen the whip used to better advantage than in the 1977 Derby at Epsom. I don't know how many times Lester whacked The Minstrel, but I do know he would not have won without it. I also know that he did the horse no damage whatever because, a few weeks later, The Minstrel came out and won the Irish Derby as if he had not had a race at all at Epsom. Then, to my personal frustration, he conjured another inspired finish from the horse to win the King George by a short-head when I was sure my own mount, Peter Walwyn's Orange Bay, was going to prevail.

Lester's split with Noel Murless occurred in 1966, for reasons which will be familiar to anyone who had dealings with him in those days. Lester always wanted to be the boss, to the extent that he was never happy being tied down to ride a certain horse, even by his retaining stable. I'm told he tried to get off one of Sir Noel's in the Oaks and that, in effect, was that. And yet, so great was his standing among trainers that he continued to ride some good horses for the Murless yard while picking up more and more from Vincent O'Brien, the partnership which was made official in 1968, the year of the great Sir Ivor.

Having won the Guineas and the Derby with Sir Ivor, I am sure Lester would not remember his ride in the Hylton Handicap Stakes at Liverpool, in March of that same year. But I am not likely to forget it in a hurry. This was the contest in which I had my first English ride, on Tim Molony's Dido's Dowry and, if that in itself was not enough to set my heart thumping, I had my hero among the opposition. It might now provide a good quiz question, though I doubt if even the greatest racing buff would readily come up with the answer if asked to name the race in which both Piggott and Eddery fell, the latter even before the tapes went up!

Too much was happening around me that day for there to be any question of a conversation with the great man but, as I began to ride regularly, I realised that one did not just start a conversation with Lester under any circumstances and that the only time he would start one with you was if he wanted to know something.

In those early days I seldom changed anywhere near him in the weighing-room, there being a strict pecking order of pegs and changing space in which he was number one and I was into the hundreds. But because I had marvelled at him from afar for so long it was only natural that I should take an interest in him.

I suppose it might have been easy for a youngster like me to be disappointed with the real Lester, for the shine to be knocked off the idolatry by his ways. He was always insular, often surly and sometimes downright rude. But for some reason I never considered this even strange, much less offensive, and I don't think this was blind worship.

Certainly, I made allowances for him because I regarded him as a superior being among us ordinary jockeys, but I think I also recognised in him a fanatical dedication which permitted nothing in the way of frivolity or even relaxation. Everything he did, everything he said, was calculated to add to the vast Piggott store of winners and, of course, money, for even by then he was a seriously rich man. I recognised that he was ruthless, not only during a race but in all his dealings, for he would never hesitate to try to jock you off if he considered your horse had a favourite's chance, and he had no scruples whatever about doing so. He was his own man and he ruled the roost, not purely in his own mind but, to all intents and purposes, in reality.

I recognised, too, the deprivation to which he had submitted in order to go on riding. I have been relatively lucky in this respect, firstly through being born about the right size and shape to be a flat jockey and then because my metabolism never rebelled to the extent that I was facing a daily battle against the scales. I have to be careful, but I do not have to starve. Lester was tall and angular. Even by the age of eighteen, he was 9 st. 7lb. He was a hopeless case really, and I expect he was regularly told as much, but such was his devotion to his chosen field that he hit upon an easy solution. He just wouldn't eat.

It is, of course, part of sporting legend that Lester has always survived on black coffee and a daily cigar but it is not complete myth. A slight exaggeration, maybe, but it is undoubtedly true that his regime is as strict as any I have ever encountered. I have no idea how much mental anguish he might have had over the years through never being able to eat and drink, socially, as most people can do without thinking and even I can do without worrying, but even if he accepted the spartan lifestyle as willingly and phlegmatically as he appeared to, it must still go some way towards explaining his personality.

Lester, in those days, was withdrawn to the point of being a complete introvert, shutting himself off from the outside world and, probably, deliberately contenting himself with his own company in order to proceed, as if in blinkers, along this regimented routine which kept him in the saddle. It did not make him compelling company, at least it did not seem so at the time. If there were two other good reasons for retreating into himself, they may have been his partial deafness and his notorious speech impediment, but I do not honestly believe he considered these social drawbacks which had to be concealed. I think he was just being Lester, living the part to the full, and if he was not exactly lovable because of it, then neither did he lose my respect.

This respect, I might say, did not extend to his gentlemanliness and acquiescence on the racecourse. Out there, Lester was accustomed to having his own way, lining up on the inner (before the days of stalls) and dictating the pace of a race. If he wanted to make the running, woe betide any young whipper-snapper who tried to take it off him. He would not forget, of that we could all be sure. Lester liked to run a race to suit himself and, all too often, he did. This particular young upstart, however, was, as I have said, similar to the younger Piggott in being hell-bent on victory, never mind the consequences, and for all my off-course admiration of Lester, I would never pull out of a scrap with him during a race if it meant the difference between winning and losing.

Lester might have been wild in his early days but by the time I came up against him he was canny. He liked nothing better than shutting you in on the rails, especially if you were on a fancied horse, and this tactic, successfully accomplished, more than once cracked his face into a rare chuckle while I was trying to keep my temper in check on the thwarted horse. At Chester one day I failed to keep control and quite deliberately barged Lester's mount ever wider on the final bend to gain myself the gap for a challenge. It was a mad thing to do and I knew I would go down for it, which indeed I did. What made it worse was the knowledge that I had first got into a position where the old maestro had manipulated me like a chess grand master, and then that I had allowed myself to be so unforgivably provoked. Predictably, Lester was smugly unhelpful in the Stewards' Room and, much as I yearned for the chance to gain my revenge while my blood was still boiling over the incident, it never came. Lester was not only very clever, he was also invariably on the better horse!

As my own success rate escalated, and I began to be perceived as a serious rival to his throne, there was always just a little needle between us on the track, but I like to think it was based on a mutual acknowlegement of ability. To ride a tight finish against Piggott was to set the adrenalin flowing and few things in the game gave me greater pleasure than beating him by a short-head, especially if he had really fancied his horse. Over the years there were any number of short-head verdicts between us, as we frequently found ourselves riding the two best horses in a race and, although I never kept count, I would be surprised if the score did not pretty much even itself out.

The good thing about it was that, Chester apart, most of our riding contests were conducted in the right spirit. We were deadly serious up to the winning post but, as soon as we pulled up, there would customarily be a 'well done' from loser to winner. I still thought he was the greatest jockey who ever lived and, hopefully, he thought I could ride a bit too, so we got along fine without ever becoming matey.

He was not entirely solemn, even in mid-race. I have already mentioned the mischievous delight he would sometimes take in keeping a rival blocked in. This was surpassed by his infuriating habit when he came past you on an obviously superior horse. You would be flat to the boards, scrubbing away unavailingly, and as Lester sailed past, bottom raised on high as if in salute, he would give a squawking kind of laugh.

I had been riding several years before I broke down the expressionless mask of the man when off horseback, though, and it might never have happened at all but for the advent of the international jockeys' team which, out of the European season, made trips to places such as South Africa, Singapore, Hong Kong, Cyprus and even America.

The idea was that we rode as a team against the host country, usually over a series of three or four races. They were good trips, part work but a sense of escapist holiday too, and well paid besides. Jimmy Lindley came along as manager and the team regulars included Willie Carson, Greville Starkey, Yves Saint-Martin, myself and, of course, the Long Fellow, more commonly known to the rest of us as 'the old man'.

We were always put up in top-class hotels, all expenses paid, and the hospitality of the hosts was invariably very generous. On the first couple of trips, Lester remained well within character, seldom emerging from his hotel room for any communal eating or drinking. But as we became, through habit, more of a real team, his barriers came down a shade, he began to join us at the dinner table if only to pick at a piece of fish, and I began to appreciate that there was a genuinely amusing man beneath it all.

His humour is essentially dry, spontaneous and sometimes cutting. He will not tell lengthy, convoluted stories but can put somebody down with a single, throwaway sentence. He is at his funniest when he is most relaxed, and that usually means after a drink. Now, I do know jockeys, especially some of the jumping boys, who can put a great deal of booze away without showing the effects at all. Lester is not among this select band. He very much enjoys a glass of champagne and, when in the mood, will not say no to a second. Any more, and his humour is likely to be decorated with regular giggles. At times like this, though, he does become very good company and those lucky enough to meet him for the first time when he is, shall we say, on a loose rein must find it difficult to equate him with the gruff, abrupt and deadpan character they had always been led to believe was Lester Piggott.

I found increasingly that, although he would not put himself down, even in jest, I could do the job for him. I took the mickey and he took no offence. He was, without doubt, mellowing a shade towards the end of his 'first' riding career but, to my eyes, he still ruled the roost. Riding for Henry Cecil made him champion jockey again in 1981 and 1982, bringing his tally of titles to eleven. Teenoso gave him his ninth Derby, an amazing number, in 1983, and then there was Commanche Run's St Leger (a classic piece of Piggott 'jocking-off' involved here), and the 1985 2,000 Guineas aboard Shadeed. When he retired at the end of that season Lester had ridden twenty-nine English classic winners, not to mention taking the Irish Derby five times and the Arc three. He had ridden winners in all corners of the racing world and, for heaven's sake, he had even ridden twenty over hurdles.

Although it might have been thought that the rest of us would have a better time of it with the old man out of the way, I was personally sad when he packed up. Consumed as he was with the game, it was natural enough that he should then go into training and there was a time when I felt he would make a real success of it.

He set up at Newmarket, where the competition is fiercest but where Lester knew the territory better than any man alive. It was obvious that he would attract some influential owners, for despite the fact that he had treated some of them in rather cavalier fashion over the years, there was an enormous residue of goodwill and regard towards him. For me, he would succeed in his new venture if he could translate his unparalleled gift for getting a tricky horse to run for him, from riding to training, and if he could overcome the frustration felt by so many ex-jockeys when they are suddenly confronted by an entirely unfamiliar set of problems.

When you are riding, your contact with the horses is confined to race-days and occasional work mornings. You will hear plenty of woeful tales of leg problems, wind problems and the dreaded virus but, within the cocooned world in which every jockey operates, such things never become personal.

Start training, and you see a different world. The daily worries about tendon strains are equalled by the hassle of dealing diplomatically with all the owners, some of whom might be difficult. I don't know how Lester coped with that, or whether he left it to his very capable wife, Susan, but I can well imagine it was a part of the job he didn't relish. All he wanted to do, or so I came to believe, was to ride the horses at exercise, get them hard and fit, and then take them to the races.

He did all of this pretty well. He still rode out every morning, which may or may not have been an early sign that he was regretting his retirement, but he certainly produced his horses looking well and he had thirty or so winners in each of his two seasons with a licence. I rode some winners for him myself and I remember, after one especially impressive run, jokingly asking him what super-juice he was giving them.

He may have grown accustomed to the routines and demands of training, but I had the impression it never really suited him. Essentially, I think he was bored. How the training story might ordinarily have developed, however, we shall never know, because it was towards the end of that second season in training that the saga of unpaid tax, publicised so greatly in advance that it can only have been to Lester's detriment, finally came before Ipswich Crown Court.

Quite how wealthy Lester Piggott had become during his riding career I just don't know, but his savings must certainly have been counted in millions. There is no doubt at all that he could easily have afforded to pay the amount the taxman claimed he must. But he didn't and so, for tax evasion on a fairly grand scale, he was sentenced to three years' imprisonment.

My gut reaction, as I digested the news in the Doncaster weighing-room that bleak October day, was that it was wrong. It had to be too harsh a penalty for the crime he had committed. There were people going around beating up defenceless old men, raping young girls and firing off guns while robbing banks, yet still being sent down for less time than Lester. How could that be right, when he had hurt nobody except the Treasury? It was a reaction, I know, based principally on emotion and, yes, the abiding hero-worship which I had for him. But even in hindsight, I feel that the court made an example of Lester because of who he was rather than what he had done.

He served no more than a third of the three years but that must still have been twelve months of unimaginable confinement for a man who had spent every day of his life out in the open with the horses he loved. I am sure there will be those who have no sympathy for him whatever, arguing that he got what was coming to him, but I can see it must have been almost intolerably hard for him.

It was not as if he was left in peace. Lester Piggott was too big a name for that. There were some vile, vicious press stories about him during his time inside and, when he was allowed home on a weekend visit, he scarcely had a moment away from prying cameras. Somehow, he managed to smile and, I thought immediately, look remarkably healthy.

I did not go to see him in prison. I couldn't face it, to be honest, and if I had, I just cannot imagine what we would have said to each other. We had become friends as well as rivals, but we were never so close that I would know what to say in that situation. I know Joe Mercer visited him, being of much the same vintage, and he reported back to us that he was bearing up very well.

Since he came out, I have never discussed prison with Lester. It is not up to me to mention it and I am not the type to be curious about the inside of a jail. If Lester wanted to talk about it to me, that would be different, but I cannot believe that day will come.

My admiration for him has held up despite it all. He may have done wrong, certainly did disastrously wrong in the eyes of the tax man, and he may have been thoroughly naive to believe he would get away with it. But this was Lester being stubborn and pig-headed, as occasionally he always could be, rather than him being a calculating criminal.

I certainly admired his attitude when he came out, because he never tried to hide himself away. It would, of course, have been difficult anyway, such was the media fascination with him, but it must still have taken some courage to be as public as he was so quickly.

He began to go racing again with his wife, who now held the training licence, and, once the initial attention had worn off, it began to strike me that people were forgetting Lester. For the first time since he had hit the headlines as a teenager, he was not the most instantly recognisable figure at any race meeting. He might still have been so to me and to other jockeys, but to the general public he was a lean, drawn man in his mid-fifties they seemed to remember from somewhere. No longer in silks, no longer in the parade ring with his runners and no longer, thankfully, the focus of notoriety, he had begun to fade as a personality.

Whether or not this can have had anything to do with his comeback I am not sure. Lester certainly enjoyed the limelight, even if he often had a strange way of showing it, and it is possible he had begun to miss it now. Much more compelling a reason, though, was that I feel sure he wondered just what he was going to do with the rest of his life. He knew, and wanted to know, nothing but horses and racing. He was still fit and surprisingly light (though prison can have done him little damage in that respect). He still had the devotion of many owners and trainers.

It was to a background of these thoughts, I believe, that Lester planned the sport's greatest comeback. Oddly enough, despite twelve months of incarceration, despite being cruelly stripped of the OBE that his services to sport in general had so richly merited, I don't think he was a bitter or resentful man. I just think he was fed up with inactivity and anxious to get back to doing what he had always done best.

I still found it hard to envisage that he would soon be back among us in the weighing-room. He was, after all, approaching his fifty-fifth birthday and had not ridden in a race for five years, a very long gap for any career to survive, let alone for a man of his age. And so, when I was told confidentially of his planned return, a couple of months before it was announced, at first I wouldn't believe it.

But, as we now know, the old man was deadly serious about riding again, and when it finally happened, his comeback was cheered as loud as anywhere in the jockeys' rooms around the country. I was at a different meeting to Lester on his first day back, but there was a real buzz among the jocks, waiting to see how he would perform. When his first winner of another new career arrived, at Chepstow, there was genuine delight among all his colleagues.

Only Lester, ten years short of the pension book and only a few weeks back in the saddle, could fly out to America and ride a winner in the Breeders' Cup. The fairy-tale was topped off by the fact that the horse's trainer was Vincent O'Brien, his guv'nor and his friend for so many years. I was present and privileged to witness one of the most emotional occasions I have known in my career. The massive stands at Hollywood Park were packed and everyone stood for Lester. He was cheered back into the weighing-room, not least by the American jocks, and when he appeared on our TV monitors, being interviewed by Brough Scott, there was an excited scrum around the set, everyone straining to hear what the great man had to say.

If Lester's vintage, pumping finish that day proved that, given the horse, the magic was still in him, then the subsequent interview hinted at what has now become very evident. Lester, starting over again, is a far more relaxed and talkative man these days. He enjoys himself, and shows it, and although I suspect the motivation and dedication are still as strong as ever, he has eyes and ears for more than just his next winner. He is better than he once was with the kids in the weighing-room, he is more open with us all and he takes greater pleasure nowadays in other people's victories than he once did.

When I won the 1991 St Leger on Toulon, the first jockey to congratulate me when I got of the horse was Lester. He just walked straight across and said, 'Well done!' Not much to ask, you might think, but to me it still meant a lot.

In his first full year back riding, Lester dodged all over the world, revisiting places and people who never expected to see him again, following his lengthy farewell tour in 1985. I imagine he still lives largely on coffee and the odd cigar but his weight is as good as mine and I have a feeling the old boy fancies riding until he is sixty. It would not be for me, but I wish him well, all the same. Whatever ups and downs he has had, Lester is still the greatest.

17

FRIENDLY RIVALS: The Sparky Scot and the Quiet American

The sparky Scot and the quiet American. It may sound like the team for yet another slightly implausible television detective series but these, in fact, are the men whose company I have come to enjoy better than almost any other these past few years. On the course, they have dogged every step of my efforts to regain and then retain the jockeys' title and, if there have been times in this regard when I have considered them too close for comfort, I have greatly enjoyed their company off the track and, in the Scotsman's case, even on holidays.

They could hardly be more different. Willie Carson, the diminutive, indestructible one from Stirlingshire, and Steve Cauthen, the Kentucky kid who charms with his manner and his riding. Their personalities are at opposite extremes: one all action, energy and occasional irascibility, the other all reserve and serenity. Their style on a horse is in character; all they have in common is the ability, proved time and again, to win most races they are expected to, and many they are not.

In background, Willie has more in common with me than Steve, not only through being born this side of the Atlantic but because it took him a very long time to ride his first winner! He was actually three years into his apprenticeship when he broke his duck in 1962, when nineteen years old. Steve was that same age when he came to England in 1979 but, by then, he had already achieved fame and considerable fortune by riding an amazing number of winners in the States. They called him the Six Million Dollar Kid and there is no doubt that he could easily have stayed at home, piling up the millions, for as long as he wished. It was a very brave move for a rich teenager to uproot and fly the Atlantic to take on a completely alien racing scene, exposing himself to scrutiny and unrealistic expectations.

I guess he probably earned a million a year in America and even with the patronage of Robert Sangster he can have picked up only a fraction of that during his initial seasons over here with Barry Hills. As will always happen when someone arrives from overseas with a big reputation, there were many eager to run him down if he did not win every race in which he rode and have the championship won by mid-August. Of course, he did neither but, fortunately for his peace of mind, neither did he seem to possess any false hopes.

Steve settled remarkably quickly into the English style of riding – which is different in a variety of ways from the norm in America – and the English way of life. To his great credit, he also visibly enjoyed both. The sceptics whooped over the fact that he rode 'only' fifty-odd winners in each of his first two seasons in this country but, to me, that was quite an achievement. Given the right horses, it was never going to be too long before Steve conquered this side of the pond as he had done the other and, after topping the hundred for the first time in 1982, he took the title – from Willie – two years later.

In 1985 he had the sort of year we all dream about but very seldom attain. To ride 195 winners in a season might not, to Steve, have been that extraordinary when compared with the staggering 487 he rode in the States as an eighteen-year-old, but it is a feat best measured against the deeds of Lester Piggott. Lester retired in 1985, never, we thought, to return, and the best seasonal winners' tally of his career, a career which included eleven jockeys' titles, was 191.

With all due respect to Barry Hills, who not only had the enterprise to employ and befriend Steve in the first place but also made him a champion in 1984, the main reason for the American's wonderful run was his new retainer with Henry Cecil. Steve had replaced Lester in the job at Warren Place and I think he and Henry were ideally suited.

Henry is an odd mix of a man. He dresses in exotic, expensive clothes, has a rather vague style of speech and could be thought a dilettante at the game. But beneath it all lies a sharp business brain and that indefinable gift, possessed by few, for producing horses at a pitch. In 1985 he did it with such regularity that he turned out 132 winners and was champion trainer for the fifth time in eight years. He and Steve seemed to get along famously from the start and their first-season relationship was topped off by winning no fewer than four classics. I had a pretty good year myself in 1985 and in the autumn I couldn't seem to stop riding winners. But my Irish commitments had meant that I missed too many big days; I think if my winners in Ireland had been added on to my British score, I would have been about level with Steve and there would have been a tremendous duel to the wire, both for the title and in search of the elusive 200. That had to wait for another year.

Although I was still riding for Vincent in 1986, the partnership was drawing to an end and, understandingly, he let me off to ride in England on a number of Saturdays. By retaining rides and contacts which might otherwise have drifted away to rivals, I had a better control of my destiny within the title race and became champion, surprisingly comfortably, for the first time in ten years.

It was a good, solidly successful year, even leaving aside the glamorous exploits of Dancing Brave. I won the St Leger for the first time, on the Duchess of Norfolk's Moon Madness, but in truth, the lasting pleasure came from regaining the title. To be number one in your field is surely what everyone sets out to achieve in life and any jockey who tells you the championship means little to him is either a liar or a fool. It is the ultimate, and you cannot buy the feeling of satisfaction which comes with looking back over a year which has gone as smoothly, and ended with the right result, as this one did.

Steve finished second to me in 1986 but the Cecil machine was firing a few unfamiliar blanks. Not so, a year later. They set off at a gallop and by the time the York meeting came around, in late May, Steve had already set up a lead of a dozen or more. I thought I had no chance. Gradually, though, I began to worry away at his lead and we went into the season's last two months on pretty much level terms. And that was how it stayed, with first one of us inching a couple in front, then the other, all the while creating increasing public interest and building up to the best finish seen in the championship for many a year. To be part of it was exciting, of course. But I must say I also found it a strain. The telephone at home never stopped, calls coming in from press people who knew nothing of racing but were jumping on the bandwagon of what was a major sporting story. I could not blame them for that and I tried to remain civil with them all, but my patience was exhausted when, on more than one occasion, the privacy of the weighing-room was violated by reporters who could see nothing wrong with marching straight in and accosting me for quotes.

Perhaps they were used to different ground rules, and more flexible territories, in other sports, but in racing the one rule that is simply not negotiable is the sanctity of the Jockeys' Room. One or two of those who barged in were not only bold but rude with it, and I am afraid they found, in me, an unwilling victim for their foot-in-door style. I just told them to back off and conduct their interviews somewhere else. In general, the title duel was conducted in great spirit. The racing press, as opposed to those from outside, were very good; the racecourses made a great fuss of us, no doubt relishing the extra publicity and income; and between Steve and myself there was never anything but friendly rivalry, despite the intensity of it all.

It became a mad scramble for winners and both of us found ourselves riding for unfamiliar trainers, and on unfamiliar courses. In the frantic final fortnight, we both went to Hamilton and Edinburgh, Scottish tracks which would never normally be on our itinerary. When the last day at Doncaster arrived, however, Steve was two winners in front, and that was how it stayed. We each rode one on the final card of the year and the curtain came down at 197–195, that 200–mark still mystically unattainable even with all the extra travel we had undertaken. My total number of rides was only four fewer than 1,000, easily the most I have ever had in a single season, and to miss out on the title after such a prolonged slog left me feeling very deflated.

For anyone who has ever lost a sporting contest, the temptation is strong to make a futile study of the exchanges that took place and come up with the moment, or moments, when luck was cruel. All ifs and buts. But in this instance there was a moment, or rather a race, which had a crucial effect on the outcome and it happened only a week from the end of the season, during the final Newmarket meeting.

Cutting short a long and painful-to-relate story, I won a race, and won it on merit so far as I was concerned, only to have a stewards' inquiry called to investigate interference. It was not the runner-up I was deemed to have impeded but the third horse, whose jockey made a meal of it in front of the stewards – predictable, perhaps, but utterly unproductive because he was never going to get the race. All he achieved was to get the race taken off me and awarded to the second horse, which had not even been involved in the incident. The jockey to benefit, in the event, was Steve, and but for that unearned winner the final score would have been a draw, all honour satisfied.

If, for a time, I felt frustrated and glum over the loss of the title, I begrudged Steve nothing, however. It was, I think, a pity that one of us had to lose and I have a feeling we were both glad when it was all over and we could step off the relentless merry-go-round for a rest. But through it all Steve had conducted himself impeccably and my opinion of him, never less than high, was enhanced still further. I don't believe I have ever heard anyone say a bad word about Steve. He is that kind of guy, instantly likeable. He does not have as much to say as some in the weighing-room, but he has a good sense of humour and is a very engaging man to be with. On the surface, he is very serene, nothing apparently able to bother him, but I can well believe that is not entirely the case.

His greatest professional problem has always been his weight. Steve is tall and big-boned for a flat jockey and it was only ever a matter of time before the scales caught up with him. I suppose he could conceivably have adopted the spartan lifestyle of Lester but, initially at least, that was not Steve's way. He is a naturally sociable chap and he had quickly become part of the Lambourn set. He enjoyed fine food and, on the good days, he enjoyed a glass or two of champagne as much as the rest of us.

The problem seemed to be taken out of all perspective one close-season, however, when he was alleged to be little short of an alcoholic. The man making the claims, at least according to certain newspapers, was Steve's father, Tex. This was manna from heaven for the tabloids, who not only unleashed news-writers but gossip columnists and medical correspondents on the sad story of the champion who had 'hit the bottle'. I just don't know whether Tex had been misquoted but I was astonished at the things he was reported to have said, not only because Steve was his son but because, so far as I am aware, they were way removed from the truth. If his motive was to give his son a shock so to prolong his career, maybe it was effective. Steve did acknowledge the danger signals of increasing weight, and decreasing choice of rides, and in recent years he has become a Perrier water man. Nature cannot be denied forever, though, and as Steve has no desire to live the reclusive life Piggott willingly adopted, I question whether he will ride very much longer.

He is now retained by Sheikh Mohammed, who owns the largest number of horses in training among the Maktoum brothers. It is a job which ensures him success and a good income and additionally means he can ease off from the constant quest for outside rides with a winning chance. It will probably keep him going as long as he wants to ride, but I have no doubt that when he does pack up it will be as a hugely popular and respected figure. Steve is an ambassador for racing, as far removed from the obsessive insularity practised by Lester as it is possible to imagine. He is also a very fine rider, a master at judging pace.

The public and the press were anticipating another titanic title scrap between us in 1988, but it did not materialise. By his own standards, Henry Cecil had a modest season and Steve was already trailing me by upwards of thirty winners when he had a horrible fall at Goodwood at the end of August, his mount clipping the heels of a horse in front and then rolling all over him when they hit the deck. Neck injuries ruled Steve out for the rest of the season; he was lucky to get up at all.

You can never have everything in this game and, although I regained the title once more and maintained a steady flow of winners, the season's classics were disappointing. We thought we had the potential 2,000 Guineas winner in a horse called Warning, trained for Prince Khalid by Guy Harwood, but after a surprising defeat in his prep race he was found to have the virus and had to be laid off. When he came right, in late season, he won the Sussex Stakes at Goodwood and the Queen Elizabeth at Ascot in the style of a champion miler.

If that was frustrating, my Derby experience was infuriating. The Prince did not have a runner, so I took the ride on Geoff Wragg's horse, Red Glow. I knew this was an irresolute animal and I had got him home at York, prior to the Derby, only by holding him up cosily, then producing him with a few cracks of the stick so that he was running almost before he realised it. I was amazed when they made him favourite at Epsom, and although I did the only thing possible and tried to repeat the same tactics, I was not surprised at all when he did not go through with his effort and finished only fourth behind Kahyasi. What did surprise and disturb me was the reaction of one tabloid newspaper writer, who laid into me and my riding of the horse so volubly that I was subjected to TV inquests concerning the race for days afterwards. I have no respect for the writer involved and he now knows better than to ask me for any interviews. Red Glow, by the way, failed to add to his one win . . .

One of the classics in 1988 did bring me some pleasure, though, despite not even riding in it myself. The pleasure came from the sheer delight exuded by Willie Carson when he won the Leger on Minster Son, a horse he bred himself. I should not think it is possible for a winner to give a jockey more satisfaction than in these rare circumstances and the whole weighing-room was pleased for Willie.

Julian Wilson, the TV presenter, once wrote of Willie that he was 'not much good at being a former champion'. I know what he means. Willie is such a competitor that any defeat hurts him and, possibly, too many setbacks are taken personally. He was for many years in the shadow of Lester, and then had to play second fiddle to me for a few seasons. For all that, he has been champion five times and, in the past twenty-one years, he has only once failed to ride 100 winners in a season. If he has finished second more often than his fierce pride would choose to accept, he has still been remarkably consistent.

He finished runner-up to me in 1988 but it was around this time that I came to know the real Willie, rather than just Willie on duty. When he is at work, at the races, he is often not at all the happy-go-lucky chap with the infectious laugh that the public so obviously enjoy. There is a serious side to him which can sometimes become morose. He can be sharp and he has a temper, which leads to some inevitable mickey-taking by the other jocks, treatment Willie will only tolerate to a degree. But he has been at this game a long time and, if there are frayed edges on show now and again, it is not exactly surprising. Away from the track, as I have now learned, Willie is a very different man.

We began going on holidays together through our respective

The most disappointing moment in my racing career when Secreto passes El Gran Senor (inside) at the finish of the 1984 Epsom Derby.

FAMILY SCENES

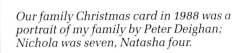

My wife Carolyn in her racing gear.

Our family Christmas card in 1988 was a portrait of my family by Peter Deighan; Nichola was seven, Natasha four.

I just pip my brother Paul (nearside) at the post of the Taylor Woodrow Handicap, Ascot 1985.

e international team challenge at Sandown. (From left to right:) S. Hawley, S. Cauthen, Asmussen, C. McCarron, L. Piggott, me, G. Duffield and G. Starkey.

ny hero Lester on the way to the ock for the 1984 Derby.

Jupiter Island comes home winner of the Japan Cup, 1986.

One of the greatest horses I have ever ridden: Dancing Brave, whom the nation had taken in its heart, cruises to victory in the 1986 Arc. After the race, I'm congratulated by Linda Gray, Larry Hagman and Mrs Rocco Forte.

...polino brings me my third consecutive Arc win in 1987.

...win some, you lose some: celebrating Trempolino's success; Steve Cauthen just beats me ...e 1987 jockeys' championship.

Quest for Fame coasts home in the easiest Epsom Derby I have ever ridden and, left, enters the winner's enclosure with Roger Charlton.

The man behind the scenes: Grant Pritchard-Gordon, Prince Khalid's racing manager.

My private plane, a Cessna.

Trainer Roger Charlton welcomes Sanglamore back after our victory in the Prix du Jockey Club.

Miranda Jane, the mare who brings up the elusive 200 at Chepstow.

Pebbles, the first British-trained horse ever to win at the Breeders' Cup meeting, canters to the start in 1985.

Two moments of triumph in my racing career: with the Queen Mother after Dancing Brave's epic victory in the King George VI and Queen Elizabeth Diamond Stakes, Ascot 1986; and after winning the St Leger in 1991.

wives, who talked regularly on the phone as friends. Elaine, Willie's wife, asked if we would like to go and spend a couple of weeks with them at their house in Barbados one winter and we took them up on the offer. We got along well and the trips have become a happy annual habit. We both enjoy living simply out there. Days will begin some time after nine, with a spot of gentle food shopping. Then there will be the first of several daily excursions into the sea for water-skiing. Willie, who reads more than I do, will contentedly dip into his book on the beach, while the rum punches are consumed during the day. When the sun goes down, the four of us will have a couple of hours on the tennis court before a good dinner with plenty of wine.

It is a blissful existence and an escape, although just occasionally we are invaded by owners and trainers who make up the yearly January exodus to what has become known as Newmarket-on-Sea. We are happy, though, with our own company and only occasionally does Willie's other side, the irrepressible competitor, come to the surface – usually when Carolyn and I are giving the Carsons a beating on the tennis court and Willie is roundly abusing poor Elaine for an inadequate shot!

He gets his own back at water-skiing, for he is much better than I am, and the noisy delight he takes in that is further evidence of what drives the wee man on. I suspect Willie would always try to beat his own boys at draughts, or at football in the garden, such is the streak within him which dictates that he must win. It may not always endear him to people, but there is no doubt it makes him a survivor in our tough game.

A couple of years back, Willie told me he was thinking about retiring. With most people of his age (he was fifty in 1991) that would not have been a surprise, but I remember thinking about him and wondering what on earth he would do with himself. I believe the reason for such thoughts was that Willie was upset by what had happened to Dick Hern, with whom he had enjoyed such a long and mutually fruitful relationship. Dick's tragic accident, which left him confined to a wheelchair, was followed by the loss of the royal horses. Willie felt his trainer's setbacks more keenly than anyone and I am sure they depressed him. But as so often happens in racing, something else soon came along. In Willie's case it was the job as first jockey to Hamdan al-Maktoum, a job which has already provided him with countless good

winners and, I think, banished all prospect of retirement for the immediate future.

Willie is not bored by his riding, I am sure of that, and he is able to enjoy it without the confinements to which most jockeys, to one degree or another, have to submit. He is the right shape for longevity and he can eat exactly what he pleases without seriously increasing his weight. Being able to ride at 7st. 9lb., as he has done for so long, is a great advantage when the big handicaps come around and Willie is very often a man to follow when he steps in to ride one with a low weight.

He has eased the stress of travelling, just as I have, by buying his own plane, but the difference in Willie's case is that he flies it himself. I admire him for it, and I believe he gets great enjoyment from it, but I think I shall be sticking with my pilot!

He likes to wind down at home, on his beautiful stud near Cirencester, but as all of us know who spend our days with him, there is no winding down for Willie while there are horses to be ridden and races to be won. Driven on by whatever his demons may be, he pursues winners with relentless determination.

His riding style may not be pretty, but it is mighty effective. Often, one could logically write off his mount at the sight of Willie in behind the leaders and pumping away for all he is worth. He seems, invariably, to be getting nowhere, yet no sooner does he pull his horse out and increase the rhythm a shade more than he is flying for the line. It is different from any other rider I know, but with his record it is beyond criticism. Horses run for Willie because he makes them run and, if he never wins the jockeys' title again, it will certainly not be for the want of trying.

18

THE ELUSIVE 200: Making and Breaking a Record in a Most Successful Year

Three weeks into the 1990 season, bookmakers were betting odds-on that I would ride more than 200 winners. I scoffed derisively at their meanness of spirit. How could it be an odds-on shot when, since the last war, only one man had achieved the feat, and that almost forty years earlier? How could it be odds-on when we were barely in sight of the opening classics, the long season, with all its pitfalls and vagaries stretching ahead? I had made a good start, a very good start, but I believed anyone who plunged on that bet had far more money than sense. Six months later it seemed the bookies had been right, after all, in their inbred caution. I was already on to 190 winners, with more than a month of the season remaining. I was about to make racing history, joining the great Sir Gordon Richards in the 200–club. When the elusive figure was reached, at Chepstow in the third week of October, I was an extremely proud man.

I had known it was possible, of course, because both Steve Cauthen and I had got within three and five respectively of the double-century when we fought out the title in 1987. But, thinking back to the rigours of that year, the miles we covered and the horses we rode in search of the crucial winners, I had also known that it would need to be a season of quite exceptional good fortune, not only in the number of good horses available but in being able to stay clear of the injuries and suspensions which are always likely to scupper such a bid. I thought it was most unlikely to be achieved by anyone while I was riding; certainly, I thought it complete folly to be considering it at all with the season barely out of its infancy.

The first hundred came quickly, so quickly that I would not

have been human if the second had not now crossed my mind. But as so often happens after a run in which a jockey can do no wrong, I suddenly hit a flat patch and in the big three-day meeting at York, I did not ride a single winner. The dream, and it was still no more than that, receded still farther from the realms of reality.

York was not, as it turned out, the end of the road. It was a quick stall before my engine started running smoothly once again and, for much of the rest of the season, I kept firing in the winners with a regularity that made me blink. Trebles were commonplace; there was the odd four on a card and twice – once, ironically, at York – even five. Into the 190s and I knew that only a cruel stroke of ill-luck could stop me, but on the very brink, on 199, I got stuck for three days. It felt like a week or more, such was the intensity of the press expectation and, truth be told, my own anxiety.

An October Tuesday at Chepstow is not, by custom, one of the most energising fixtures in the calendar, but I shall always remember this one. The course executives plainly felt completely confident that I would find the missing winner, because I knew they had an engraved decanter awaiting the moment. They might so easily have had to sell it as an unused curiosity, because from six booked rides that day, I just salvaged the necessary one win.

It came on a filly called Miranda Jane, a name I shall probably recall as easily as Golden Fleece. She was trained by Michael Jarvis who phoned up a couple of days before the meeting to try to book me. He said the filly had needed her last run, that she would win and I had better get on her. There was a problem, as we had already taken another ride in the race but, fortunately, the trainer let me off and Michael was as good as his word. It was a great moment, and a great relief. There is a sequel to this episode which I tell against myself, for exactly a year later precisely the opposite happened. Chepstow had decided to name the corresponding race after me, which was a gesture I really appreciated. I also felt I wanted to ride the winner. Barry Hills was going to run a filly of Prince Khalid's, which normally I would automatically have ridden. I had ridden a piece of work on her a week or so earlier and she struck me as a sharpish sort, but Barry assured me that she was not fancied and I was duly given leave to seek a likelier ride. We settled on one trained by Henrietta Knight, with form which looked rock-solid, and we went off favourite, with Barry's filly among the 33–1 outsiders. Needless to say, that was the one which came to beat me, and won going away by eight lengths! It was a galling experience, especially as I had to present the trophies, but if there was any consolation it came in the pleasure of a rare winner for the jockey, Bob Street.

Although a fair proportion of my 200 winners in 1990 were owned by the Prince, I had no one big provider as a trainer. The winners came from everywhere and I am pretty sure I did not ride more than thirty for any one stable. Three of those who regularly put me up on winners, however, were Michael Stoute, Jack Berry and Richard Hannon. This is as unlikely a trio as you could come across, linked only by doing their job exceptionally well. They train hundreds of miles apart and their lifestyles are as distant from each other as their homes.

Michael has been a heavyweight among trainers for many years. He has not been out of the top three in the money-earnings list since 1978 and only his near neighbour, Henry Cecil, has prevented him achieving a domination. I don't pretend to know how the two of them get on together but I do know there is as much rivalry between them as, for instance, there is between Willie and me. I am constantly aware, year after year, that Willie is going to be the toughest little terrier to shake off if I want to be champion, and similar thoughts must always be in the minds of Henry and Michael. It is too easy to say glibly that they annually get the pick of the yearlings for their principal owners, but this misses the point. A trainer has to earn the right to first pick and the only way he will then guard that entitlement is by maintaining his standards, season after season. It may be very tough getting to the top, but it is no sinecure staying there, either. I have ridden for Michael, on and off, since I was a kid. Nowadays he has a lot of horses for Maktoum al-Maktoum, my second retainer, and he also puts me up on a few more now that he no longer engages Wally Swinburn full-time. Michael is Barbadian by birth and, unsurprisingly, he is a cricket nut; he gets his relaxation from the racing game by focusing on another – and he is the type who needs some diversion. He has never shown his temper to me, but his eyes betray that it is lurking, somewhere near the surface. He is a volatile man who badly wants to win and has Willie Carson's dislike of finishing second. He works tremendously hard for his success and achieves his results with extraordinary consistency; if ever there is a slack period in the Stoute fortunes it never seems to last much longer than ten days.

Jack Berry, on the other hand, titled his autobiography *It's Tougher at the Bottom* which, for some years, is where he was stationed. His rise and rise equates to that of Martin Pipe in jump racing and, having ridden for them both and observed their methods, I think they are similar men, essentially working-class, efficient and innovative, willing to work every hour God sends to achieve success. Pipe has somehow kept training more winners each season over jumps since he took out a licence in 1977, and although Jack has been around a few years longer, and spent rather more time getting off the ground, he too is now dramatically improving his returns every season.

The greatest thing about Jack is that he is always the same, always happy and smiling. He simply cannot be as relaxed as he seems but, day after day, he will just tell his jockeys to go out and enjoy themselves and to win if they can. Nothing seems to upset him. More than once I have jumped off a horse of his and explained that if I had done something a bit different, we might have won. He never moans, never holds it against you, just continues on his contented way.

Only five or six years ago, Jack was struggling to turn out twenty winners a season. In 1991, he reached his century before I did – a rare and remarkable feat, because a top jockey can have six or seven decent rides a day, whereas even the very best trainers cannot match that.

Well over half of his winners these days are two-year-olds, and he has made a profitable speciality out of producing sharp juveniles fully ready to do their job. A lot of Jack's will win their race without being the best horse because they are the fittest and the best prepared. He teaches them well and he knows their trip; they are primed for it, to the last few yards. Jack's horses will jump off smartly, run straight and get to the line. They never pack up at the furlong pole for lack of a piece of work or because they don't truly appreciate the trip. If you are in front a furlong out and you still get beaten, the winner must be in a different league, because Jack's don't stop.

To Be a Champion

Jack trains a very long way from the fashionable centre of Newmarket, way up in the north-west at Cockerham, but this certainly does not seem to discourage potential owners, and his string is building annually, both in numbers and in quality. He had a good two-year-old in 1990 called Distinctly North, owned by Robert Sangster, and another called Paris House the following year but, as yet, there has been no classic horse at Cockerham. I don't think it will be long in coming because Jack has demonstrated that he is ready and able to train the best horses, in addition to getting the best out of moderate ones. Of one thing you may be sure – even if Jack has the favourite for next year's Derby, he will be wearing his trademark red shirt in the parade ring at Epsom. Quite how the superstition started I am not sure but it has become a habit which Jack doubtless enjoys as a private joke. Whoever sells him his shirts is a lucky man because he must have dozens of them!

I enjoy my rides for Jack because he is such an easy-going man and because the horses always know their business. I enjoy riding for Richard Hannon, too, not least because he makes me curl up laughing. He is a genuinely funny guy and he can turn the customarily uncomfortable few moments in the parade ring with anxious owners into a comedy routine which instantly relaxes everyone. To ride for Richard is to be sure of having a laugh, but nowadays it is also invariably to be on a horse with a very good chance of collecting.

As with Jack, there is no set arrangement for when I might ride for Richard. Jack has his own stable jockey, John Carroll, and he is very loyal to him, but when he has runners split between meetings in the north and south, he will usually offer the ones coming south to me. Richard has all manner of people riding for him, including his own capable claimer, Richard Perham; Brian Rouse, Bruce Raymond, Michael Roberts and Willie all ride for him a fair bit and I think generally he tends to nominate the best available, although certain jockeys obviously strike up a partnership with one or more of his horses. There is certainly no danger of there being insufficient to go round – in 1991 Richard had a lot more runners than I had rides!

Although his father trained at Marlborough before him, Richard had an unusual route into the game, via a spell as drummer with the chart-topping sixties pop group, The Troggs.

He then became assistant to his father and took over the licence in 1970. Three years later he won the 2,000 Guineas with a 50–1 shot, Mon Fils, and aptly called it his meal ticket for life. It undoubtedly helped him build up the strength and facilities of the yard, but for a long time he was no more than a middle-of-the-road trainer, averaging between thirty and forty winners a year. Latterly, he has twice done the Guineas double, winning in England and Ireland with Don't Forget Me and Tirol, and the time has come when he is attracting top owners and more expensive horses. His talent down the years, however, has plainly been a great eye for a horse, because he has done most of the buying himself and has never paid over the odds. He has then consistently made the best of the available material and, although he keeps his horses on the go a long time, he has the happy knack of also keeping them fresh and enthusiastic so that, more than once, I have ridden one of his with very unpromising form figures and he has suddenly begun winning, maybe two or three times, towards the back end. I was never more pleased for anyone than I was for Richard when he reached 100 winners for the first time and I think he will now go on from strength to strength.

Jack and Richard are two who run their horses a fair amount and like to win the two-year-old races. A greater contrast one could not hope to find than Roger Charlton, Jeremy Tree's successor and former assistant at Beckhampton. It does not always follow that when the assistant takes over he will train in the same way as his old guv'nor, but it certainly applies to Roger. Just as Jeremy did, he regards the two-year-old season as a time of learning and strengthening; the juveniles from Beckhampton will invariably not have more than one or two runs, as evidenced by the statistics from last season when Roger had fewer than fifty two-year-old runners as compared to almost 400 from the Hannon yard and closer to 500 from Berry.

Jeremy never ran a lot of horses in search of small prizes around the gaffs; he was a man who always had the Group races and the classics in mind. I am sure his enduring ambition was to win an Epsom Derby and, with no disrespect to Roger, I found it sad that he retired a year too soon. Roger Charlton's training career began, in 1990, like a fairy-tale, for he not only won the English Derby but also the French, and he came close to an unbelievable hat trick in the Irish. The recognition was rightly his but Roger would have been the first to point out how fortunate he was to inherit such a legacy from Jeremy, who had left him three very nice maiden three-year-olds in Quest for Fame, Sanglamore and Deploy.

When the season began we had no way of knowing that any, let alone all, of the trio would be Derby material. Jeremy had given them one run each at two and they had all acquitted themselves satisfactorily without winning. All three were in the ownership of Prince Khalid and I looked forward to riding them as three-year-olds, but at that stage I would have nominated Deploy as the one most likely to go on to the classics. He, ironically, was the only one to miss out on a big prize. Deploy was, however, the first to win and he also provided Roger with his initial winner. Knowing Roger, and liking him, for so long, I had been itching to get him off the mark and it was nice that it came on a decent course, Haydock Park, and with a potentially very decent animal. Quest for Fame then bolted up in his maiden at Newbury, and Sanglamore, although not so impressive as the other two, won his first race at Nottingham. We now had to be thinking in terms of a serious campaign for all of them and Roger was already planning their likely programmes so that they would not clash. Disappointment, however, was lurking around the next bend. Quest for Fame went to Chester, for what is usually a pretty reliable Derby trial, and was beaten fair and square by Henry Cecil's Belmez. The other two went to Newmarket and I thought they were both good things but, on ground probably a shade too firm, they too were beaten. Deploy also encountered a training setback and was off the course for some weeks. Our options had narrowed significantly, but two things then happened to restore our optimism.

Sanglamore was sent to York, for the Mecca–Dante and there, encountering the soft ground which obviously suited him best, he once more looked a good horse in victory. His reputation salvaged, he was then aimed for Chantilly. Quest for Fame, in the absence of Deploy, was to be our Epsom horse and our chances were improved when Belmez was injured and taken out of the race. He had been made favourite on the strength of his win at Chester and, although I felt the longer straight at Epsom might have given my horse a chance of reversing the form, we would have been up against it, as Belmez demonstrated when coming back later in the summer to win the King George.

With the obvious danger eliminated I went to Epsom feeling quietly confident, a mood my horse fully justified. I have ridden some very fine horses in the Derby – some of them, it must be said, better than Quest for Fame – but I have never been carried around Epsom more easily. The turns and undulations of the course, and the number of runners jostling for positions, are such that an entirely trouble-free trip is very rare in the Derby, but on this horse I can honestly say that I never had a moment's anxiety. He carried me round on the bridle and I only had to shake him up a furlong and a half from the line to go on and win. Precious few races go so perfectly to plan as this.

Quest for Fame was one of Prince Khalid's home-breds and, because we knew he could gallop, we did not worry about the undeniable bow in his legs. If he had gone to the sales as a yearling I don't suppose he would have made much money, because people simply will not pay for crooked-legged horses. But he proved, as many others without perfect legs have done before him, that it is no barrier to winning good races. He has been a hard horse to keep sound, though, and he was sore after the Derby despite the driving rain which had softened the ground. He is probably destined to be labelled the winner of a sub-standard Derby, but that will not worry Roger Charlton, and why should it?

If I had been optimistic going to Epsom, I was never more than hopeful about winning the French Derby on Sanglamore. I knew he was improving, but I had serious doubts whether he was improving quickly enough to beat some of the decent French three-year-olds. Sanglamore, unlike Quest for Fame, was also a difficult horse to ride. He hated the stalls and he pulled too hard for his own good. The Chantilly mile and a half was, additionally, plenty far enough for Sanglamore. I always thought he was essentially a ten furlong horse and I knew the race would have to be run to suit him if he was to get the trip. All in all, I was not exactly boiling over with expectations as we went down to the start.

We were allowed to go into the stalls last, which was a major aid, but what helped my horse more than anything was the pace of the race. Very often, in France, the first six furlongs of a mile-

and-a-half race are dawdled and the last six sprinted but, for some reason, they went off at a really good gallop. I was able to drop Sanglamore to the back, stone last, and he settled well for it. I waited until we turned into the straight and then waited a bit longer, anxious to conserve his run as late as possible. When I did ask him, we got a great run through and got up to beat the favourite. I was delighted, because there had been so many things which might have gone wrong with this horse, but it did not change my view of his best trip. Over ten furlongs, against the same opposition, I think he would have won more easily.

The hat trick for Roger was only narrowly thwarted, though I would not have been responsible for the final leg. We ran two in the Irish Derby and, although I knew how good Deploy could be, I felt I had to remain loyal to my Epsom winner. Quest for Fame could only manage fourth, but it looked for some way as if Deploy would win. Eventually, he was just touched off by that brilliant filly, Salsabil, and the disappointment was compounded when Deploy broke down. I felt he would have won the St Leger because he was strong, he stayed and yet he could quicken, too. But that was one race destined not to come our way. I could hardly complain. With two Derbys and more than 200 winners, the year of 1990 must go down as the most successful of my life.

19

THE BREEDERS' CUP: The American Way and British Victories

The British flat-racing season goes out, nowadays, with a whimper rather than a bang; even the traditional closing meeting at Doncaster being illogically succeeded by a nondescript November Monday, invariably cold and foggy, at Folkestone. But since 1984 there has still been a fitting climax for us all to anticipate, even if it has meant flying the Atlantic to enjoy it.

Breeders' Cup day is as exciting as any in the racing calendar, not only for the coming together of Group One horses from across the northern hemisphere but for the inimitably American glamour and presentation. It is a travelling extravaganza, awarded to different tracks each year, and while we all have our personal favourites – and mine are those in the south with the sunshine thrown into the bargain – none have yet fallen down on the job of staging the richest, if not the most important, race-day anywhere in the world.

For the British, the annual jaunt is, paradoxically, ever more irresistible for the annual failures. It is said you always most want what you can't have and I think it applies in this case. There have now been eight Breeders' Cup days, six or seven mouth-watering races each day, yet the British winners' tally stands at a miserable two.

The French go there and win races; in 1990 the Irish took an event, even if it did owe much to the very English riding of one L. Piggott. But the English-trained horses, sent there each year with rock-solid form and cheerful optimism from the stables, annually come home defeated. Any number of our best horses have been sent, although not until Quest for Fame went to Churchill Downs last year and finished a good third, was an Epsom Derby winner in the raiding party. It has mattered not a jot. The Americans thought up the event and funded it. Up to now they have been winning their own money, year after year.

Many varying theories have been advanced for the British failure. Some believe it crucially unfair that American horses can run on medication, such as Bute and Lasix. This occurs in all states except New York, where such drugs are banned, and the medication can be given openly to improve a horse's performance. There is, though, no direct evidence that it regularly improves a horse, and mostly it is used as an anti-inflammatory treatment. Any horse running in the Breeders' Cup can be given Bute or Lasix, provided it is declared to the stewards and applied no less than four hours before a race, but British trainers have not exactly flocked to use it and I personally believe it is an invalid excuse for defeat.

A far more plausible reason is, to my mind, the time of year when the Breeders' Cup is run. British horses will have been on the go since the spring, trained to peak for their classics and Group One races in May, June, July and August, then frequently given a break before being brought back for Arc day at Longchamp. To ask them to remain at their best until early November is to ask an awful lot indeed. All too often a horse will still appear to be well, looking superb and even working pleasingly; it is not until he actually gets on to the racecourse that he tells you he is over the top, and then it is too late.

A British trainer will also be worried about travel arrangements, which can so often develop a hitch; about whether his horse will recover from the journey in time; whether he will acclimatise; and whether he will settle into unfamiliar quarters. All these are potential drawbacks and they help to explain why, in the years prior to the Breeders' Cup, so few British horses were sent for races in the States. The purses have always been good, but the complications discouraged almost everyone until the unique international nature of Cup day, allied to phenomenal prize-money, made it an offer few could refuse.

My first trips to America were made in the days of the international jockeys' series. We went to California two or three times, racing at Bay Meadows, but this was always to ride American-trained horses. It was not until 1983 that I got to ride a British horse in the States and that still ranks among the greatest thrills of my career. I rode Tolomeo, for Luca Cumani, in the Arlington Million in Chicago and, getting a wonderful run through on the inner, I beat the great American horse John Henry.

One British trainer who was brave and enterprising enough to take on the Yanks in their own backyard, long before the enticements of Cup day, was Clive Brittain. Clive loves a new challenge and he certainly broke new ground, but it was 1986, and two Breeders' Cups had been run by the time I linked up with him to ride that good horse, Bold Arrangement, in two big races at Kentucky. We were unlucky not to win the Bluegrass at Keeneland, then we went on to Churchill Downs for the Kentucky Derby and ran a blinder to be second to Ferdinand.

If that particular venture was thwarted, however, Clive fittingly has his place in the trans-Atlantic racing record books for being the first, and for six years the only, British trainer to have a Breeders' Cup winner. The year was 1985, the horse was Pebbles and I can vouch for the fact that, for the jockey, it was a dream come true.

As a three-year-old, Pebbles had been an outstanding miler, winning the 1,000 Guineas and finishing runner-up to Katies in the Coronation Stakes at Royal Ascot. A training setback then kept her off the course until the Champion Stakes at Newmarket, in which she was again second. Having had only four runs as a three-year-old she was still a fresh filly when she came back in the spring of 1985. She won twice at Sandown, including the Eclipse Stakes in which she beat the subsequent Arc winner Rainbow Quest, and she was again second at Royal Ascot. In all three races she had been ridden by Steve Cauthen, and I envied him.

My chance to ride her came when she was again brought back from a mid-season lay-off with the Champion Stakes in mind. This was also the target for that year's Derby winner, Slip Anchor, and Steve was claimed to ride him under his retainer for Henry Cecil. I went up to Clive's yard at Newmarket one morning and rode a bit of work on Pebbles, confirmed that I was available for the ride and duly took it on the agreement of Pebbles' owner, Sheikh Mohammed.

The Champion is a ten furlong race, which might just have been Pebbles' best trip, and I thought she had a good chance despite the presence of both Slip Anchor and the previous year's

Leger winner, Commanche Run. Pebbles was strong and fresh and I knew she could pull like a little monkey, so I was content to drop her out early on. She took a bit of holding but I saved the challenge for a couple of furlongs out and then switched to the stands rail. She went past them all on the bit, still hard-held, and I don't think I have ever ridden an easier Group One winner.

After that, we had to be optimistic about the Breeders' Cup and I was delighted to keep the ride. There were doubts, of course. The Turf race, in which she was entered, was over one and a half miles, which she had never attempted, and as she was a particularly difficult filly to settle I was not wholly confident she would stay.

Cup day was at Aqueduct that year and I flew out three days beforehand. I rode Pebbles on the track, slightly with heart in mouth over her demeanour, but I could not believe how relaxed she was. She seemed to be enjoying everything about the place, and I was very encouraged by it. It was still not going to be an easy proposition because I could not risk her stamina by having her too handy, but Aqueduct is even sharper than the usual American track and to come from off the pace was an undeniable gamble.

Cup day was, as it always has been, breathtaking. The build-up is greater than that for any race-day in the world and the occasion itself never proves a let-down. Every race is worth at least a million dollars, with one worth two million and the Classic worth a cool three million. Unfailingly, money cannot buy quality but, each year so far, the Cup has produced top-notch horses from Britain, France and Ireland, as well as the best of the Americans, and the result has been a day of unrelenting excitement for everyone.

The Americans do these things well. Their staging may lean towards razzmatazz but there are times when that is no bad thing and they certainly have some very effective little touches. There are TV screens all around the stands and, before each race, replays are shown of the recent runs of the principal horses. It all helps to create an atmosphere and build to a climax.

There are always thousands of people around the paddock and, just occasionally, during the pre-race parade, I have glanced across at the packed stands and quietly drunk in the sense of anticipation for a moment. Once I am down at the start, though, everything else is blanked out. It does not matter whether it is Epsom, Ascot, Longchamp or Santa Anita, I hear and see nothing once we go into those stalls, other than the horses around me and my best route to the finishing post. The stands may be bursting with noise and excitement; I honestly would not be aware of it.

I had plenty to think about as we circled at the start that day. Clive, as usual, had been tremendous, not burdening me with fussy orders, just telling me to ride the race as I saw it. He knew I planned to try to come late and he did not try to discourage or dissuade me. But it was one thing making a plan and quite another carrying it out. For that, I would need some good fortune in running.

Pebbles pulled hard when the stalls opened, as I knew she would. She kept pulling as we came past the stands, a circuit ahead of us, but to my huge relief, she dropped the bit as soon as we started into the first turn. I tucked her in on the rail and waited, just hoping that the gap would come when I needed it. As we went into the last turn, heading for the straight, we were really racing and although I was stopped once as I made a move, the opening came when Teleprompter, tiring in front, moved off the rails.

Pebbles, asked to quicken and seeing daylight at just the right moment, was through in a trice and that devastating turn of foot she had shown to win the Champion Stakes was once again decisive. She had first run on the favourite, Strawberry Road, and although the margin was down to a neck by the line I was never worried.

There was a special feeling about winning a championship race in America and it had little to do with the vast sums of money involved. It was like an England football team winning an international match in a far-off land where the odds were stacked against them. It was an away win, and the subsequent barren years have proved what an achievement it was. I had plenty more Breeders' Cup rides in the next five years, and some good ones too. They do not come much more attractive than Dancing Brave, for instance, but he did himself no justice at Santa Anita in California. He lost a lot of weight before the race and seemed to wilt in the very hot weather. He may have won the Arc in great style but he had had a tough race and a demanding season; the Cup was just one step too far. I was second on Trempolino after he had won the Arc, and runner-up again on a filly of André Fabre's a year or so later. But these were French-based horses and they have consistently performed better than the British in the Breeders' Cup. For us, there have been all manner of disappointments, hopes raised and then dashed year after year.

Our main hopes have often been in the sprint but, although some outstanding British speed merchants were sent across, the nature of racing on dirt, and on tight American tracks, was all against them. British sprint races are almost all over a straight course; in America, you sometimes have to complete virtually a full circuit of a course as tight as a greyhound track. They go very quick, right from the stalls, and unless you break well you will inevitably suffer the kick-back of the sand, to which our horses are completely unaccustomed.

In 1990 it seemed that the long spell without a winner had finally been broken. Willie Carson and Dayjur were in front in the sprint, a few yards from the line. It seemed they could not be beaten. But they were, and in the most bizarre circumstances. Dayjur jumped a shadow, not once but twice, and the time lost in performing this unnatural action at the end of a flat-race sprint meant he was touched off on the line.

I was watching the race on television and could barely believe what I was seeing. Dayjur was a nervy sort of horse and had spooked at a shadow when winning in France on Arc day. He had got away with that and, indeed, he might have got away with jumping just the once in America. But not twice. It was heartbreaking for Willie, especially when the extent of the misfortune became clear. The shadow, spreading down from the stands, was not in that crucial place fifteen minutes before the race and was not there again fifteen minutes afterwards. It is not often that a million dollars is won and lost on such a freak of nature.

Twelve months on, the venue had changed to Kentucky's Churchill Downs and the British representative in the sprint, the first race on the card, was now Sheikh Albadou, a three-year-old trained by Alex Scott. I had ridden him whenever available during the season and he had picked up a couple of nice prizes, but in my heart I would not have put him in the same class as Dayjur.

And yet, this game being so endlessly unpredictable, Sheikh

Albadou succeeded where Dayjur so unluckily failed. He has always broken well in his races, and although we were a little way off the pace he was always going very nicely and, something of a departure for a British horse, relishing the dirt.

I knew as we went into the turn before the straight that I could beat all those in front of me and he just quickened up and left them for dead. He is a well-balanced horse, which you need on the American tracks, and a real pleasure to ride. The plan is to go back for the 1992 Breeders' Cup in Florida and, who knows, he could provide my own, and Britain's, third winner in this unique championship.

20

AT THE DISTANCE

The regular disappointments which afflict us all in the precarious world of horseracing demand a caution which, at times, can breed unmerited pessimism. As I approached the 1991 season, however, I felt it was not pessimism but realism which persuaded me I had little chance of remaining as champion jockey.

The bookmakers had no such doubts – I was odds-on for the title once again – and if their judgement was based on the previous season's 200 winners, I could hardly blame them. I was the 'form bet' and I suspect there were few, inside or outside racing, who confidently opposed me. Still, my doubts persisted, and I felt they were far from groundless. The most obvious problem besetting me was my own contracted rides. Sure, 1990 had been a golden year for the Prince's horses and he might easily have ended up with three Derby winners. But although both Sanglamore and Quest for Fame were, after some debate, to stay in training, I feared that the new season's crop of three-year-olds were well below standard. They had shown us at two that they weren't much good and, surveying the list back in early March, I felt that we simply didn't have a good enough hand to maintain the level of success achieved in recent years.

Then there was the opposition to consider. Willie's retaining owner, Hamdan, had carried all before him with Salsabil in 1990 and their two-year-olds also looked a cut above everyone else's. He had some phenomenal ammunition. Steve Cauthen had taken a retainer with Sheikh Mohammed, who has the small matter of 700 horses in training; plenty to choose from there. I felt they both had more aces than I did and that they would be hard to beat over the course of the season, especially if, as I anticipated, my commitment to the Prince took me to midweek meetings in France and America more often than before.

But to admit that I was prepared to lose the title does not mean I was resigned to it happening. Anything but, in fact. The sense of honour and achievement I have always felt from being champion has not diminished with age or repetition. It is still the biggest thing on my mind at the start of each new season. Of course, we all want to win the classics and the Group races, we all love to pick up the prizes in those rich and prestigious events in France. But the jockeys' title is to me like the league title to a First Division footballer: it is the assessment of achievement over eight months and, for all my fears, I was not lightly going to allow someone else to displace me at the top of the ratings.

We kept the title by getting down to it and working on it. It's as simple as that. I was not outlandishly wrong about the quality of our three-year-olds because, Toulon apart, they were a pretty disappointing lot, and although Sanglamore did win a Group race first time out, neither he nor Quest for Fame trained on as four-year-olds in the style one would hope for from Derby winners. In general, it was not a year for the glamorous, high-profile winners, it was a bread-and-butter year, the type in which contacts and judgement of the form book must keep producing winners at the downbeat midweek meetings if you are to stay ahead of the game.

Willie was always in determined pursuit, as I knew he would be, but perhaps Hamdan's horses did not fire quite as consistently as in 1990. As for Steve, he passed his usual century and rode sufficient winners to keep Sheikh Mohammed in his accustomed position as leading owner, but he did not appear to give himself as good a chance of the title as I had done. Outside his contracted rides, Steve took it easy. His strike-rate was the best of any leading jockeys, but he had fewer than 500 rides during the season; Willie, whose enviable feather-weight means he invariably has the most, rode almost 900. My ratio of winners to rides was 20 per cent, a figure I always find satisfactory. The punter, studying his *Sporting Life* over the breakfast cuppa, may see you with five good rides on a card and leap to the conclusion that, because you are champion jockey, they should all win, but as a rule, if you come away from a day's racing with more than one winner it is a bonus.

A winner can usually console and compensate for whatever other setbacks might have littered the day. And there are those days when, with half a dozen rides all potentially favourites, I would not be human if I did not begin to anticipate two, three or even four winners. So when they all get beaten, as sometimes they inevitably will, the journey home is not exactly jolly and the evening which follows can be downright miserable.

Frenchie was always good for me when things had gone wrong. 'Don't worry about it, boy, there's always tomorrow,' was his familiar rallying call if I had been beaten on a good thing. His words have stuck with me over the years and they still help now. You have to live with the bad days, because everybody has them. You must just get out there the following afternoon and hope things pick up.

Easy to say, of course, but not always so easy to put into practice. I do get down, I do have evenings when the day has depressed me and I find it hard to talk civilly to anyone. Fortunately, only Carolyn sees me this way and she is far too sensible to let it worry her or to interfere with the healing process. It never takes that long. The following day usually has something to commend it in this job, and it will never be long before I have Terry's indomitably cheerful voice on the phone telling me of some booked rides that will turn the tide.

The 1991 title was a credit to Terry as well as to me. He is my third arm, the one which does the vital telephoning and pieces together the often complex jigsaw of possible rides. He cannot always get me on the winner, nor will we always choose correctly between various options in a race, but I believe the results overall speak for themselves. Apart from a very occasional day when the office paperwork has got too much for him, Terry will be with me at the racecourse throughout the season, including Sundays in France. He does not waste his time at the races, either. Every conversation he has might have a winner or two at the end of it, which is why I impressed upon him, soon after he took on the job, how important it was for him to be there. He has to be available to trainers at the races, because with the best will in the world he cannot speak to them all on the phone in the mornings, and now that they all know him so well, much of his business is actually conducted during racing hours.

It is not just a question of asking trainers what they might have for me. Terry will go armed with a mine of information about recent races so that he has a very good idea which horses I would want to ride. There are times when he will even end up advising trainers about where and when to run their horses to avoid clashing with a good horse from another yard, so it is a mutually beneficial system. Additionally, Terry knows quite enough now to be able to assess a race he is watching and note down one which looks a likely winner next time out. He can't do that if he is sitting at home.

He is a friend and he is family, quite apart from being an indispensable member of the team, but I can't help chuckling when I think back to Terry's complete lack of knowledge about racing when he set out on the job of driving me. Neither of us thought that his role would develop quite as it has, and his racing involvement enjoyed a new peak in 1991 when he had a horse in training with Roger Charlton. On the morning of the St Leger at Doncaster, Terry arrived at my house as usual and we were going through the day's arrangements when he broke off, looked at his watch and told me he would see me later that evening. I looked, and felt, perplexed. 'What do you mean, you'll see me tonight? Aren't you coming to Doncaster?' I asked. I had forgotten all about it, but his horse was running at Goodwood, and this was one occasion, Leger or not, when he would not be at my side.

It turned out to be quite a day. Toulon won the St Leger and Terry's horse won at Goodwood. There were no long faces in the Eddery household that night.

Terry's good intentions during the learning process did, briefly, include riding. I used to go hunting a lot, packing up only when the Vincent O'Brien job meant that it was no longer worth the risk of injury, and for a short time Terry would come along as well. Usually, the Master of the Hunt would make sure he was given a pretty placid animal to counter his lack of riding experience, but this notwithstanding Terry is a bloke who will have a go at anything and the size of the hedges and brooks never seemed to daunt him.

His hunting days ended one day when I found myself on a real monkey of a horse, a great bull of a thing I was having great difficulty holding. Mischievously, I suggested to Terry that we should swap mounts to see what he thought of mine. Oblivious to the motives, Terry agreed and, sure enough, was very quickly run away with. I couldn't stop laughing as I watched him standing up in his irons, yanking on the reins with both hands to try to restrain the animal as he galloped relentlessly towards the highest hedge in the county.

He managed to pull him up and came back apparently unscathed, though not beyond aiming some well-justified abuse in my direction. The next morning, though, the tops of his arms were in a dreadful state and he was in agony enough to go to a doctor who, to Terry's alarm, pronounced that he had a thrombosis. It wasn't anything of the kind, of course, but the muscle damage was still sufficient to remind him that hunting was a pretty treacherous business. He has not participated since, although he did venture on to horseback again. It was a pony, actually, which belonged to his daughter and was in one of our paddocks at home. One summer Sunday, when I was in France and Terry had for some reason stayed behind, he got on the pony for a laugh but ended up back at the doctor's again when he not only had a fall but broke his ribs when the pony rolled on him! Enthusiast he most certainly is, but this second painful warning was enough to put Terry off any further riding exploits.

One, more critical, barrier Terry has had to overcome in doing his job is a basic fear of flying. He used to be shocking when we went up in our light plane, but now he loves it, habitually sitting up front with Jan, the pilot. There have been times when it has been just as well that his flying constitution, like mine, has become pretty solid. Some of the gale-force winds we tend to encounter each autumn now make quite an impression on a Cessna. We set off for the last big Newmarket meeting last season with gale warnings ringing in our ears. It is the cross winds which can make life almost impossible at the landing end but, on this particular day, we had a tailwind on the journey out and a headwind coming back. It made quite a difference: our flying time to Newmarket was fourteen minutes, but coming back it took well over an hour. Apart from these occasional, hairy days, flying takes all the hassle out of the travelling side of my job and even makes the midsummer period, in which I will usually be riding at two meetings each day, very much more comfortable. We fly almost everywhere now but if there is one destination I would cheerfully scrub from the flying plans it is Brighton.

We have a lot of very good racecourses in Britain – Ascot, York, Ayr, Newbury and Sandown to mention but five – but I personally believe we have too many. There are a few which could productively be eliminated, partly because nobody ever attends and partly because they aren't great tracks anyway. I could not claim, hand on heart, that nobody goes to watch at Brighton, because the holiday meetings pull in pretty large crowds, but it is the one track in the country at which I will actively try not to ride.

I am partly prejudiced against it by having been present when a young jockey named Joe Blanks was killed during a race there, but my arguments are not strictly emotional. It is all downhill, the ground is invariably not only firm but also rough, and there are three places where roads cross the track. We are in a high-speed profession and, as jockeys, our bodies, even our lives, are at risk each time we ride. But in so far as I can, I try to avoid conditions which I fear may increase the risk of serious injury. A well broadcast example is the infamous incident during the Portland Handicap at Doncaster a couple of years back when horses were going down because there were huge holes in the track. I believe the ground had not been properly filled in after drainage work, which was the probable cause of several accidents that day. Everyone survived with their lives, thank goodness, but not everyone came away with their livelihoods. Two jockeys, Paul Cook and Ian Johnson, were forced to retire due to the injuries received on that dreadful day and nothing can compensate them for that. This, remember, was a Grade One track during a classic meeting. It was a very bad advertisement for our racing and it must never happen again.

The state of the ground, the going, is always a trainer's greatest grumble and, leaving aside such extremes as we encountered at Doncaster, it is more a trainer's concern than a jockey's. A trainer will need to know accurately, more accurately than the going reports often indicate, what sort of ground he is going to find before deciding whether to invest the weeks of preparation in actually running a valuable and precisely trained horse. For a jockey, it scarcely matters whether it is as hard as a road or knee-deep mud, because he just turns up to ride the horse – he doesn't have to take him home afterwards.

A more pressing problem for jockeys, certainly if my

experiences are a guide, is the inconsistency of stewarding around the country. I can almost hear the cry go up that here is Eddery moaning through his pocket, having missed eighteen days of last season through suspensions. It is true that I would have won the title by a far greater margin but for those 'holidays', and might even have closed in on 200 winners again, but my complaint does not stem from this. Only the last, and the lightest, of my four suspensions was open to any great dispute. The point at issue is that jockeys cannot, under the present system, know where they stand with the stewards, because discretionary interpretation leads to so much inconsistency that I might lose a race for coming marginally off the straight at Epsom one day and keep one after barging a couple of horses aside at Yarmouth the next.

Racecourse stewards have to give up a fair bit of time to do the job and I am sure all of them are honourable, well-intentioned men with the good of the sport at heart. They are not, however, full-time professionals. The way the Newmarket stewards assess an incident can differ from the way it would be judged, say, at Kempton because different people are involved, all with their own personal opinions to air. I believe there must be some consistency of personnel, with maybe two full-time stewards present at each meeting.

I am certainly not seeking greater leniency. In France and America, where the stewards are professionals, the judgement of interference in a race is stricter than in England. If you break the rule as a jockey you will lose the race, and cop a fine and probably a suspension, too. But the jockeys there all know where they stand and respond to the situation. The public appreciates the consistency and racing proceeds with far fewer divisive arguments than one hears in Britain. I would prefer that system, stricter as it is, to what we have now.

My determination to ride winners, coupled with the sheer volume of rides, makes it well-nigh inevitable that the season will not pass without a few visits to the Stewards' Rooms for possible interference. It is not something I seek, certainly not something I welcome, but although my style is certainly more refined and less cavalier than in my younger days, contentious moments will still occasionally occur, usually in big fields and at some point after the two-furlong pole where everyone seeks to make their challenge.

If I am obliged to regard this as a penalty within the job, and swallow the punishment when it comes, I feel somewhat different about the issue of the whip. Until 1991, I had never been suspended for a whip offence in more than twenty years of riding. I do not consider that a happy coincidence and nor, it goes without saying, do I believe my whip style infringes any technical or moral constraints. So when I was stood down for two days after beating my brother, Paul, a short-head in a desperate finish to a race at Newmarket, I felt aggrieved, to say the least. This was a race in which my horse unarguably responded to the whip. I do not believe he would have won without it. It was, indeed, just one very good example of why the current rules leave the jockey in a no-win situation. He is there to win a race; if he loses it by being demonstrably easy on his horse, the public who have backed it will have suffered an injustice and the stewards might have the jockey in to explain himself. If, as I did, he wins the race through strong but not excessive handling, he is still prone to the whims of the stewards. The Newmarket stewards told me that I had not used the stick properly. This hurt. I have been riding twenty-two years without a problem and they tell me that. I asked them to examine the horse, for I knew him to be completely unmarked. Still, they suspended me.

The existing regulations stipulate that a horse must not be hit in front of the saddle. This, I feel, is unnecessarily stringent. Nobody wants to see a horse thrashed down the shoulders but it is educational for a young horse to get a tap in that area, keeping him straight and teaching him his job.

Good jockeys will never abuse a horse, for the simple reason that they love them too much. No animals are better looked after than British racehorses and I believe that goes for their time in action as well. Some control over use of the whip is obviously essential, but I believe the Jockey Club is misguided in its current actions. They need only look at certain other countries, where the whips dwarf ours and are used with impunity, to see how reasonable everything is over here. My own view, and I know it will be a controversial one, is that the whip issue is one example of how too much television coverage can be a bad thing for racing. I have great admiration for Channel Four, for the extensive and professional approach they have given to racing, but when the personal hobby-horses of members of their team are repeatedly aired live, is it any surprise that the public is influenced and the authorities feel empowered to act dramatically in matters which really do not merit such attention?

I feel our racing is as scrupulously fair as any in the world. Sadly, it is also among the most under-funded and there is only one overriding reason for that. Far too little of the millions which are punted on the races every day actually finds its way back into the sport. Too much remains in the bookmakers' satchels and too much is retained by the Government.

Virtually every other major racing nation operates the equivalent of a Tote monopoly, and the results are there for all to see in terms of prize-money and racecourse facilities. In an ideal world, Britain would follow suit, but the bookmakers have been around for generations and they are too powerful simply to be eliminated. But accepting that they are here to stay is one thing, accepting their notion of a fair financial return is quite another.

It seems scandalous to me that major bookmaking firms are buying casinos and racetracks in America with the money they take out of British racing. Just think of the potential if they were willing to invest in the product they are currently bleeding dry: a purpose-built track near London, maybe, with floodlights for night racing; elevated indoor dining and viewing areas for spectators who want to make a decent night out of it. These things are done in other countries and only a lack of finance, and occasionally enterprise, prevents it happening in Britain. It may be thought that our climate is against floodlit racing, but if they can do it in the States when the temperatures are below freezing, then why not during the winter months in England? I would love to see it attempted, and I am excited and intrigued by Ron Muddle's scheme for floodlights at Wolverhampton. But how much more realisable such dreams would be if the bookies paid a fair return for their gains. They can, of course, only be forced into increasing their payments by the government of the day and although, as I write, the next Levy scheme has gone to the Home Secretary for arbitration, recent trends would not encourage optimism. The Government shows no sign of any interest in protecting the welfare of the racing industry, adopting the attitude that the sport must sort out its own problems. They forget, or would appear to ignore, that racing is far more than a sport. It is one of the country's biggest employers, when all branches are taken into account, and the unemployment which would result from a continuing economic crisis in racing hardly bears thinking about. This aside, the Government takes a lot of money out of racing, certainly enough to encourage the view that they might be taking a little more interest. The problem with racing is that when it comes to the need for united action on essential issues, the sport is so fragmented, and each department of it jealously protects its own interests. So, all too often, many words are spoken but nothing gets done.

I do not see myself switching departments, in the short or long term. The obvious move a retiring jockey makes is into the training ranks, but I have long since discounted that. I see enough of the worries and hassles encountered by every trainer I know to be certain that it would not be for me. The breeding side, which has fascinated me ever since I became close to Vincent O'Brien, will occupy me rather more in the coming years, but that does not mean I am close to hanging up my riding boots.

Life is too good to think of changing anything just yet. I enjoy my riding and I can come home each evening to a lovely home and a growing family. My two daughters are now riding ponies, successfully too, and Carolyn throws herself into that each weekend, ferrying them to shows and, I think, thoroughly enjoying the involvement. She gave up race-riding a couple of years back and, although she was a successful amateur, I am glad she stopped. However good a woman rider may be, I am one of those who consider it too dangerous a pastime for them. Quite apart from that, now that she has retired there is not the awful possibility of her beating me if ever we came to ride in the same race!

The Eddery family, Irish born and bred every one of us, is now predominantly based in England. My eldest brother John works with me, running the stud at home; Michael is in Newcastle selling his horse feeds; Robert works in a yard; Paul and David are both riding here. Of my four sisters, all are married, two each living in England and Ireland, but only one of them has any interest in racing. Perhaps, in the case of the other three, they saw and heard more than enough of it as children!

Of the two brothers who have joined me in the riding ranks, David is working in Newmarket, for James Fanshawe, and as yet has had only a few rides. I would love to see him do well, but he is not the best of shapes for a flat jockey and may struggle. I delight in Paul's success. He is a real worker, never sitting about and waiting for the rides to come to him but going out and grafting for them. He rode more than seventy winners in 1991. I may begin to worry if he keeps improving like this!

There are, of course, any number of new kids on the block queuing up to take my championship. Some of them are immensely promising. Frankie Dettori could, in my view, be the best of the lot, but he seems destined to have trouble controlling his weight, a big drawback for any would-be champion. Alan Munro, who has one of the flattest riding styles seen in this country, does not have that problem as yet and the successes of Generous should ensure him plenty of patronage in the coming years. He knows his own mind, does Alan, and certainly has the character to carry off the pressures of title-hunting. The same, I think, may be true of the discovery of 1991, Darryll Holland, whose feet are kept firmly on the ground by his guv'nor, Barry Hills. But for Darryll, as with any successful apprentice, the big test will come when he completes his indentures and steps out on his own. I was lucky, finding the best of jobs with Peter Walwyn as soon as I left Frenchie, but all too many have no such good fortune and fall by the wayside.

It seems a long time now, a very long time, since that September morning in 1967 when I set off from Ireland in search of a riding career. But, though I may have plenty to reflect upon, I believe I can still look forward with optimism, too. I may have been champion nine times, but a fellow called Piggott has eleven titles to his name. I have a few years left in me yet and, of all the things I would like to achieve, that figure of Lester's (and beyond?) is high among them.

Appendix

1966   Apprenticed at the age of thirteen to Seamus McGrath in Ireland.

1967   Indentures transferred to Frenchie Nicholson (Prestbury, Glos.) with whom he served the rest of his apprenticeship 1967-72.

1968   First ride in England (at Aintree) on Dido's Dowry.

1969   On April 24th, rides his first winner, on Alvaro at Epsom. Rides his first Royal Ascot winner on Sky Rocket in Wokingham Handicap.

1970   Rides first five-timer, at Haydock on August 22nd.

1971   Champion apprentice, with 71 winners.

1972   First ride in Derby, finishing third on 50-1 shot, Pentland Firth. Retained by Peter Walwyn.

1973   Top jockey at Royal Ascot. Rides his first 100 winners in a season, ending with 119 successes.

1974   First Classics winner, (Polygamy in Oaks). At twenty-two is the youngest champion jockey for fifty years.

1975   Rides first Derby winner (Grundy). Champion jockey.

1976   Champion jockey.

1977   Champion jockey.

1980   Rides first Prix de L'Arc de Triomphe winner (Detroit). Parts from Peter Walwyn after riding more than 800 winners for the stable.

1981   Becomes first jockey to Vincent O'Brien, succeeding Lester Piggott.

1982   Wins Derby on Golden Fleece.
       Champion jockey in Ireland.

1983   Wins Arlington Million (USA) on Tolomeo.

1984   Wins Irish Derby on El Gran Senor.

1985   Wins Prix de l'Arc de Triomphe on Rainbow Quest.
       Breeders' Cup winner on Pebbles.

1986   Winner of Prix de l'Arc de Triomphe on Dancing Brave.
       Equals British record of six winners in a day (three at Nottingham and three at Windsor).
       Champion jockey.

1987   Winner of Prix de l'Arc de Triomphe on Trempolino.

1988   Champion jockey.

1989   Champion jockey.

1990   Wins Derby on Quest for Fame.
       Rides winner of French Derby on Sanglamore.
       Passes Fred Tucker's total of 2,748 winners to go into sixth place in British all-time list.
       At Kempton on June 27th achieves his fastest ever century of winners from 389 rides. (Fastest ever: Sir Gordon Richards on June 17th, 1949).
       Another six-timer on July 17th. Passes Joe Mercer's total of 2,810 winners and moves into fifth place in jockey's table.
       Champion jockey, and ends the season with best ever total of 209, first flat jockey since Gordon Richards, in 1952, to amass more than 200 in a season and only fourth flat jockey to reach double century, the other two being Fred Archer and Tom Coates.

1991   On July 22nd achieves the fastest ever 3,000 winners in British Turf history, in a period of 22 years 3 months; the fifth jockey to reach this domestic target. And the Champion jockey.
       Breeders' Cup winner on Sheikh Albadou.

Pat Eddery

2. ENGLISH CLASSICS WINNERS

THE DERBY: GRUNDY (1957); GOLDEN FLEECE (1982); QUEST FOR FAME (1990).
1,000 GUINEAS: NONE.
2,000 GUINEAS: LOMOND (1983); EL GRAN SENOR (1984).
THE OAKS: POLYGAMY (1974); SCINTILLATE (1979).
ST LEGER: MOON MADNESS (1986); TOULON (1991).

YEAR-BY-YEAR WINNING TOTALS

1969... 23	1976...176*	1985...162
1970... 57	1978...148	1986...176*
1971... 71	1979...123	1987...195
1972... 69	1980...130	1988...183*
1973...119	1981...109	1989...171*
1974...148*	1982... 83	1990...209*
1975...164*	1983...122	1991...165*
1976...162*	1984...107	

* = CHAMPION JOCKEY.